MW01123116

THE CALL OF
THE NORTH

To Dave & Judy
Love Bill

THE CALL OF THE NORTH

WILLIAM STANLEY

Archway Publishing books may be ordered
through booksellers or by contacting:

Archway Publishing
1663 Liberty Drive
Bloomington, IN 47403
www.archwaypublishing.com
844-669-3957

ISBN: 978-1-6657-2402-9 (sc)
ISBN: 978-1-6657-2401-2 (e)

Library of Congress Control Number: 2022909176

Print information available on the last page.

Archway Publishing rev. date: 05/13/2022

THE CABIN IN
THE WOODS

CHAPTER 1

The trapper's cabin sat abandoned, stripped of its past by a lone trapper who had occupied this structure for twenty-five years. He had died while warming himself by the fire after a cold day on his trapline. His family, not hearing from him for an extended period of time, feared the worst. The cabin was located around two hundred miles from Yellowknife in the North West Territories and was accessible only by air. A bush pilot was hired and family members, armed with a GPS location, accompanied him on the trip. The young couple chosen were the great-niece of the trapper, Jean, and her new husband, John, their love of the bush making them willing volunteers for the trip.

The plane circled, landing on the frozen surface of the lake without incident, and taxied toward the now visible cabin. John and Jean exited the aircraft along with the pilot, and with troubled thoughts made their way to the cabin, silence enveloping them. The pilot had made many trips like this before, none of them ending positively. The bodies of missing men were ordinarily never found, as they typically died in the bush, usually by accident.

The cabin looked forlorn and empty. When they opened the door, they never expected to find the body of the trapper and his loyal dog frozen in place where they had last rested. A sense of sadness and mourning overtook them as they thought about the circumstances that surrounded this scene. The bodies were wrapped in blankets and taken to the plane. The trapper's furs were collected and stored on board the aircraft. The sale of the furs back in Yellowknife would guarantee a proper burial for the man in the spring.

The return to Yellowknife was made in silence, the bodies creating an uneasy feeling among the passengers. The coroner was called upon their return and the trapper's body was picked up and taken to the morgue for an autopsy. The results indicated the cause of death was a heart attack. The trapper's dog was cremated, and its ashes would be buried with the trapper in the spring. A return trip to the cabin would be made to retrieve the trapper's personal belongings. This trip would prove to be a life-changing experience for John and Jean, one that would shape their lives for years to come.

Spring arrived and the trapper, with his dog, received a proper burial. Plans were made for John and Jean to return to the cabin, an adventure they were looking forward to. Their love of the bush would allow them to stay for two weeks, to enjoy the beauty and solitude of nature. A tribute to the trapper and his hard life would be recognized. A good night's sleep would be needed, as their fly-in was scheduled for early tomorrow. Their dreams were of the trapper and his life at the cabin, and their future plans. Tomorrow would be the start of that adventure. A message from the trapper would seal their fate in a positive way, leading them to believe that this was their destiny.

CHAPTER 2

The day was sunny and bright as the bush pilot's plane lifted off the runway. Its destination was Gold Lake, where the trapper's cabin was located. The plane was dropping John and Jean off and when they were ready to return, they would call the pilot to be picked up. In what seemed like a short time they were landing on the open water, the plane taxiing toward the cabin. A sense of euphoria, unlike anything they had experienced, filled them as they took in the beauty of the pristine water and the surrounding forests. The pilot helped them unload their supplies and with a handshake and smile he boarded his plane, taxied out on the lake, and was soon in the air dipping his wings in a final farewell. As the plane disappeared out of sight the silence was overwhelming. Collecting their thoughts, the couple retrieved some of their supplies and headed for the cabin.

The trapper's spirit was everywhere, creating the feeling he was still here. With the help of the pilot John had boarded up the cabin on their previous trip, leaving no path for animals to enter and damage the building inside. They removed the barriers from the doors and windows and entered the cabin. A feeling of complete grief overwhelmed them as memories of their last visit here entered their minds. They stood in silence for a moment collecting their thoughts, John finally telling Jean they had better collect the rest of their supplies, store them, and have lunch.

Most of the food the couple brought with them was canned or smoked. There was a spring that remained open year-round, providing water for the cabin. After a lunch of soup and sandwiches, they cleaned the cabin and put fresh sheets on the bed. They laid down and slept soundly for the rest of the afternoon, waking only when they heard a noise outside.

It was just coming on dusk when John got up and went to the window. To his surprise two deer were browsing on foliage about twenty feet away. They had no idea John was watching them. He thought of the trapper whose reputation with the family was one of being a hermit and recluse. The spirit of the trapper overwhelmed him, beckoning him to live this life, and at that very moment he made his decision. With the blessings of his wife, they decided to start a life here, knowing the trapper would guide them and look out for their well-being.

The cabin was well stocked, as the trapper had supplies flown in twice a year to supplement what nature could not provide. The dwelling was quite large, about eight hundred square feet. It had a double bed, an eat-in kitchen, and a wood stove for cooking. The stove provided heat and had an oven and a reservoir for water. The cabin had four windows which allowed plenty of sunlight to enter. On the outside of the structure there were a large shed and an outhouse, and a small woodshed had been built onto the back of the building.

John and Jean decided to stay for two weeks, allowing them to get a better idea of what would be needed for a permanent life here. Soon they were back in Yellowknife, telling their shocked family of their future plans. They would stay in town long enough to settle their affairs and take a six-week course on wilderness survival and trapping. By late August they planned on moving to the cabin on a permanent basis, which should allow enough time to prepare themselves for the long winter. Time would not be on their side.

CHAPTER 3

＋ ◆ ＋ ◆ ＋ ◆ ＋ ◆ ＋

Time flew by as John and Jean prepared for their new life. Their house was sold, and a good profit was made. They completed the survival course which proved helpful in teaching them about trapping and living in the wilderness. They realized trial and error would also be a large part of the learning process. Supplies were ordered and delivered to a warehouse where they awaited being transported by plane to the trapper's cabin, which would require two trips. Everything was set to go.

After wishing a tearful farewell to family and friends, the couple boarded the plane along with their new dog, a Siberian husky named Bow. They had acquired him shortly after returning to Yellowknife from the cabin in the spring. He was a trained sled dog, capable of pulling heavy loads. The plane became air-born and after banking sharply, was on its way to the cabin. As they flew, the conversation turned to the lake.

The pilot shared the story of the legend of Gold Lake. Following World War Two an influx of trappers moved into the area, as the popularity of fur caused prices to skyrocket.

The men that came were a hardy breed and many of them ended up around Gold Lake because of its reputation as a prime fur-bearing region. Many perished during the hard winter, having failed to properly prepare for the conditions. Their decaying cabins can still be seen dotting the shores of the lake. However, some men survived and successfully trapped for many years. It was rumoured, that in addition to his furs, one of these men had gold to sell each spring, the gold worth five times more than the furs. This was a well-kept secret around Yellowknife. However, a few men having heard this tale took it upon themselves to investigate this claim. They were unsuccessful and no other reports of gold being found in the area were ever made.

Soon the lake came into view. The plane landed on the water gracefully and taxied to where the cabin stood. After an hour of hard work, the supplies were unloaded and moved to the cabin. A canoe stored above the plane's pontoons also made it there safely. The pilot stayed to eat and then left, assuring the couple he would bring the rest of their supplies the following week. Both John and Jean were exhausted and chilled. It was near the end of August, and it was starting to get cold. A fire was soon going, and a warm glow filled the cabin. Bow seemed quite happy sleeping on the floor in front of the stove. They would relax for the evening, and tomorrow they would get organized.

CHAPTER 4

John awoke as it was just coming on daylight. He pulled himself out of bed and started a fire in the stove. The nights here were much colder than in Yellowknife, making him think about preparations for the winter. The cabin needed some work to make it airtight and comfortable. The trapper had let the maintenance lag, as this was not an important issue for him. John had bought new stovepipes for the cabin which were coming in the next load from Yellowknife. The trapper had ignored the fire danger the current ones possessed. Four new windows were purchased, which John, being a carpenter by trade, would be able to install himself.

As the fire in the stove grew, a warmth enveloped the cabin. Bow awoke and was let outside while John got his food ready. Jean woke up and John cooked her a breakfast of canned beans and fried potatoes with toast. After eating, they decided to take the canoe and explore their surroundings, saving their work for later. Leaving Bow in the cabin, they were soon paddling in the pristine wilderness of Gold Lake. The only sounds they heard were the raven piercing the silence with its shrill call and the sound of the canoe paddles in the water, adding to the serenity of the moment. Hawks flew overhead, scanning the ground for a meal. John found the trapper's spirit was with him, filling him with joy and perseverance for the future.

After taking in the beauty of this wilderness lake for a couple of hours, the couple found themselves back at the cabin being greeted by their loyal dog. They relaxed and talked about their future here and decided that after lunch they would start work. The first order of business was to clean and organize the shed, another log building where the furs would be processed. A small woodstove sat in the corner, and a partition divided the fur processing area from another large room which was used for storage of materials needing protection from the harsh environment. The trapper had kept his two pieces of mechanical equipment, an ice auger and a chainsaw, and his sled in this part of the shed. After close examination, the sled was found to be in fine condition, with a new set of harnesses to go with it.

The trapper had built an underground freezer, complete with a secure entrance that could not be breached by any animal. This is where meat and fish would be stored in the winter, and it provided cold storage for vegetables in the summer. A few small modifications needed to be made, but it was solid and well-constructed.

The woodshed was well stocked, as if the trapper's hobby had been cutting and splitting firewood. Another pile of wood was stacked along the side of the storage shed leaving John and Jean with a winter's supply. Keeping enough wood ahead was important, and a job that could not be neglected.

The pair checked the spring and found a steady stream of water pouring from it. This would be supplemented by lake water, which would require a hole be kept open in the winter ice. Year-round water was vital, as without water there would be no life.

Returning to the cabin, they moved some of their supplies to the storage shed, and then had an afternoon nap. Being on the lake in the fresh air had relaxed them and made them feel lazy. Bow felt the same way, joining them in sleep, dreaming about adventures in his new home. He was glad he was here, instead of Yellowknife, where he would be living in a small doghouse and kept on a chain. He felt great affection for his owners and would work hard for them.

Night comes early this far north in the fall and winter. John was aware of this and had bought lanterns that lit the cabin almost as well as electric lamps, allowing John to read and Jean to do her knitting in the evenings. These replaced the oil lamps the old trapper had refused to give up. After dinner they went outside, including Bow, and marvelled at the night sky. To the observers on the ground, it was filled with what seemed like a million stars reaching out in infinite space.

The first sense of loneliness gripped the couple as they felt small and insignificant while staring at the sky and the wilderness that surrounded them. Tomorrow, with Bow, they would take a hike and search for areas that looked promising for trapping. They entered the cabin, read, and then went to bed falling into a deep sleep, not awakening till the morning's early light.

CHAPTER 5

The new day dawned cloudy and cool. The couple had an early breakfast; an exploratory trip to get familiar with their new surroundings on their agenda. Their trapline this year would be small, running only twenty traps, as this was a new way of life for them. They were soon ready to leave, especially Bow who sensed an adventure was about to happen. The old trapper, after years of working these forests and woodlands, had left well marked trails that led to his traplines. In an abundance of caution, they had brought trail signs to mark the route, making it less likely for them to get lost. Getting lost, especially in winter, meant almost certain death.

The area was heavily wooded, with open meadows and wetlands. The trails led to beaver dams and a large cave, where the remnants of a campfire indicated the trapper had used it for shelter. This cave brought back memories of the story that the pilot told about the legend of Gold Lake. John noticed outcroppings that harboured caves, and maybe in the future they would explore them. Continuing their journey, they saw little signs of wildlife except for bear scat, meaning a good food supply was evident. This was a good sign, as they needed a moose or a couple of deer to get them through the winter. Bears in the area usually meant there was food for these large game animals as well.

Two hours into their trip, Jean and John were surprised to come upon another cabin. It had been built along the trapline for use as an emergency shelter, when getting back to the main cabin was not possible. This could be due to weather conditions or broken equipment, like a problem with the dog sled. The cabin was bare bones, but if needed could well be a lifesaver.

The wind was cold and there was a hint of frost in the air, not unexpected for this time of year. This brought John's thoughts back to the cabin. He had used his satellite phone to confirm the delivery of the rest of their supplies. The most important items John was waiting for were the stovepipes and windows. The pilot was also bringing them fresh bread, and baking supplies so they could learn to bake in their woodstove.

The trip back home was uneventful, until they reached the cabin where they found a fox sleeping in their front yard. They startled him and he left in a hurry, more surprised at this disruption than they were. Lunch was made and after a nap, John and Jean thought they would try their hand at fishing. Fish would make an enjoyable dinner, something that was fresh rather than being out of a can. The sleep was short, and soon they were heading to the lake, fishing gear in hand. Within one hour they had caught six fish, including whiting, the most abundant fish in northern lakes. Pickerel and Jack perch, which could grow to multiple pounds, were also caught. They happily returned to the cabin, cleaned the fish, and ate the first dinner that nature had provided for them. They listened to their satellite radio, talked, and John wrote in his journal before retiring for the night.

CHAPTER 6

John and Jean were beginning to settle into a routine of life in the bush. They continued cleaning and organizing the house, exploring the area, and enjoying the peace and tranquility. They went canoeing and hiking to see what resources could be found, including noting trees that could be felled for future firewood.

The pack of wolves that called this territory home made themselves known; loud howling heard in the distance nightly. John did not know how to view the wolves' behaviour. He wondered if he should look at them as a threat or something that could be ignored. Wolf attacks on humans were rare, as they perceive man as a danger and try to keep their distance. John knew the couple's presence would become known to the wolves, and eventually they would come to investigate, most likely at night while they were sleeping. Bow was also feeling uneasy. He too worried about the wolves, sensing these animals would soon find him. He knew wolves viewed him as a mortal enemy and would kill him immediately if given the chance.

Their first week at the cabin had flown by. John awoke to the smell of breakfast cooking and coffee brewing. At Jean's urging, he pulled himself out of bed and sat at the table to eat. They discussed the day's events, the most important being the arrival of their supplies. John decided to chink the cabin while waiting for the plane's appearance. This chore needed to be done before winter set in. Chinking is the process of sealing cracks or holes that develop between the logs, keeping the cold air out of the cabin.

John's eyes scanned the horizon, his hearing on high alert for the sound of an engine. The plane finally arrived, and the landing was uneventful. John and Jean exchanged pleasantries with the pilot, as they made their way to the cabin for lunch. After conversation and a good meal, they returned to the plane to unload their supplies. Along with the new windows and stovepipes, a chainsaw and twenty traps were also in the load. The traps that had been at the cabin were old and appeared unusable to John, but not to the old trapper who had used them for the last twenty-five years.

The plane was soon unloaded, and fond farewells were said. The plane taxied out into the open water and with a roar from the engine was soon flying out of sight, not to return until the spring. John and Jean packed their supplies away and decided the rest of their afternoon would be spent marking the trees to be cut down for firewood. Trees cut in the fall are dry enough to burn the following summer. This job would have to be completed before the arrival of winter.

Before long, the sun was setting, and the warm cabin was beckoning. Their dinner was beef brought by the pilot from Yellowknife, a special treat as fresh meat was scarce.

Jean baked an apple pie for dessert, another gift from the pilot. John would start replacing the windows and stovepipes in the morning, important tasks to accomplish as snow could arrive at anytime.

The trapping season would start shortly, and John needed to be ready. Tomorrow would be a busy day, so they retired to bed early. Their dreams of the trapline and the furs they would harvest, pointing to a future of hard work.

CHAPTER 7

John awakened early; he was ready to get to work. Replacing the windows in the cabin was now a priority for him. After breakfast, and with Jean's help, the project was started. A cold wind blew off the lake, once again reminding them that winter was approaching. His measurements for the custom-made windows had been followed precisely, and with little trouble they were installed and weather-proofed. Just as the sun dipped below the horizon, they finished the job. A sense of accomplishment was felt by both John and Jean as they retired inside the cabin for dinner and to get warm.

Tomorrow they would install the new stovepipes. John had bought them for both the cabin and the shed. The following day dawned cloudy and cold, and with little trouble the stovepipes were in place and operational by noon. Snow began falling shortly thereafter.

Their home felt cozy and warm, as the new windows allowed no drafts to enter the cabin. The snow continued falling, and by morning a measurable amount was on the ground. The landscape had undergone a sudden transformation, going from dull brown to brilliant white.

The trees were beautiful, clad in snow. Bow was let out of the cabin. He bounded through the snow like a child enjoying a new gift. Being a husky, he loved the snow, his breed having adapted to working in the cold.

John prepared the sled for a test run. He harnessed Bow to it and they went for a short jaunt. Bow proved to be a strong dog, well suited for his responsibilities. John, Jean, and Bow then went for a walk to the lake, the beauty of the landscape overwhelming their senses They were grateful for their good fortune so far.

The freeze was now here, diverting John's attention to putting meat in his freezer for the winter, a deer or moose a must have. Tomorrow he would take Bow and the sled to look for sign, prints left in the snow, and areas where these large animals had been feeding on limbs of trees. The next day dawned sunny and cold. Snow had continued to fall, laying down a suitable surface for the sled to operate efficiently.

John and Bow were soon off, following the trapper's well marked trail. There were many rabbit tracks, mostly snowshoe hares and some cottontails. The snowshoe, a meat rabbit, was a staple of many trappers' diets. The rabbits could be caught with snares fixed on runways in the deep snow, leaving them vulnerable to ending up on the dinner table. Fox tracks were plentiful, along with the prints of other fur bearing animals, showing John promising sign for their first trapping season. Bow was pleased, knowing he was doing a good job and making his owner happy.

As the pair approached a line of cedars, they saw deer tracks. Deer live in groups in the winter, finding shelter near viable food sources. If it is safe in the area, they will stay for an extended time before moving on. John felt certain he could shoot a deer here, and as it was close to the cabin transporting the meat would be fairly easy. Satisfied with this outing, the pair turned around to head back home.

Suddenly Bow was whining and acting nervous. A quick look around showed John why. They were being followed by the wolves that called this territory home. John counted eight wolves led by a black wolf, a rare animal that, according to folklore, possesses powers special to nature. The wolves followed from a distance until John and Bow reached the cabin, and then they disappeared into the bush. John felt sure the pack would visit the cabin tonight under the cover of darkness.

Over dinner John shared his day with his wife and discussed his high expectations for their future. The couple read for an hour before falling into a peaceful sleep, rejuvenating their bodies for what would turn out to be an eventful day tomorrow.

CHAPTER 8

————— ✦ ✦ ✦ ✦ ✦ ✦ —————

It was just coming on daybreak when John left the cabin, his rifle in hand. He had decided last night he should seize the opportunity of shooting a deer that had been offered to him. He planned to walk the mile to where they were sheltering, find a place where he would not be seen, and wait for the deer to come out of the trees. This should provide a clear shot and a good chance of success.

John arrived in the area and found appropriate shelter. After four hours of waiting patiently he finally saw movement. Two deer walked out of the cedars, stopped, and looked around. A shot rang out and the buck fell, taking a bullet to the heart. John was thrilled, his worries about providing meat were temporarily solved. After examining the deer, he returned to the cabin where he hooked up Bow. They were soon off to finish the important task of field dressing his kill.

John arrived at the deer and was soon butchering the animal. Four hours later he was done, the meat piled high on the sled, and thoughts of a venison dinner filled his head. The remnants of the deer were left for the scavengers. They were soon back at the cabin, where John dressed and stored the meat, sharing his excitement with Jean. With fish from the lake, rabbits they could catch, and deer in the freezer, the couple's food issues had been taken care of.

Turning his attention away from the hunt, John had noticed large animal tracks around the cabin. The wolves had investigated the previous night. If they became aggressive towards the couple or Bow, John would have to shoot and kill one of them. By doing so, the rest of the pack would know the danger he presented. John also noticed fox tracks in the snow around the cabin. He wondered if this was the same fox they had startled soon after they had arrived. It was rumoured the old trapper had kept a wild fox as a pet, the animal having learned not to fear the trapper's dog.

The wind picked up and dark clouds moved in, signaling to John and Jean that bad weather was on the way. John checked the weather report on the radio, which confirmed the first major blizzard of the season would be arriving soon. Extra food, water and wood were brought into the cabin from outside, as these storms could last for days. Around dinnertime the storm hit with a vengeance, the wind so intense it seemed to rock the cabin, the fury of the storm making the couple feel vulnerable to nature's wrath. The wind howled all night; John and Jean got little sleep.

Daybreak found the winds calming, and the snows finished, leaving grey sky and a fresh coating of white snow covering the landscape. The couple spent the day in the cabin talking about their trapline. It was agreed that tomorrow they would set half of the traps and some snares for rabbits. Jean would accompany John and help in this venture. A second dinner of venison was prepared, and an early bedtime followed. The thought of starting their trapline brought about anticipation and anxiety. The cabin became quiet as sleep took over, casting them into a pleasant state of mind, which would only be broken by dawn's early light.

CHAPTER 9

A sense of excitement filled the cabin as today the trapping season officially starts. The day was perfect, with sunshine filling the sky, a light wind, and moderate temperatures. After a hearty breakfast of venison stew, they loaded the sled and, with a sense of elation, the couple and their dog started down the trail. They had decided to set traps about every quarter mile until they reached the emergency shelter. Once this route was established, more traps would be added until they set a total of twenty traps. Two beaver traps would also to be set once the ice thickened. The goal was to keep their trapline between the main cabin and the shelter. This was their secure area, as travelling beyond this point could be risky. Being new to this venture, safety was a big concern, as one misstep could spell disaster or even death. This winter would be a learning experience, with no expectation of making a lot of money. Survival during the harsh winter would be their top priority.

Using the knowledge from the trapping and wilderness course, the couple set their first trap. The bait was the remains from the deer and fish. Most fur bearing animals, excluding the beaver, will eat both. They continued along the trail, setting traps in areas that showed promising sign until all the traps were deployed. The couple decided to make a fire at the shelter, eat a lunch of smoked meat and beans, and on the way back to the cabin set snares for rabbits. The rabbit population was healthy, with heavily travelled runways abundant, indicating an ample supply of meat for eating and bait for their traps. Ten snares were set on the way back home. They would check them daily, as a dead rabbit in a snare was easy pickings for a variety of animals, including hawks and eagles.

The trio soon found themselves back at the cabin with John stoking the fire, bringing warmth to their cold bodies. Today had been a success, and they were hoping that more like it were in the future. After dinner, John and Jean decided that a game of cards was in order. They had grown up playing cards resulting in them being familiar with a number of games. After an enjoyable evening, their eyelids grew heavy, and soon sleep would be upon them. They snuggled together in their warm bed excited about what they might find tomorrow in their traps.

CHAPTER 10

✦✦✦✦✦✦

The couple woke early, the new day's light filtering in through the cabin windows as the sun rose. Looking out the window, John saw the fox standing alone in the yard. Maybe there was truth in the story about the trapper and his pet. John grabbed a small piece of smoked meat while Jean held Bow. He opened the door, and with a low whistle summoned the animal. To his surprise it warily approached, and with coaching from John, the fox took the meat and happily pranced off behind the cabin. John now knew he had another friend.

Hearty helpings of fresh bread from the oven and left-over stew from the night before were eaten for breakfast. Stew was a mainstay of a trapper's diet, with many animals caught on the trapline providing a good source of protein. Early trappers used edibles from the forest to add flavor and body to their stews, while modern trappers now order enough root vegetables and spices to last them through the winter.

The couple left the cabin, loaded some supplies, and hooked Bow up to the sled. The silence of the bush and the brightness of the sun's reflection off the snow generated a feeling of being one with the earth. This was the trapper's spirit providing protection on their journey. Arriving at their first trap, they found it empty. As they continued down the line they were faced with similar results. The couple's hopes were fading, until they came to the second to the last trap. A loud growling and hissing could be heard. It was a bobcat with its leg caught in the trap. John picked up his rifle knowing what he had to do. One shot to the head and the bobcat lay dead. John felt some remorse at taking this beautiful animal's life, but also exhilaration at having a handsome fur. It was the only fur they harvested that day.

Heading home, the snares proved more productive. Four rabbits were caught from the ten snares they had set. Overall, the couple agreed it was a good first day. Rounding the last corner, their cabin came into view. The fox was standing in the yard as if waiting for them to return. Loud barking from Bow made him retreat to the woods behind the cabin. With hope, the pair would get to know each other and become friends.

The sled was unloaded, and the rabbits and bobcat were locked up in the skinning shed. Tomorrow a roaring fire in the woodstove would thaw these animals so they could be processed. Bedtime came early, but sleep would be fleeting, as an incident during the night made them realize how alone they really were in this wilderness.

CHAPTER 11

A low growl from Bow woke John from a pleasant sleep. He could hear activity outside, when suddenly it sounded like something was attacking the cabin. The wolves, with insistent growling, howling, and barking swarmed the cabin, jumping and scratching at the door trying to gain entry. Bow cowered, terrified at what the outcome of this event would be. Were the wolves behaving like this because they knew the dog was in the cabin, or was it because they felt John and Jean were trespassing on their territory and they wanted the intruders gone? In disbelief, John quickly made the decision to stop this encounter. He went to the window and in the moonlight saw the black wolf standing, watching his pack, seemingly instructing them on what to do. The wolf's eyes glowed red in the moonlight, making this terrifying ordeal surreal.

Quietly opening the window John positioned his rifle for a shot. The black wolf should have been his target, but John's superstitions told him otherwise. He was afraid killing this wolf would unleash this beast's evil, changing their luck forever. John took aim at an unsuspecting wolf close to him. A shot to his head, brought instant death to this menace. As soon as he fell, silence dominated the scene. The wolves were stunned by this sudden change of events. Now sensing danger, they scattered into the darkness. A sigh of relief came from the residents of the cabin. If not for the dead wolf laying in their front yard this would all seem like a nightmare. Getting back to sleep was not an option.

Morning soon came, and it was decided they would process the bobcat and wolf pelts today. John walked to the skinning shed and prepared a fire in the woodstove. The bodies of the frozen animals were placed nearby, once thawed they would be skinned. Quiet permeated the shed as John's thoughts kept turning to the previous night's encounter. The dead wolf served as a reminder to the pack that man presented a grave danger and should be avoided. With the animal's bodies thawed, and Jean's help, the furs were processed, the rabbits cleaned, and the shed secured for the night.

With their work completed, the couple returned to the cabin to cook dinner, rabbit being the main course. The remaining rabbits were put in the freezer. The couple reflected on the events of the past twenty-four hours, realizing the struggles to make this new life work were daunting. For the first time thoughts of ending this adventure after one season were discussed. The encounter with the wolves made them keenly aware of how vulnerable they were here in the wilderness. Maybe a good day on the trapline tomorrow would help a sense of normality return. They decided one bad experience would not destroy their dream, and perhaps spiritual help from the trapper would block the memory of the wolf attack. Tomorrow, they planned to check the trapline and set the beaver traps, hoping to catch this desirable and valuable animal. Emotionally and physically exhausted, the couple went to bed early, their dreams sending them back home to Yellowknife.

CHAPTER 12

The new day dawned bright and sunny. The sled was loaded, and off they went with Bow down the trail. With the wolf episode behind them, their thoughts turned to the trapline. John sensed a good day was in store for them. As the sled pulled up to the first trap, they saw a marten, the most common fur-bearing animal in the north, waiting for them. After collecting it and resetting the trap they moved on. The second and third stops yielded nothing, but the fourth trap held a red fox, a valuable pelt and lucky catch. At the fifth stop the trap had been set off and the meat taken, the same result awaited them at the next stop. A mystery was in the making. What animal was responsible for this? The next four traps yielded one marten and a weasel. After removing the animals, they reset the traps and made their way to the emergency shelter where they would eat lunch, rest for a bit, and then move on to set their beaver traps.

The ice on the river had grown thicker and an axe was needed to chop a hole large enough to pull an adult beaver through. This wetland area was vast and contained many beavers. Unless they expanded their trapping area, only a limited number of these animals would be caught here, leaving an ample supply of beaver to breed and produce offspring for future years of trapping. With trial and error, the traps were finally set. John, Jean, and Bow continued down the trail, planning to check their rabbit snares on the way home. John was worried. It had clouded over, and the wind had picked up, a sign that bad weather was coming their way.

Knowing a storm was imminent, the decision was made to skip the snares and return to the cabin as quickly as possible. The snow started when they were a half hour from home and was intensifying as they pulled up to the skinning shed. The sled was unloaded, the shed secured, and extra meat was retrieved from the freezer along with wood from the woodshed.

John appreciated the new windows and stovepipes he had installed, making the cabin warmer and eliminating the threat of fire. The blizzard lasted for two days. The little cabin stood its ground, protecting the residents from certain death. On the third day the sky cleared, and the sun shone brightly. More hard work was now facing the couple. The traps would have to be dug out of the deep snow and reset. Today John would process the furs that were still in the shed, and, if time and daylight permitted, they would try to replenish their fish stocks from the lake. This was a hard, but satisfying life, promoting spiritual and physical well-being, a state of mind difficult to find.

CHAPTER 13

+ + + ◆ ◆ + + +

Yesterday's fishing trip had been successful. A total of six fish were caught, cleaned, and stored for future consumption. Today Jean and John dealt with the trapline and rabbit snares. After a hard day's work, the trail had been broken and all ten traps dug out of the deep snow and reset. A surprise awaited them at the beaver traps. A large adult beaver was caught, yielding a valuable pelt, and providing a sense of accomplishment to the couple. The rabbit snares, after being dug out of the snow, offered up two snowshoe rabbits. They had been laying frozen under the snow since the last time the couple checked the snares, so were still edible. On the return home, John managed to shoot two grouse, which they planned to have for dinner. Food was plentiful at this time of year, but as winter wore on that may change. John, Jean, and Bow made their way back to the cabin satisfied with the day's events.

Arriving back at the cabin, the fox was in the yard. Once again Bow made a fuss and the fox retreated out of sight, wary of the dog. John and Jean were tired. Feeling caught up on needed chores, they decided they could relax for a couple of days. Jean had some knitting she wanted to get to, and John wanted some time to write in his journal. He had been keeping a detailed account of their activities since they arrived at the cabin.

The grouse for dinner was a treat, serving up a taste as sweet as candy. They had been eating venison, rabbit, and some fish, making fowl a positive change. Jean had been feeling depressed, the isolation of the bush bothering her. Arrangements were made for Jean's mother to call the satellite phone to speak with her daughter. John was hoping that this would make Jean feel better. The stress of this wilderness life was starting to put a strain on her mental health. John worried about Jean, wondering if she would make it through the winter. Total mental breakdowns were a common occurrence for men and women living in the far north. However, John had faith in Jean as she was a strong woman and not someone to give up easily.

As the weeks went by a routine was established. Jean and John decided that using ten traps were enough for this season, until they gained experience and became faster at the job. Their trapline produced many furs, including two more beaver, fishers, martens, foxes, and weasels. However, there had been a thief occasionally robbing their traps. They suspected it was a wolverine. Fearing nothing, including bears and wolves, this animal was so smart it was rarely caught in a trap. Christmas was fast approaching, and it was decided a two-week vacation from their trapline would be planned. It was a time for rejoicing and resting before the coldest part of the winter fell upon them.

CHAPTER 14

━━━━━━━ ✦✦✦✦✦ ━━━━━━━

It was Christmas day, and a celebration was in order. The cabin had been adorned with decor from the forest. A small tree had been cut, and with Christmas items Jean and John had brought from home, the cabin boasted a festive atmosphere. The radio was tuned to a station that played Christmas music, for the trappers and the other people that lived in this wilderness with no easy means of communication. John and Jean had brought extra batteries just for this occasion. Christmas gifts had been brought from Yellowknife. John gave his wife knitting supplies, and Jean gave John a book and a new knife. Bow received a large beef bone to chew on. Prayers were spoken, and then dinner was served, venison roast with potatoes and carrots and fresh bread from the oven. Bow shared the same meal, and the little red fox, always begging for food, was also treated to a share of the feast. The little cabin, full of warmth and coziness, was the perfect venue for this Christmas party.

As day turned into night, the northern lights filled the sky with brilliant colors. Watching this show through the bedroom window while lying in bed, created a feeling of joy. Sleep came easy that night, the only disturbance was a howling wind, which awoke everyone, including Bow. Another blizzard was raging, once more keeping them isolated in the cabin. The blizzard was a reminder of how fast storms can blow in, leaving little time to get to safety if caught out on the trapline. Being aware of the signs that nature sends about an approaching storm is important and could save one's life.

The storm lasted twelve hours, and soon the sun came out and much-needed light shone into the cabin. However, the light was short-lived, as night descended upon them again, bringing peace to the cabin. The sky was clear, the wind calm, and the temperature outside frigid. The coldest part of the winter was fast approaching, with temperatures sliding as low as forty below zero at night. This kept John and his wife in the cabin, as prolonged exposure to these temperatures may cause frostbite or death.

The couple were hopeful that after New Year's Day they would be able to return to the trapline. All the traps would need to be reset, as they had been gathered up and stored for the holiday. John and Jean had decided to add two more traps and relocate them, hoping to improve their catch. The wolves, usually howling nightly, had not been heard for over a week, making John think they had moved on to another area. If that was the case, they would not be missed.

A fishing trip was planned for tomorrow morning, with a grouse hunt in the afternoon. The venison supply was quickly being depleted, making John think another deer or moose would be needed soon. The couple retired to bed knowing tomorrow would be another busy day.

CHAPTER 15

A north wind blew across the lake, dropping the temperature to twenty-five below zero, which was too cold for fishing. However, the grouse hunt would go on. The forest would act as a windbreak, making it at least tolerable to be outdoors. John would go hunting alone, leaving Jean and Bow to enjoy the warmth of the cabin. He planned to walk the trapline to an area where he had seen a healthy population of the birds. With a kiss good-bye and a wish for good luck, he left the safety of the cabin and was on his way.

After a trek of about one mile, John reached a cedar bush, prime habitat for these birds. As soon as he entered the cedars, he had two grouse to put in his pack. Over the next hour, six more birds were added. He decided to head home, as he had been out long enough in the frigid air. While exiting the cedars he noticed something was following him. It was a stealthy animal that kept its distance and was probably not aware that its presence was known to John. A wolverine, the most dangerous and unpredictable animal in the north, was stalking him. He decided to leave the cedar bush, take cover, and see if the animal would follow. If it did, he might be able to get a clear shot and add this animal to his furs, eliminating this danger to his trapline, himself, and his dog.

The excitement mounted as John waited. Then, in a matter of minutes the wolverine showed itself. John took his shot and the animal lay dead, taking a bullet to the head. John was shocked. He had just done something that was rare in a trapper's world, he had shot and killed a wolverine. These animals rarely left themselves open to this option. The wolverine would have to be left here, as it was too heavy for John to carry home. John headed to the cabin. He wanted to drop off the grouse, get the dog and sled, and retrieve the wolverine.

Two hours later the job was done. Jean had started cleaning the grouse, which would be dinner, and John began processing the wolverine fur. John finished his job just as the sun was going down. He was still basking in the glory of killing his most elusive prey. Tomorrow the trapline would be his priority, getting back to trapping the goal.

Dinner was served, and cards were played, with bedtime coming early. The snow, blowing in whirlwinds around the cabin, interrupted their sleep but made them realize what a safe, cozy home they had. Working outside was becoming more of a challenge, as the cold and wind became more intense. John and Jean once again questioned their life here, dreaming about their past in Yellowknife.

CHAPTER 16

The deployment of the traps was uneventful, with a total of twelve set. Changing the location of the traps would help avoid over trapping, which can lead to a catastrophic decline of wildlife. Leaving some animals to breed guarantees the survival of the species that call this place home. Two beaver traps were also set, as the couple had only caught half of their personal quota. John hated trapping beaver. He admired their social structure and work ethic, which is unmatched by any other mammal. Unfortunately, the value of their pelts contribute greatly to a trapper's successful season.

The following day was so beautiful that John and Jean decided to interrupt their routine. They wanted to explore the surroundings beyond their safe zone, as it was their plan to expand the trapline next year. After exploring the area, they found it similar to the one they were currently trapping. The best thing to come out of this trip was stumbling upon another deer location. The meat from the first deer John had shot was almost gone, so this was a lucky break for them. He had plans to return tomorrow and hunt the animal.

The day was getting late, so they decided to return home. The thought of finding more meat occupied John's mind, making him think back to when he shot his first deer. This time it would have to be done differently. He would take Jean and Bow with him. Jean would stay with Bow, keeping him a safe distance from the deer. This would allow John to walk in and surprise them.

Soon they found themselves back at the cabin. The sun was setting as they finished unloading the sled. A dinner of beaver stew that Jean had prepared yesterday was waiting for them. The fire was set in the woodstove and soon a warm glow filled the space. The little cabin in the woods was their comfort zone, providing safety from the outside elements. At times things were difficult, but at times like this they could see their lives no other way. The stew was delicious, especially for Bow, who regarded this as his favorite meal.

The night was dark and silent, only the hoot of an owl could be heard. Bedtime beckoned and soon sound sleep followed. The couple were awakened in the night by Bow growling. John got up and looked out the window but saw nothing. He would check for tracks in the morning. Going back to bed he soon fell into a deep sleep, oblivious to the strange events tomorrow would bring. The forest, the silence, and the comfort of having his wife beside him were all that mattered to John.

CHAPTER 17

John awoke, wondering what caused Bow to growl the night before. The morning sky was just beginning to lighten as John dressed. Jean started cooking breakfast while he prepared the supplies for today's deer hunt. As soon as John was ready, he accompanied Bow outside and looked around. He was shocked at what he saw, which did not make sense. There were giant footprints in the snow, much larger than those of a human. He went inside the cabin to summon Jean, shaking with excitement and fear.

After a short conversation they agreed it could have only been one thing, Bigfoot. These mythical beings are said to live in the forests of the far north; a creature that walks on two legs, can stand eight feet tall, and is covered in hair. They are elusive, humanoid, and rarely seen. They are not considered a threat, as no attacks on men have ever been reported. The old trapper had made comments about seeing large footprints around his cabin, and at times he would see them when he was out on his trapline. These stories were perceived as just an old man's tales. John now realized there was credibility to these stories.

After a hearty breakfast they were off, with Bow leading them down the trail. The plan was to ignore the trapline today and concentrate on trying to harvest a deer. They would go to the emergency shelter where Jean and the dog would wait. John would snowshoe the mile to where the deer were and hopefully shoot one. If the hunt was a success, he would return to pick up Bow and the sled, retrieve the deer, and dress it at the shelter.

The stand of cedar trees came into view, a secure area for the deer, providing thick cover and a plentiful food supply. John again had to wait until the deer came out so he could get a clear shot. Two hours went by, and finally three deer made their way out of the cedars, unaware of John's presence. A shot rang out and one of the deer fell dead in the snow. John, with much elation, checked the animal and then headed back to the shelter with the good news. Thirty minutes later he was at the shelter, drinking hot coffee, waiting for lunch, and sharing his story with Jean.

The decision had been made to spend the night here. Jean had prepared the cabin for a sleep over when John had left earlier that morning. The couple and Bow went to retrieve the deer. A short time later they were securing it to the sled and returning to the shelter. Upon arrival, a raven on the roof gave out what sounded like a greeting, knowing some of the spoils from the deer would be his.

John got to work, and with Jean's help the deer was quickly dressed. The remains were taken a distance from the structure, and the meat was stored inside, protecting it from predators. They had venison for dinner, with Bow getting seconds for being an obedient and reliable dog. Sleep came easy that night, only the sounds of the tree limbs creaking in the wind could be heard. Tomorrow another surprise would await them, but for now rest was their priority.

CHAPTER 18

Staying in the emergency shelter was uncomfortable. No matter how much wood was put on the fire it was still cold, the air coming in through large open cracks in the logs. John would work on solving this problem in the summer. Packing up and leaving early was their plan, returning to the cabin and warming their cold, aching bodies would be a priority.

They left the shelter as soon as there was enough light to see the trail and before long their cabin came into view. As they drew near, they noticed a dark, inanimate object lying in the front yard. The remains of Roxie, their somewhat domesticated fox, lay in a pool of blood surrounded by wolf tracks. The wolves had returned the night before. Sensing that no one was in the cabin gave them free reign, and upon finding Roxie, they had immediately attacked her. Sadness prevailed, and then anger. John decided at that moment he was declaring war on the wolf pack. Any time a wolf was seen it would be shot. Maybe killing a couple more wolves would convince the pack to leave for good.

What was left of Roxie's body was placed in the freezer and would be given a proper burial in the spring. Jean went in the cabin to start a fire while John unloaded the sled, taking extra care to make sure the deer meat was secured in the freezer. Upon returning to the cabin, the warmth from the fire could already be felt. Bow found his favorite spot on the rug in front of the stove and immediately went to sleep, his snoring heard throughout the cabin. Jean worked on making a venison stew, which would be for lunch and dinner. After they ate a large lunch, a nap was in order. The trapline would be checked tomorrow, leaving them to take care of the smaller chores around the property later today.

John decided a cleanup of the skinning shed was a priority. Their annual inspection by the game warden was coming soon, and he wanted to make a good impression. The visit was a combination of a wellness check and an inspection of his furs, traps, and even the health of his dog. Their living conditions were also important, as survival was foremost in the minds of the gamekeepers. Wardens had been known to close trapping operations with numerous safety violations. One time an old trapper was so angry at being forced out of his home, and having his trapping license suspended, that he took his rifle and shot the game warden in the leg. The warden returned fire and, unfortunately, the trapper was killed.

John was to check in with the ranger station on the first of every month to see if his appointment date had been set. These inspections were the wardens' hardest job, as trappers often bucked authority and failed to follow the rules.

Twilight was approaching as John finished his work. Locking up, he went to the cabin for dinner. He told Jean that he had decided to set a trap for the wolves. He would leave the remains of the animals he processed in a clearing, hide nearby, and wait for the wolves to come in to feed. Revenge was now the plan for killing their harmless pet, Roxie. After dinner, a game of cribbage was played until heavy eyes sent them to bed for a peaceful night's sleep.

CHAPTER 19

John and Bow headed down the trail, the sled breaking a new path through the fresh snow they had received the night before. Jean had stayed home today. John was worried about her, as Jean's depression had worsened. He was thinking that if things kept sliding downhill, she would have to return to Yellowknife. The isolation, brutal cold and hard work just to survive was taking its toll on her. John's mind was not on his work, it was on his wife and what the future held for her. Decisions would have to be made before she got sicker. Getting her out of the bush and sending her back to the city was becoming a real possibility.

The first trap John checked yielded a fisher, a small animal but a valuable fur. Continuing on, more fur was collected until they reached the end of the trapline. The last trap held a big surprise, the black wolf with his leg caught. John approached him warily, gun in hand. The wolf was growling and snapping, knowing his end was near. John cast aside his superstitions and with one shot from the rifle, the wolf lay dead. An eerie silence followed. John's thoughts about this wolf were disturbing. Out of respect, and wary of the mythology surrounding this animal, he decided to take its body into the bush and let nature dispose of it, hoping he had not brought a curse upon himself. After this task was completed, the beaver traps were checked, but they yielded no prize. Getting low on rabbit meat, John reset his snares on the way home, and within a short time Bow and John were back at the cabin.

Over the next two days, Jean's condition worsened. She exhibited symptoms of cabin fever, a mental health condition that if not treated could lead to death. She refused to eat, and if left alone might wander off into the frigid cold or burn herself on the stove. The decision was made to call Yellowknife and have her picked up and taken to the hospital to get medical care. John and Bow would be left to finish the season alone.

Preparations were made for a plane to come tomorrow. A nurse would accompany the pilot to take care of Jean until they reached the hospital. John made dinner, put Jean to bed and with great sadness thought about this change of events. The worry over his wife, and the loneliness of not having her here, terrified him. He went to bed, dreading tomorrow when his wife would leave, knowing their dreams were crushed.

Depending on medical advice, new arrangements might have to be made for their future. John drifted off into an uneasy sleep, knowing that morning would come too quickly. His wife would be gone, and he and Bow would be left alone to tackle the daily hardships together. Time would tell how this would work, but John would try to finish what he had started. As a last resort he would pack up and join his wife in Yellowknife, giving up the trapping life forever.

CHAPTER 20

The sound of the plane's engines could be heard as it was getting ready to land. Jean had no idea she was leaving. She was laying under the blankets, looking like a former shell of herself. John went outside and watched as the plane taxied toward the cabin. The pilot and nurse stepped out and made their way to John. A simple greeting was exchanged as they entered. The nurse immediately went to Jean to check on her condition. After a quick examination it was decided a sedative should be administered for her return trip to Yellowknife. John and the pilot would carry Jean to the plane. Her belongings, which John had packed the night before, were loaded first.

Jean, being a petite woman, was moved easily to the plane without incident. John wept, wondering how he was going to make it without her companionship and help. Bow, sensing something was wrong, rubbed against John whining. John watched the plane leave, silence following. He cried as the plane disappeared over the horizon. An overwhelming sense of loneliness enveloped him as he and

Bow made their way back to the cabin. His main concern now was his wife, not his trapline.

A call from John's father confirmed Jean had made it back safely to Yellowknife and was resting comfortably in the hospital. A sense of relief lightened John's spirit, as he knew Jean was receiving the care she needed. He would make it work and would see his wife in the spring when he returned to Yellowknife.

Tomorrow he would get back to his trapline and try to bring some normality back into his life. Sleep did not come easy that night, as thoughts of Jean dominated John's thoughts. He hoped tomorrow would be a better day, allowing him to face a life he had been forced to accept. John finally drifted off to sleep, his faithful companion Bow snuggled next to him. The little cabin in the woods and the trapper's spirit comforted him, as he faced the bitter reality of his life in the bush alone.

CHAPTER 21

John awoke to the sound of water dripping off the roof. During the night, the temperature had risen to forty degrees, melting the snow, and causing the drip. The pilot had mentioned that unusually warm air was on its way to Yellowknife, but he was unsure if it was projected to reach this far north. The warmer weather made John happy. It was uplifting compared to yesterday's tragic events. Climate change had affected the weather here. There were fewer blizzards, shorter periods of prolonged frigid temperatures, and even unheard-of temperature swings, such as what was happening today.

After breakfast, John hooked the sled up to Bow and they were soon on their way down the trail, the trapline their focus again. The warmer weather would increase animal activity, which should be beneficial to the number of animals caught. The first trap yielded an ermine. As they moved down the trapline more animals were caught, including a fox, a marten, a fisher, and another weasel. The beaver traps were empty, so John decided to change their location. The rabbit snares yielded three rabbits, a welcome addition to their meat supply. After finishing their work, the pair started on their way back to the cabin.

As they rounded the last corner on the trail and the cabin came into view, a flood of emotion swept over John. This was where he was going to miss Jean the most, the cabin felt empty without her. He would phone Yellowknife later to check on her health. The sled was unloaded, and John decided to process the furs tomorrow. With Bow following, they returned to the cabin. The outside air was still warm, but the cabin was damp and cold. The woodstove was started to warm the home.

The rabbits were cleaned, and both John and Bow enjoyed a good meal. After dinner, John, using the satellite phone, was able to get information about Jean. She was stable, responding well to medication, and was expected to fully recover. After her release from the hospital Jean would live with her mother who would care for her. Knowing his wife was safe made John happy, but still did not make up for the loneliness he felt without her.

Retiring to bed to read, John remembered he had dropped his book behind the headboard the night before. Reaching down he felt something metal. Pulling it out he realized it was a gold pan. Memories flooded back to him about the legend of Gold Lake. Had the old trapper been panning for gold during the summer months? If he had, he kept it a secret. John put the gold pan aside, found his book and read until he drifted off into a deep sleep, dreaming of panning for gold.

CHAPTER 22

＋ ✦ ✦ ✦ ✦ ✦ ＋

As the weeks went by the steady grind of checking traps, processing furs, and braving the elements kept John and Bow busy. Jean had recovered from her illness and was communicating with John on a regular basis. Their love for one another had been growing stronger with time. The trapping season would soon be over, as March was fast approaching. There was much work to be done before the season ended, and many decisions to be made. The game warden had come and John had been approved for a new license the following year. However, if he was not able to have his wife with him, he probably would not come back.

Returning to the cabin one day after running the trapline, John was surprised to see the message light flashing on his satellite phone. Returning the call, he was shocked to learn that a magazine was interested in writing an article about trapping life. John willingly agreed to participate, looking forward to the activity it would bring. It was agreed a photographer and writer would spend the first week of March with John, staying with him in the cabin. As these men were experienced in winter survival,

John had no concerns with the arrangements. With much excitement, John contacted Jean to let her know of this new development. She wished him the best of luck, looking forward to seeing the magazine spread.

John decided in preparation of the photo shoot, he would reset his beaver traps. He had already caught four beaver this season, his personal limit. However, he hoped to show the journalists his entire trapping operation and figured fresh beaver would make a good meal. He also wanted to clean up the shed to make room for the reporters' gear. When the men arrived, John would keep a fire burning in the shed's woodstove to keep it from getting too cold.

The trapline had produced a lot of fur and this wilderness lifestyle was starting to take a hold of John. He loved running the trapline in fresh snow, with Bow happily breaking new trail. The cold air piercing his lungs, and the beauty, silence and tranquillity of the surroundings brought serenity to John's tortured soul. He now realized what kept old trappers in the bush until their lives ended; they would have it no other way.

Checking his trapline on another beautiful day, John was shocked to find a lynx with its foot caught in one of his traps. The lynx was a beautiful animal with limited numbers living in the bush. As much as John hated to do it, he shot the lynx and loaded its body on the sled. That day held yet another surprise, a young wolverine had lost his short life in a trap, something an older, more experienced animal would have avoided.

John and his dog soon found themselves back at the cabin enjoying the warm fire and eating venison stew filled with the root vegetables the warden had brought for him. John spent the evening reflecting on how much he missed Jean; her companionship, snuggling together to keep warm at night, and their passionate love making, which he longed for the most. Soon he would have all that back.

CHAPTER 23

John awoke to a raging storm going on outside. He would be stuck in the cabin all day if the heavy snow continued. He had been thinking about rearranging the cabin to suit the needs of three men. The journalists would be coming soon, so maybe it was a good day to tackle this job.

After breakfast, with the snow easing somewhat, Bow was let out of the cabin. Howling and barking soon filled the air. John, sensing something was wrong, grabbed his gun and in a moment was facing a wolf pack. They had circled Bow, getting ready to attack. John fired two shots in the air and the wolves quickly dispersed. The brazenness of these wolves surprised him, making John realize these animals posed a danger to him as well as Bow. The wolves would have to be hunted down and shot. He knew where they lived.

After calming down, John got to work. He packed Jean's personal effects and stored them, as well as some un-needed furniture, in the shed. He wanted to clean under the bed, a job that probably had not been done in years. The bed sat on a frame that the trapper had built, with an old rug underneath. John had wanted to discard the rug since he moved here. He moved the bed, being careful not to damage the frame. He removed the rug and immediately took it outside. Sweeping the dirt from where the rug had been, he noticed something unusual. The old trapper had cut out a section of floor and then replaced it, creating a hiding spot concealed by the rug.

The gold pan flashed through John's mind. He wondered if these two discoveries were related. He retrieved a large screwdriver to lift the cut section of floor. Underneath was a cavity that had been dug out, a box now occupying the space. John picked up the box, shocked at this strange chain of events. He opened it and discovered the old trapper's valuables. There was a considerable amount of gold he had apparently panned, bonds he had purchased with his fur money, and old coins, including a 20-dollar gold piece. It also contained the trapper's wedding ring. The trapper had been married for five years and had two daughters. He had left his wife because of his love for the bush. His two daughters lived in Yellowknife, but he had little contact with them because of his strained relationship with their mother.

The box also contained several papers. Looking through them, John found the trapper's last will and testament. He also saw what looked like a hand-drawn map, of a river or creek with X's marked on various sections. The map appeared to indicate where the trapper had found his gold. John returned the box to its hiding place, keeping the will and map out to be studied later. He sat back astonished, not knowing what to do. He would sleep on it and maybe after reading the will he would have a better idea of what the trapper's last wishes were, not knowing another big surprise awaited him.

CHAPTER 24

John awoke with yesterday's memories fresh in his mind. This morning he would check his trapline, collecting the furs that had been caught over the last couple of days. Bounding down the trail with Bow in the lead they came across a dead animal. It was a deer that the wolves had killed and fed on until full. They would be back over the next couple of days to finish this bounty.

This discovery gave John an idea. Tonight, he would be waiting, in hopes that the wolves would return. He would hide a distance from the kill, so as not alert the wolves he was nearby. He had a powerful scope on his rifle, and if the skies were clear there should be enough light to take down at least one wolf.

As spring approached, there seemed to be less fur being trapped. This was probably a result of over trapping. With only two animals caught, Bow and John headed back to the cabin. They picked up two snowshoe rabbits from the snares on their way home. John thought that rabbit was what they would eat for dinner tonight.

After arriving at their destination, the sled was unloaded and everything was put away. The animals caught today would be processed tomorrow, except for the rabbits, which would be thawed on the door of the oven so they could be cleaned and eaten for dinner. For John, the most important event of the day was reading the trapper's will, something he had been thinking about all morning.

John sat on his chair and reached for the envelope that contained the will. He removed it and started reading, "To the finder of this will, all that I have accumulated over my lifetime is now yours. This includes the cabin and the one hundred acres of land adjoining it. My hope is that trapping will continue to be the mainstay of this property." John pondered this, wondering if this discovery should be kept a secret for now, not even telling his wife. It was the decision he made.

After a mid-afternoon dinner, the valuables John had found the day before were retrieved and examined. The gold consisted of small nuggets and powder. It had probably been panned, and there was a sizable amount, weighing close to a pound. There were bonds of various denominations dating back to the late nineteen thirties, some of them being war bonds. There was the twenty-dollar gold piece, and many five- and ten-dollar pieces as well. There were also two rings, one the trapper's wedding ring and the other appeared to be a woman's gold band.

John was unsure what to do with the jewelry. He felt certain if he gave the rings to the trapper's daughters, the will would be contested. He felt it would be better if he did not reveal a will had been found, avoiding all the chaos it might bring. John felt no guilt with this decision, as the daughters had disowned their father twenty-five years before.

CHAPTER 25

John left the cabin before six p.m., hoping to get himself in a good position before the wolves arrived. He figured they would leave their den shortly after nightfall and make their way to the remains of the deer. John would be ready. He positioned himself in a clump of trees about fifty yards from where the wolves would be feeding. Clear skies, using his scope, and the kill being out in the open, gave him a good chance for success. John waited, looking through the scope of his rifle, watching as the wolves exited the woods and made their way to the deer. Through observation, he was able to pick out the new leader, his primary target. If circumstances allowed, he would try for a second shot.

John watched the wolves feed, letting down their guard as feasting dominated their thoughts. Two sharp cracks rang out in quick succession. One wolf went down, the shot killing him on impact. John missed with the second shot, as the remaining four animals ran off into the bush. John approached carefully, making sure the wolf was dead.

Surveying the scene, he noticed a significant blood trail leading off into the woods. He must have wounded the second wolf, and by the amount of blood loss it would soon lose its life. John followed the blood trail, searching for the wounded wolf. He walked only one hundred feet and there was the wolf dead in the snow. John dragged the body to where the other one lay. He headed to the cabin to pick up Bow and the sled.

The bodies were retrieved, with a nervous Bow trying to keep his distance. The animals would be processed in the morning and the remains would be taken back to the wooded area where they had been shot. This should serve as a grim warning as to the fate of the remaining members of the pack if they returned to the cabin. John was happy with the way things had turned out. The other wolves would leave the area. With their numbers down to three, they would look for another pack to join.

John put the wolves in the skinning shed and returned to bed, soon falling into a deep sleep. He would call Jean tomorrow and tell her about the wolf hunt. They would talk further about their plans to spend the summer here together. Jean's heart was longing for her husband. She enjoyed the solitude of living in the bush but knew she would never again be able to spend the winter there. John would come to Yellowknife in less than a month, which seemed like an eternity to Jean.

CHAPTER 26

John stepped outside when he heard the engine of a small plane approaching. He walked to the lake, arriving as the plane landed and taxied toward the cabin. It was the warden completing his last wellness check of the winter. John, happy for human interaction, welcomed him and the pilot with an invitation for coffee. They were much obliged, the three men heading to the cabin. Their conversation turned to the hardships and dangers of the trapping life. John updated them on Jean and shared his adventures with the wolves. In turn, the men told John about their close experience with death. Their plane's engine died, and an emergency landing was made on a wilderness lake. A search and rescue plane was sent from Yellowknife to rescue them. They also told John that two trappers in their district had disappeared this year, apparently, they went missing and had not yet been found.

It was soon time for the men to leave. They left a box of root vegetables with John, which he greatly appreciated. He watched as the plane flew over the horizon and out of sight. This reminded him of Jean's departure, sending a wave of emotion and loneliness through his soul. The men from the production company would be arriving in a few days, which John was looking forward to.

John was not running the trapline until the journalists arrived. He had not been catching many animals, so he wanted to have something in the traps when he took them out on the run. Today, John and Bow would take the beaver traps and reset them. He hoped they would be successful, as this animal was a favorite to photograph and discuss.

On the return trip home from the river, the wind picked up; the makings of a storm was in the air. The snow started in earnest just as they arrived back at the cabin. Putting the sled away, they retired to enjoy the warmth of a roaring fire. John realized that he was lucky to have this cabin, which had served them well this winter.

Just as quickly as it began, the snowstorm abated, leaving clearing skies, a glorious exhibition of the northern lights, and brilliant stars. This always reminded John of the beauty of nature, a display that man could never duplicate. He would catch up in his journal and then read through it, marking the writings he thought might be of interest to the journalists. Tomorrow he would hunt grouse in the morning and fish in the afternoon, assuring a variety of food for his company. John's excitement was mounting about sharing his trapping life, regretting his wife was not here to be part of the story.

Sleep came easy, the silence of the night sending John into a dreamful sleep. He dreamed of his wife, the found treasure, and their reunification. He soon would be back in Yellowknife with Jean, and this life in the bush would seem like a dream, an existence he was not sure would be repeated.

CHAPTER 27

John picked up his shotgun and a box of buckshot and headed out the door. The area where he hunted grouse was about a mile away from the cabin. Using snowshoes made the walk easier in the deep snow, allowing him to reach the cedar bush quickly. Under the cover of the trees, grouse were able to conceal themselves well and a good meal was always within reach. This allowed for large numbers of this bird to congregate in one area. John stepped into the trees and almost instantly two grouse were scared into flight and shot. One hour later four more grouse were in his bag for a total of six, the number he had hoped to shoot. Not being greedy, he decided the hunt had been a success and headed home.

Bow was waiting for him, not happy about being left alone while John was gone. John rewarded him with a venison bone, his favorite snack, for being a patient dog. The birds were cleaned and put in storage. John had lunch and then prepared for the fishing trip. John took Bow, the dog sled, and the ice auger out to the lake, and with some luck they would be eating fish for dinner.

After drilling multiple holes in the ice, John set his lines and was soon hauling in a large number and variety of fish. After two hours of braving the numbing cold wind on the lake, John gathered up the catch and headed for the warmth of the cabin. Bow was looking forward to a dinner of fresh pickerel, his favorite fish to eat.

John spent the remainder of the day preparing for the journalists, who were to arrive tomorrow. He wanted to make sure he was ready and had developed a calendar of activities. Of course, weather would dictate if every item on his list would be accomplished.

The days were getting longer and the sun was growing warmer, melting the snow on the roof of the cabin, causing it to drip and form icicles. When they fell from the roof Bow would immediately pounce on them and lick them like candy until they were gone. John was looking forward to the summer weather, as it seemed he spent most of his time just trying to stay warm. Spring would bring life back to this far northern landscape. Green would prevail, if only for a short time, as winter was the dominant season here, with snow and ice prevailing for up to seven months of the year.

John was looking forward to his weekly phone call with Jean tonight. These conversations helped him cope with being alone, for as much company as Bow was, he could never replace Jean. Darkness was approaching as dinner was served, the fish being delicious. John was in a good mood, speaking with his wife and the thought of company coming tomorrow made him happy. He settled into reading until his eyes would no longer stay open. He was tired as he crawled under the warm blankets on his bed and fell into a deep peaceful sleep.

CHAPTER 28

The sound of a small plane could be heard approaching Gold Lake. John had been waiting since early morning for his company to arrive. He went outside with Bow, the dog being apprehensive, sensing something special was about to happen. The plane landed and taxied to the shoreline. John walked down to the lake to meet the plane and welcomed the two men to his domain. The men introduced themselves, Joe being the photographer, and Bob the journalist. They said they were freelancing for a trapping magazine out of Edmonton, Alberta. Their equipment and supplies were unloaded, and the plane soon took off, on its way back to Yellowknife.

In short order, the non-essential equipment was stored in the shed, while the cameras, which were extremely cold-sensitive, were brought into the cabin. The men entered the structure, looked around, and were happy with their arrangements for the week. The living space would be tight, but they would prevail. John put water on the stove for coffee and they sat around the table, talking, and getting to know one another. The men explained they would take still photographs, and interview John about trapping life, which would be recorded. The men had brought a surprise for John, twenty pounds of beef and five pounds of bacon, a special treat for this trapper.

After lunch, the men joined John on a tour to help them get acquainted with their surroundings. Bow went with them, pulling the sled, in case it was needed. He showed them part of the trapline, and the river where the beaver traps were set. After a two-hour exploratory trip, they arrived back at the cabin. The two men were pleased with the prospect of a successful venture.

They told John of their various adventures, including a story about polar bears in Churchill, Manitoba, and wildlife in Banff National Park, their two favorite assignments. They were looking forward to this experience, as they did not often get to live the life of the person they were interviewing. John gave Bob his journal to read, as it contained details of his adventures of this fall and winter. He told them about Jean getting cabin fever, and how she ended up in a hospital in Yellowknife. The men asked if she had a successful recovery and John, with a smile, told them she was fine, and he was reuniting with her in Yellowknife when the trapping season ended. The men remarked on how cozy the cabin was, and how comfortable John made them feel.

A dinner of venison stew had been prepared the day before and was much appreciated by the visitors, who rarely got to eat such a meal. The full moon shone through the windows of the cabin giving it a light rarely seen at night. The conversation turned to their plans for tomorrow. They would start with the homestead; the cabin, skinning shed, pictures of the fur-bearing animals John had trapped, and the identification of the different species. Bedtime beckoned and with little trouble the men fell into a deep and restful sleep, preparing for a busy day tomorrow.

CHAPTER 29

+ + + + +

The day dawned sunny and mild, a perfect day to start the magazine feature. The story would be called *A Trapper's Life*, about one man's struggle to work and survive in the far north. Joe started by taking detailed pictures of the inside of the cabin. Moving outside, more photographs were taken of the spring, the lake, and the hole that was kept open in the ice to ensure a supply of fresh water. Pictures of the outside of the cabin were taken and Joe would talk to the editor about using one of these pictures for the magazine cover.

Joe moved on to the skinning shed, where photos of John's work areas were taken. It had been decided that when they brought fur back from the trapline, John would demonstrate how furs were processed for Bob. Joe would take more pictures of the animal furs at this time. They moved to the outside freezer where the winter meat was stored. Joe was amazed at the ingenuity of this. Next was the woodshed with its dwindling supply of firewood. Almost forgotten was Bow, a mainstay to keeping this homestead going. Pictures were taken of Bow, hooked up to the sled with John. This picture would be Joe's favorite when the job was done, and they were putting the copy together.

After lunch it was Bob's turn, interviewing John about how he ended up living in the bush. John told the journalist about finding the old trapper and his dog frozen to death in the cabin, and how he and his wife, because of their love for the bush, had decided to continue the old trapper's legacy. He spoke about their dreams being put on hold when depression overwhelmed his wife, and she had to return to Yellowknife. He described his fight with the wolves, but never mentioned the giant footprints he saw around his cabin.

When the interview was complete, they relaxed with some Canadian whiskey, a special treat Bob had brought from Yellowknife. After dinner, fatigue set in and sleep came easy, the effects of the whiskey on the men helping to send them off into an undisturbed slumber.

Work continued in the morning, the day being all about the trapline and collecting the furs. As the three men stopped along the route, Joe took pictures. The traps yielded a special gift, a silver fox, its fur worth its weight in gold. Two martens and a fisher were also added to the catch. Heading to the river, they were in luck, as a beaver had been caught, necessitating more photos to be taken.

They stopped at the emergency shelter for lunch. John explained to the men the value of such a shelter, as it could save one's life if caught in a blizzard far from the cabin. Heading back home, John picked up two snowshoe rabbits that had been caught in his snares. Rabbit would be on the menu tonight. On the way back to the cabin, because of the excess weight, Joe and Bob took turns jogging beside the sled until they reached their destination.

The animals went to the skinning shed, where photos were taken of the variety of furs there, including the beautiful silver fox they had just brought in. After John talked about processing the fur, they retired to the cabin where Bob continued interviewing John until their story was complete. The plane was to pick up the two men in the morning, taking them back to Yellowknife, ending this memorable adventure. A big surprise awaited John tomorrow, once again changing the direction his future would take.

CHAPTER 30

The men were up early. Joe and Bob packed their belongings, ate a hearty breakfast that John prepared, and were now waiting for the plane to arrive. A feeling of loneliness washed over John as he realized his company would soon be gone and he would be alone again. The trapping season would be over in a week, and there was much work to be done before ending the season and returning to Yellowknife.

The sound of a small plane could be heard in the distance. Soon it landed and was making its way to the landing where John and the men were waiting. The plane stopped, shut off its engines and the people on board disembarked. In shock and disbelief John's emotions took over, there was his wife. They flew into each other's arms hugging tightly, tears flowing freely, as their love for one another brought about feelings that overpowered them.

Jean had hatched this plan one evening while longing for her husband. Her family helped convince her to go, as she had made a complete recovery and the cold dark winter season would soon be over. She thought that returning to the cabin would be beneficial, not only for her emotional well-being, but also as a help to John who would be packing up for the season.

Good-byes were said and soon the plane was gone, leaving the couple together and alone. Hand-in-hand they returned to the cabin with a happy Bow in tow. To John the events that had just taken place were more like a dream than reality. The couple were soon on the bed and long desired passion took over. Except to get up and eat the fried chicken Jean had brought as a special treat for John, bed was where they stayed until the next morning.

John woke with his wife asleep beside him. He pulled her close and hugged her gently, not wanting to let go, his emotions overwhelmed with love for her. The bright sun shone in through the window, filling the cabin with a warmth that matched his feelings of having his wife back with him.

Jean had also brought eggs, bread, and potatoes with her, and with the bacon left by his recent company John was able to make a homestyle breakfast in the wilderness. During this meal, the couple discussed all that had happened since Jean's departure. However, John kept the biggest secret of all, the hidden box, until after dinner.

The weather was changing. It was early March, and the most intense cold was behind them. The Increased daylight and a warmer sun meant more snow would melt. The furs would have to be taken to Yellowknife soon to avoid spoilage, especially if the weather got too warm. John was worried about his wood supply. He assumed they would spend another trapping season here. Trees had to be cut, limbed, and left to dry over the summer, ensuring them enough fuel to get through another winter. This was a trapper's biggest and most important undertaking.

The couple decided to tackle the woodcutting, and after a backbreaking day of work they returned to the cabin and ate dinner. John presented Jean with the box, telling her to open it. With a gasp she stared at the contents, speechless. John handed her the will which she read, a flood of emotion taking over. She hugged John tightly, knowing what was in this box would change their lives.

John explained this had to be a secret between them, as they did not want this to become gossip in Yellowknife. Jean agreed, once again hugging John tightly. Sleep came easily, as the couple enjoyed the comfort of being together. Tomorrow decisions about their future would be made, but for now sleep would rule.

CHAPTER 31

Jean awoke, it was the middle of the night, and she was sure she had heard something outside. She woke up John just as the doorknob rattled. It was as if somebody was trying to open it. Bow was at the door, a low growl emanating from his throat. John was now fully awake, and in silence they listened for more activity, but there was none. The large footprints John had seen outside the cabin earlier in the winter came to mind. Had the bigfoot returned? Without John saying a word, Jean knew that was what he was thinking. She snuggled into John as he hugged her tightly, making her feel safe. They both went back to sleep, not to awaken again till morning.

The smell of breakfast cooking greeted Jean's senses as she awoke. Her thoughts turned to last night, wondering if their suspicions were correct. During breakfast the couple discussed following the bigfoot's tracks, taking Bow with them. They were curious if they would lead to one of the caves that dotted the area. With some hesitation Jean agreed, not sure how she would react if they actually saw the creature.

They set out on snowshoes, following the prints at the back of the cabin directly into the forest. John carried his shotgun in case they saw some grouse, as fresh fowl would be good for dinner. Following the tracks to higher ground, they stopped briefly to admire the panoramic view. After another hour of walking, they decided to turn around and go home, fearful bad weather could blow in. Two hours later, they were back at the cabin, with two grouse in their bag. They warmed their feet on the oven door of the woodstove discussing their plans about packing up and getting their furs back to Yellowknife.

John and Jean decided they would ship their furs to the auction in North Bay for the May sale. Then they would go to Edmonton to sell the items from the trapper's box, if a reputable dealer could be found. They would come back to the cabin for the summer if they made enough of a profit.

The following day, the traps were picked up, cleaned, and stored for the summer. The emergency shelter was sealed tight to keep out unwanted animals. The couple spent a few days cleaning the cabin and securing any foodstuffs. John arranged for the plane to come and pick them up.

Their last night at the cabin came quickly. Jean had brought a bottle of wine for the occasion, to celebrate a successful trapping season. When the bottle was empty, they went to bed, both excited and nervous about leaving in the morning.

CHAPTER 32

John and Jean were packed and waiting for the plane to arrive from Yellowknife. There was little conversation as they both reflected on their experiences in the bush. The sound of the plane approaching startled them back to the present as it circled the small lake and landed. They were soon loading the plane with the furs and their personal gear. John had retrieved thirty pounds of venison from the freezer, left over from the last deer he shot. He planned to give some to the pilot and the rest would go to family and friends in town. The pilot readied the plane for takeoff. With a roar from the engine the plane sped down the lake, lifting gracefully into the air, giving the passengers a breathtaking view.

The cabin and Gold Lake soon disappeared, leaving John and Jean with only memories. Holding hands tightly, they wondered what the future held for them. They were unsure they would return for another trapping season but knew they would spend the summer here. They would try to find the areas on the map the trapper had left and pan for gold. John would construct a sluice box from materials bought in Yellowknife. Over the course of the summer, they would decide about their winter plans.

The two-hour plane ride was uneventful and soon the city came into view. The small plane made a smooth landing and taxied to its hangar. John's father met them and was going to help them take the furs to the exchange. There they would be evaluated for quality and shipped to the auction.

John hugged his father tightly; he had missed him greatly. Unbeknown to John, his father was going to try to talk him out of returning to the cabin this winter. He loved his son and worried constantly about him being alone, knowing one minor mishap could result in his death.

Jean, John, and his dad loaded the contents from the plane into his truck. Everyone was happy except for Bow, who would have preferred staying at the cabin. He hated the city, missing the freedom to run he had at the lake. He wondered about his future, which hopefully would not be at the end of a chain. The furs were unloaded at the exchange. In about a week, they would receive an advance payment for the pelts, with more money coming after the auction.

They drove to the storage unit where the couple's car had been left. Having their own vehicle would prove to be an asset while in Yellowknife. John's father, who had a large house, had offered to let them stay there while they were in town. John's mother and his two sisters were there to welcome them home upon their arrival. His sisters jokingly said they did not recognize him because of the beard he had grown. Happy conversations followed until dinnertime. John's mom had made his favorite meal, meatloaf, mashed potatoes, and carrots, with chocolate cake for dessert.

The family visited a while longer, and after having a night cap, John and Jean retired to their bedroom for some privacy and a discussion about what to do with the valuables. The gold would be put in a safety deposit box and the bonds and coins would be sold in Edmonton. Being mentally and physically exhausted, they collapsed into bed and slept fitfully until the morning light signaled the start of another day.

CHAPTER 33

John and Jean showered, dressed, and made their way downstairs. John's mother offered to make them breakfast. After eating a light meal of toast, served with hot coffee, John and Jean left for the bank to open a safety deposit box. They then went to the gun shop to buy a twenty-two-caliber rifle, for shooting small game such as rabbits and squirrels. During the summer they would have to harvest fresh meat at the cabin. Along with fish caught from the lake, root vegetables, and canned food from Yellowknife, they would have no problem feeding themselves over the summer.

The couple were already anxious to return to the bush; life in Yellowknife now seemed foreign to them. Neither John nor Jean had slept well. They were kept awake by the noise coming from the street. John's dad lived close to a network of roads that had sprung up around him in the last twenty years. The couple preferred the silence and tranquillity of their cabin.

It was mid-April, and the signs of spring were everywhere. This was the first warmer weather Yellowknife had experienced in a long time. John looked skyward letting the warm sun hit his face, bringing life back to his tired soul. The cold was hard on the human body, aging it years ahead of its time.

They next went to the fabric shop to purchase material for new curtains. Jean felt it was time to replace the original ones the trapper had put up in the cabin. Jean and John had arranged to meet friends at their favorite burger joint. They were happy to see the couple they had met years earlier, with whom they had a lot in common. Their conversation centered around Jean and John's adventures in the bush. John shared their experiences with Bigfoot. The friends told John other friends of theirs had had their own encounter with this creature while hiking in the wilderness.

After lunch John and Jean went for a drive and then returned home and relaxed for the rest of the day.. The week flew by, and it was soon time to go pick up their check from the fur exchange. The prices were good, with the couple making a little over five thousand dollars. John was happy with this, especially because of the small number of traps he had put out.

The last thing Jean and John needed to do before they could return to the cabin was travel to Edmonton to sell their bonds and coins. John had found a reputable dealer who would look at their valuables, and if interested make them an offer. Reservations were made for both the flights and a hotel stay. They planned to shop for new clothing and boots, as well as enjoy some vacation time. After retiring to bed early and reading, their eyes soon became heavy and they both drifted off to sleep, thinking about their upcoming trip tomorrow.

CHAPTER 34

John and Jean ate a big breakfast, knowing they would be offered little food on the airplane. John's father had agreed to take them to and from the airport so John could avoid paying for airport parking. After saying goodbye to John's mother and Bow, who had taken up residence in John's parents' house, they left for the airport. After arriving they said their farewells to John's dad and parted company. With excitement mounting they found their gate, and after a short wait were seated on the plane. They became engrossed in conversation about the next three days they would be spending in Edmonton.

The two-hour plane ride went smoothly, and as the Edmonton airport is not large, they had no trouble grabbing a bite to eat and picking up their rental car. John had booked a Holiday Inn close to the airport, making it easy to find. After checking in, they laid down in the bed, where they stayed until dinnertime. Finally, getting up they decided to find a good Chinese buffet for dinner. Edmonton had a reputation for good Chinese food, which neither John nor Jean had eaten in a long time. The front desk clerk told them about a place close to the hotel, which turned out to be an excellent choice. With stomachs full, they returned to their room and watched TV, and within a short time they were both asleep and did not awaken till the alarm went off the next morning.

The couple made their way to the hotel breakfast room where they enjoyed coffee and Danish. Today they had an appointment with the dealer who was going to appraise their coins and bonds. They left the hotel and went directly to his office, growing anxious as they pulled into the parking lot. John clutched the bag of valuables as they headed to the office of Jack Spade, a well-known and credible buyer of old coins, paper money, bonds, and valuable political signatures.

Mr. Spade examined the articles closely. He had good news. The twenty-dollar gold piece was uncirculated, making it worth upwards of twenty thousand dollars. John and Jean were both shocked, having no idea the coin would be that valuable. The rest of the items were collectively appraised at nearly thirty thousand dollars. Mr. Spade offered them thirty thousand dollars for everything, knowing he would easily turn a profit. They gratefully accepted the offer and within two hours the money was transferred to their bank account in Yellowknife.

Jean and John decided that since they were downtown, they would take a ride on the High Level Bridge Streetcar and explore Old Strathcona. There they stopped in a few shops, admired the art, and had lunch in a small café. Returning to their hotel in the late afternoon, they opted to skip dinner and relax in their room for the evening.

Jean and John both awoke before sunrise. Today they were headed to the Edmonton mall to purchase new coats and boots, as well as anything else they might need for life at the cabin. John bought a new chainsaw and ice auger, not trusting the trapper's twenty-year-old models. These he had shipped to his parents' home. They took their other purchases with them. They stopped at the local U-Haul store and picked up packing supplies to ship these items to Yellowknife.

After dropping the boxes at the post office, they returned to the Chinese buffet, knowing it might be a while before they would enjoy this privilege again. After dinner, John and Jean returned to their room and packed for their return flight, capping off a successful trip. Their dreams of getting back to the cabin, would soon become a reality.

CHAPTER 35

Early morning found John and Jean at the airport waiting for their flight back to Yellowknife. Their plane had been delayed and was not expected to leave for at least an hour. They had arrived late at the airport due to a long wait at the rental car office. Because of the flight delay they now had time for breakfast. Finding a quiet spot, they purchased and ate their food, discussing their return to the cabin.

They had decided to sell their gold and put the cash into their bank account. It would be sold in Yellowknife, as gold brokers dominated the city. Many prospectors lived in the area, bringing their riches to cash in at these businesses. The plane arrived as they were finishing up breakfast, and soon they were in the air. In what seemed like a short time, their hometown came into view.

As the pilot was making his final approach, he aborted the landing. The landing gear had failed to lock into position. The plane circled the airport, the pilot trying again to get the wheels down but to no avail. The plane was relatively small, carrying only seventy passengers and crew. An emergency landing would be imminent.

A sense of panic gripped the airplane. John and Jean held hands tightly, not knowing how this would end. They prayed to God for a miracle. On their final approach, the pilot tried once again to lock the landing gear down and it worked perfectly, their prayers answered. The people waiting on the ground, including John's father, let out a cheer when they learned the plane had safely landed.

After placing their bags in the truck, the three drove back to the house in silence. The events of the last hour overwhelmed their thoughts and made them realize how quickly life can change. Jean's worst fear was losing John, and the thought of him being by himself in the wilderness was one of her greatest worries. She would not be willing to leave him alone again after what happened on the plane.

The following day John and Jean took their gold to a reputable dealer; it weighed fifteen ounces and brought them about twelve thousand dollars. This money was deposited into their bank account. They planned on returning to their cabin at the end of May. They were organizing what would be needed for gold panning and sluicing; gathering and packing their supplies so they could be flown to the cabin. As in the past, there would be two full loads.

The ice was finally out of the lake, allowing them to set a date to leave. They were ready, having reserved a plane the week before. They were to leave in the morning. Sleep came easy and their dreams were pleasant. Tomorrow would bring a big change in their lives again, one they were looking forward to, a summer together in a place they loved.

CHAPTER 36

————— ✦✦✦✦✦ —————

John and Jean arrived at the airport early. They met the pilot, who was happy to see them again. After the plane was loaded, they made their way down the runway and were soon in the air. Silence filled the aircraft, only the sounds of the engine could be heard, as everyone seemed to be caught up in their own thoughts. The pilot informed John they would soon be reaching their destination. Within minutes the cabin came into view, and a safe landing was made on the lake. The pilot taxied to the landing, parked, and shut off the engine. The first one out was Bow, who instantly ran for the cabin, sniffing and marking his territory. The other occupants proceeded to unload the plane, piling all the belongings and supplies on the shoreline. With a farewell, the pilot left promising to return in a week with the rest of their load.

John and Jean watched as the plane disappeared, leaving them alone once again in this vast wilderness. They made their way to the cabin, removed the bear protection from the door and entered. A fire was made in the stove, and soon the chill was gone, replaced by a warmth that was more familiar to them. Their supplies were brought from the lake and stored in their rightful places, and then a late lunch was served.

Time was spent around the cabin, Jean putting up the new curtains she had made and John re-chinking any gaps that appeared in the logs over the winter. They decided after their chores were finished they would take the canoe and go for a ride on the lake. They had bought a new camera and wanted to start keeping a record of their life at Gold Lake. These photos, along with John's journal, would someday be a helpful when he wrote his planned book.

The lake was calm; paddling along the shoreline they observed ducks, beaver, osprey, and an eagle. Out further in the lake a loon could be heard calling. Silence surrounded the canoe, only the paddles splashing in the water could be heard. After spending time in the city, this was a welcome change for both John and Jean.

As twilight approached, they made their way back to the cabin to prepare dinner and let Bow get some exercise before dark. The days were getting longer as spring was slowly advancing toward summer. After dinner John studied the map the trapper had left. He figured it was about a two hour walk to the site. Tomorrow they would pack a lunch and try to follow the route, making a day of it. They had purchased camping gear in Edmonton and hoped to spend some time tenting this summer. Tomorrow would come early, so bed was in order. Soon the silence of the forest was lulling them to sleep.

CHAPTER 37

Jean was up early making sandwiches with bread she had brought from Yellowknife, a treat that would soon be a memory. John packed the rest of the gear and supplies they would need. Soon they were ready to go, the three of them heading out. Their hike took them through forests and meadows, which were turning green after a long winter's sleep. The walk was uneventful, and within a few hours the sound of water could be heard. Arriving at the river, they noticed the water was high and moving fast. John thought that in another week the water levels would drop, allowing them to use their gold pans. Today, they would walk along the river exploring the shoreline.

John and Jean thought they had found the trapper's favorite spot to pan, as it was marked with a double "x" on the map. They also found the two other areas indicated on the map and explored them. It was decided they would eventually camp near the first spot they had come upon, as that part of the river was perfect for the sluice box and provided large areas for panning.

A spring was found nearby which would provide an ample supply of fresh water. The biggest discovery was a cave close to the sight, obviously used by the trapper, as remnants of a fireplace and numerous empty food cans littered the area. John surmised it would be a place they would utilize during their summer adventure.

A large, hollow tree nearby was occupied by a mother porcupine and her two babies. Showing no fear of their visitors, these animals would provide entertainment for John and Jean. However, Bow would have to be watched closely as their quills can be painful and cause infection. They found a suitable area for their tent close to the fresh water source and cave. Satisfied they could learn no more here, they headed back to the cabin.

On their walk back, they spotted a deer with her fawn, the fawn being young and unsteady on its feet. John thought about having to harvest a deer if he planned to stay over the winter, glad to see a healthy population in the area. The cabin soon came into view, the raven on the rooftop letting them know he was glad to see them back, as his treats were greatly missed.

The next few days passed quickly. John worked on repairing a wheeled cart that Bow could pull in the summer. Jean thoroughly cleaned the cabin. They fished in the lake and gathered fiddleheads, young ferns that are delicious. The couple also found time to relax and enjoy the serenity of the bush, glad to be away from the city and its inhabitants who seemed to live in a constant state of turmoil. The peace and quiet allowed them to feel as one with God.

Tomorrow the rest of their supplies were to arrive. Hopefully these would take care of their needs for the summer. Another unexpected discovery would shock them, once more changing their thoughts about was going on here.

CHAPTER 38

The sound of an airplane could be heard approaching; John went outside just as the plane was landing on the lake. With Jean in tow, they made their way to meet the pilot and retrieve their supplies. They quickly unloaded the plane after the pilot told them he had an emergency at home. His wife had radioed on his way here. Their daughter had fallen and broken her arm. She was fine; her arm was being put in a cast at the hospital. She was expected to be released and should be at home when he returned. With handshakes, and wishes of good luck on both sides, the pilot left and soon the plane was out of sight.

The supplies were moved to the cabin and skinning shed, including the materials for the sluice box, which would be constructed on site. The rest of the day was spent packing and getting ready to move supplies to their gold panning site. They were planning on leaving in the morning to set up camp near the river.

John and Jean left early, Bow pulling the cart full of supplies. They decided to forego the tent and use the cave as their shelter. Among their supplies were the sluice box kit, a small gas burner, some butane cylinders, and sleeping bags. John's father had sent some beef and home-baking, which were also included. They had brought some larger pieces of wood with them but would gather more firewood near the cave. They planned to build their campfire outside the opening, tying Bow up there in the evenings. This would allow him to give the couple fair warning if danger approached.

The day was sunny and warm, the trip to the cave taking a couple of hours. They unloaded their supplies and got to work. Jean set up camp while John assembled the sluice box. After the work was done, they ate lunch and relaxed in the solitude of the moment, drifting off to sleep in the warm sunshine. The couple were awakened by Bow's barking. He had caught sight of the two baby porcupines. John and Jean loved nature and were happy to have these prickly creatures as their neighbours.

John thought they should hike up the river to see if they could find other spots suitable for panning. The water was still high, therefore identifying appropriate areas was difficult. After a long walk over rough terrain, they realized the preferred spot of the trapper was the best, with a flat open area, easy to maneuver around in. Returning to their camp, they prepared for dinner and set up their campfire.

Moving the wood from the cart to the fireplace, John noticed an anomaly in one of the logs. It appeared an area of rot in the center had been removed. Upon further inspection he found an old canvas bag containing another bag of gold dust and nuggets. The couple could not believe their eyes, so thankful they did not burn this piece of wood in the fire.

The old trapper had obviously thought this was a secure place for his gold, being at the bottom of his now depleted wood pile. John wondered if there were more hidden gold they would unexpectedly find.

The couple ate dinner, started the campfire, and enjoyed the evening. Countless stars filled the night sky as they listened to the river's water hitting the rocks on its journey to the lake and the crackling of the fire. Tiredness soon swept over the couple, sending them into their sleeping bags and a peaceful night's sleep. Tomorrow would bring more adventure, but not the kind they hoped for.

CHAPTER 39

The sounds of the songbirds singing and the chattering of the chipmunks woke John early. He pulled himself off the hard floor of the cave, struggling to get his legs moving. He stoked the coals of the fire and added more wood. The mornings were usually cool this far north, even in summer. After warming himself by the fire, John decided it was time to get Jean up, prepare breakfast, and return to the cabin. Bow's cart would have to be left here because of a flat tire. They would return tomorrow to fix it and retrieve the cart. They each packed a backpack, and John took his rifle, starting the walk back to the cabin with Bow leading the way.

An hour into their journey they rounded a corner, and there, not fifty feet away, was a mother bear and her two cubs. Instinct took over leading the bear to charge, the safety of the cubs her only priority. Unfortunately, Bow, feeling the same way, charged at the bear. The bear stopped, rose on its hind legs, and with a hard slap of its paw sent Bow flying. John was shocked, but his reaction was fast. Just as the bear was about to pounce on Bow, he fired two shots in quick succession, driving the bear away, saving Bow's life.

Bow was whimpering, not so much from being hurt, but from being scared. Further examination revealed no major injuries, only a scratch to his shoulder, which they would treat when they got back to the cabin. It had been a close call, making John and Jean realize they could have easily lost Bow, which would be devastating. It served as a reminder to always be aware of their surroundings, and never let their guard down.

The trio soon reached the cabin and found a note on the door from the ranger who visited last winter. He had stopped by to see how they were doing, having been informed that John and Jean were spending the summer here. John was surprised, and sorry they had missed him. They started a fire in the woodstove and laid a blanket out for Bow, who was still shaking from his encounter with the bear. Jean tended to his wound, putting antibiotic on it to starve off any infection.

The couple ate lunch and took a nap, sleeping until the raven's piercing call woke them. The bird was an annoyance more so than a pet, and John knew if he did not feed him, he would not stop with this noise. As John fed the bird some of Bow's dog food, he noticed how beautiful the lake was, prompting him to get Jean and go fishing in the canoe. Fresh fish for dinner would be a treat.

They were soon paddling the shoreline enjoying the beautiful scenery and peacefulness. After an hour of leisure time, they turned their attention to fishing and within a half an hour had enough fish for dinner. They ate their fish and enjoyed a bottle of wine they had brought from Yellowknife. It was an early night. The day's trauma emotionally drained the couple causing them to sleep soundly till morning.

CHAPTER 40

John awoke thinking about the phone call he had received from his father last night. The trapper's daughters had gotten wind that John and Jean were using his cabin and they wanted them out. They claimed it was rightfully theirs, as the trapper's only offspring. John's father surmised the trapper had claimed crown land as his own, and there had never been a legal deed to the property. In the past, the government overlooked cabins built on such land, but perhaps they should engage an attorney to look into the matter. John asked his father to proceed, but still did not reveal the existence of the trapper's will.

The new day was full of worry, John and Jean now not knowing whether they would even be able to stay on the land. They hoped a lawyer would be able to give them some answers. A walk to the cave to fix the tire on the cart and bring it back home would hopefully take their minds off their troubles. They kept telling themselves everything would work out. A plan was forming in John's head, but he would wait to get the lawyer's report before he acted on it.

The walk was pleasant and the cart was fixed. Before heading back, the couple ate lunch on the riverbank and enjoyed watching the water as it flowed over the rocks toward the lake. As Jean stared into the water, she caught a glimpse of a yellow flash. Without thinking she reached in and pulled up what appeared to be tiny gold nugget. John examined it carefully, confirming that was exactly what it was. The couple wondered if this incident was a fluke, or an example of what was to come when they started panning.

Feeling better than when they left the cabin, the couple headed back, stopping on the way to pick edible plants to enjoy with dinner. Until John was able to kill fresh game, they were eating canned meat and vegetables, making anything fresh a treat. The cabin came into view and when approaching, they noticed deer tracks in the front yard. There seemed to be an abundance of deer, which would provide valuable meat this winter, if John were to stay. Darkness descended on the little cabin in the woods, a relic of the past, and a hope for the future.

CHAPTER 41

The next week was spent cutting firewood and hauling it to the woodshed. One hundred carts of wood were moved from the bush. As the wood needed further drying, they would split it in the fall. Living in the north, this was one of the hardest, but most important jobs. Running out of wood during the winter meant spending your days trying to find enough fuel to keep warm, not allowing time for anything else. Declaring this job done for now, John and Jean's attention shifted back to the gold panning. They wondered if the water levels had dropped sufficiently for them to start working. They decided to return to the site tomorrow and spend the night.

The following day dawned sunny and warm and the trip to the site, which they had named Gold Creek, was uneventful. The water levels had dropped enough to allow them to set up their sluice box and try some panning. Hopefully, a fortune was to be made. They ate lunch and had a short rest, then went to prepare the sluice box. Through trial and error, they finally figured out how to work it. The first few buckets of dirt showed nothing for their trouble, but the fifth bucket yielded gold flakes and one small nugget. The afternoon wore on, but the rewards were few. Tomorrow John would move the sluice box to a different location, and they would try panning for gold. Giving up for the day, and before it got much later, they decided to explore the cave they slept in.

The couple had bright flashlights to allow them to see anything unusual. This was a large cave system, with numerous rooms and tunnels, which they soon discovered. After crawling through a tight space, they entered a large room. Standing up, they shone their flashlights around and were surprised to see signs of humans having been here, an old jacket lay in the corner, tin cans, even a full can of beans. Realizing this was going nowhere, they returned outside, started a fire and prepared dinner. They had bought a bag of marshmallows and some chocolate in Yellowknife to make s'mores, a treat John and Jean enjoyed immensely. Canned meat and beans were for dinner, with even Bow indulging.

The campfire provided much needed comfort, as the uncertainty about the cabin's status troubled them greatly. Maybe John would hear from his dad soon, hopefully with good news. The s'mores were delicious and soon the campfire burned low, sending them to bed.

Around midnight Bow started barking loudly, warning them of imminent danger. John grabbed his rifle and rushed to the front of the cave just as a loud crashing could be heard running off in the forest. John praised Bow for his actions and returned to bed, telling his wife it was probably a bear. John was puzzled, as it sounded more like a person crashing through the forest than a bear. He would sleep on it and investigate further tomorrow.

The full moon shone on the river making it shine like a jewel yet to be discovered. Soon this magic would disappear, as another day of life prevailed. Now, a sound and peaceful sleep overtook them, leaving their worries for another time.

CHAPTER 42

John awoke at dawn, the bird activity and the sound of the river reminding him where he was. It was going to be a hot day. The warm air caressed John's face as he stood in the cave opening, a rare event this early in the morning. John woke Jean, having a good feeling about what the day was to bring. The events of last night returned to his head, drawing him to the area where he had heard the crashing. His search for broken limbs or hair left on a branch, offered nothing that proved what type of animal had been there. Beans and bread, that Jean had baked at the cabin, were served for breakfast; the chickadees begging for any unwanted crumbs. After finishing eating, they returned to the river to move the sluice box to a different area.

The first pail of dirt was put through the sluice box and two small nuggets were found; gold fever was now affecting the couple. The second and third pail revealed gold flake, and by the end of their day the couple had accumulated about a half-ounce of gold, making them feel successful. Since it was getting on in the afternoon, John and Jean decided to pack up and return to the cabin, hoping to go out in the canoe and fish before dark. As the summer progressed the days grew longer, with daylight lasting until eleven p.m..

Arriving at the cabin they were greeted by the waiting raven. With nonstop screeching he let them know how he felt about them leaving, and that he was hungry and wanted to be fed. John regretted ever starting to feed the bird, now wishing he would just find a girlfriend and go away. The supplies they took to Gold Creek were put away, Bow was put in the cabin, and the canoe was readied for their excursion. A short time later Jean and John were on the water, only the paddles could be heard quietly propelling the canoe forward. A feeling of peace and solitude came over them, making them forget anything else in life existed in this moment, except for their love for one another. With little effort six fish were caught, which would provide them with a nice dinner and a treat for Bow.

Returning to the cabin, John wrote in his journal while Jean cleaned and prepared the fish for dinner. Bow slept soundly on the new rug by the bed. John was keeping his gold in the trapper's original hiding place under the bed and out of sight. There had been rare incidents of thieves coming by plane in the summer, looking for empty cabins to break into and stealing anything of value they could find.

John, waiting to hear from his father, checked his satellite phone and found a missed call marker; it was his father. He would return the call tomorrow, hoping he would have good news. Anxiety and worry returned, as John and Jean went to bed. They were hopeful that what they heard tomorrow would solve their biggest problems. Sleep overtook them and dreams of gold dominated their thoughts, but reality would catch up with them soon, as news from John's father was revealed.

CHAPTER 43

John was up early, nervous about what his father was to tell him. He cooked breakfast, rousted Jean out of bed and fed Bow. When done, he reached for the phone, and soon was talking to his dad, who said that he had met with a lawyer. The attorney had completed research, and the land that the trapper claimed as his own was not his. It was crown land owned by the government, which issued licenses for trapping wild fur. The trapper could renew this license annually for his lifetime. Upon his death, his immediate family would gain possession of the license, which they could choose to give to other family members. A recent change in the laws regarding live animal trapping for fur, which was slowly being eliminated by the government, would limit the renewal of this license to a five-year period. At that time, ownership of the cabin and land would return to the territory and trapping would not be allowed.

The lawyer met with the trapper's daughters, explaining the circumstances to them. The trapping license was the only thing of value, as their father did not own the land. The daughters, who had no interest in trapping, decided to sign the license over to Jean and John without compensation. Little did they know that a gracious thank you and a monetary gift would be given to them for their generosity. John and Jean were jubilant about how things had turned out. Even if they did not trap, but merely renewed the license, they would have access to the cabin for the next five years.

A date was set to meet the trapper's daughters at the Ministry's office to complete the transfer paperwork. John made reservations for the plane to pick them up tomorrow, taking them to Yellowknife, where they would spend a couple days with family and tend to their business. The rest of the day was spent getting ready for tomorrow's trip. John and Jean decided to return the trapper's wedding rings to the daughters, along with a check for five thousand dollars. They knew if they trapped it would only be for one more year but having the rights to the land during the summer was a priority.

Morning came early and the sound of the plane's arrival greeted them. It taxied to the landing, their belongings were loaded, and they were soon in the air making their way to Yellowknife. Conversation in the plane was robust, which seemed to make the trip shorter, as they were soon landing, and John's dad was greeting them. They paid the pilot and went on their way, stopping for a lunch of hamburgers and French fries, a treat they had not enjoyed in a long time and one Bow greatly appreciated. Arrangements had been made to meet at the Ministry offices tomorrow to finalize the transfer of the license. The rest of the day would be spent at with John's parents. His sisters were coming to visit, and they would have dinner together this evening.

The events of the last twenty-four hours occupied John's thoughts. The sooner this matter was taken care of, and he could get back to his little cabin in the woods, the better. Dinner went well. It was followed by an after-dinner liqueur and a few games of cards. Bedtime soon arrived, leaving Jean and John wondering if tomorrow would bring an easy ending to what could have been a difficult situation. Their minds drifted as sleep overtook them, and they did not wake until the bright sun shone in the window, helping them clear their minds for another day.

CHAPTER 44

The morning found the young couple at the Ministry's office. The trapper's daughters were already there and greeted John and Jean graciously. All necessary legal documentation was presented, and the trapping license was legally signed over to John and Jean, making them the sole owners of the trapping rights and the use of the cabin for four more years. The previous year, when John had used the cabin, was included in the five-year renewal period. It was decided they would all go to breakfast together and get caught up on old news. The trapper's daughters were shocked when John presented them with their parents' wedding rings and a check for five-thousand dollars, this being the last thing they expected. They parted company, their stomachs full and their spirits high, wishing each other well. This was a perfect ending for everyone involved.

After breakfast, John and Jean went shopping for supplies to take back to the cabin, mostly food related favorites like sandwich bread, cooked meat, fresh fruit, and chocolate to name a few. They had reserved a plane for the morning and were looking forward to getting back to their cabin and their undisturbed lifestyle. They had sold the gold they brought with them, and the money was deposited into their bank account.

John planned a special gift for Jean, a diamond ring they could not afford when they got married. They went to the mall where John steered her into the jewellery store. He got on one knee and jokingly begged her to let him buy the most beautiful ring in the store. Jean rushed into his arms, crying on his shoulder, and holding him tightly, not believing this moment. She proudly wore her new ring as they left the store. They went to show Jean's mother the ring before they returned to John's parents' house.

The next morning came quickly and after breakfast they found themselves at the airport loading their belongings into the airplane and saying good-bye to John's dad. They would be back to purchase their winter supplies in two months, so they would see him soon. Shortly after takeoff the pilot asked a favor from his passengers. He had a part to deliver to another trapper that was living on a lake a lot like their own. The man had been patiently waiting for two weeks, as the part had to be shipped from Edmonton. The trapper also loved company and would be surprised and happy to see John and Jean.

They were soon landing on a little lake and taxiing up to where a cabin could be seen through the trees. An old, grizzled man met them, excited to see other people, as he lived alone year-round. His name was Jack and he had been living this lifestyle for thirty years. He Invited everyone to his cabin for tea, which was brewed from a plant known for its medicinal qualities. Jack said his greens came from the forest, and he believed they were responsible for keeping him from having to visit a doctor for all the years he lived here. After a quick tour of the property, they headed back to the plane and were soon in the air heading to Gold Lake. In what seemed like only minutes they were landing and heading toward their cabin.

Jean and John unloaded the floatplane with the pilot's help. They then wished the pilot well, said goodbye and made their way to the cabin. The welcoming committee was there, the raven telling them how happy he was to see them home. John's annoyance at this bird was building. He was hatching a plan to capture him, take him to Yellowknife on the next trip and release him at the airport.

They entered the cabin, lit a fire, and relaxed; John started reading and Jean was knitting with the new wool she had purchased in Yellowknife. A large weight had been lifted from their shoulders, knowing a major problem in their life had been resolved. The cabin now was theirs to enjoy as their legal home. Darkness fell and the forest turned black, the silence deafening, only the loon from the lake could be heard calling. John and Jean snuggled in their bed, glad to be home. Their sleep was peaceful until a disturbing incident woke them in panic, something that would be talked about for years to come.

CHAPTER 45

John awoke to the sound of a small aircraft engine, just as it was growing light outside. Although it was not unusual to hear these bush planes, it was not normal to hear the engine sputtering and failing. John woke Jean and informed her that it sounded like a small plane with engine problems was about to make a crash landing, probably in the lake. They threw on their clothes and rushed outside just as the plane hit the water, sending pieces of the aircraft flying in all directions. John's first reaction was to phone in the location of the accident, not knowing if the pilot had been able to do so.

The couple jumped in the canoe and made their way to the crashed plane. The cockpit was underwater and there was a man clinging to the tail of the plane, apparently in shock.. They transferred him to the canoe. Not seeing anyone else, they returned to the cabin, wrapping a blanket around the shivering man, and offering him coffee. He soon started to regain his senses, telling John the pilot had hit his head on impact, knocking him unconscious. He was still in the pilot's seat as the plane sunk into the lake. The passenger was not hurt and was able to escape the plane before suffering the same fate.

There was a buzz of activity outside, a search and rescue plane, a helicopter and a RCMP aircraft all arrived at the scene. The front yard of the cabin became a hub of activity, as it was being used as a staging area for the recovery efforts. The dive team recovered the body of the pilot, taking it to Yellowknife for an autopsy. The passenger was transferred to the hospital to be treated for his minor injuries. By early evening everyone had left, only the half-submerged plane in the lake stood as a reminder of what had taken place. The RCMP told John there would be a large lift helicopter coming to remove the plane and place it on land, where it could be examined by accident investigators. The plane would then be abandoned, which was a common practice when these bush planes crashed in the wilderness.

John and Jean were physically and emotionally drained, this day being worse than when they had found the trapper and his dog frozen in the cabin. John called his parents to tell them what happened. His father had heard that a bush plane had gone down and was surprised it was in Gold Lake. John told him about the death of the pilot and witnessing the aircraft crash into the water. After a few more minutes of conversation, they said good-bye, John's father wishing his son did not live so remotely.

The dinner atmosphere was somber, as the day's events returned to haunt them. John's journal entry was the longest to date, a solemn reminder of the challenging elements of the north. Darkness overtook the landscape, and the forest became quiet, only the rustle of the leaves in the breeze could be heard. A disturbed sleep prevailed, but tomorrow would prove to be a better day. A sense of normality would return, reminding John and Jean why they were here. For now, their weary minds were healing, getting ready for another day, in this adventure they had chosen for themselves.

CHAPTER 46

The end of summer was fast approaching. The seasonal change began in August with the hardwood trees starting to change colours, reaching their peak by mid-September. The prospecting at Gold Creek had not gone well, only another quarter ounce of gold had been found. John and Jean attributed their early success to an inordinate amount of gold being washed down river in the spring. It had been deposited in the catch basin where they had the sluice box set up. They were in the right place at the right time, adding to their wealth for their eventual return to Yellowknife to start a family.

The sluice and gold panning supplies were stored in the cave for the winter, hopefully to be retrieved and used again next spring. The firewood had been split and stacked in the woodshed, a task that had taken two weeks, but ensured enough to last through the winter. The airplane had been removed from the lake and placed out of sight, no longer a daily reminder of the incident.

John and Jean's trip to Yellowknife to purchase winter supplies was fast approaching. For their second trapping season, Jean would stay in the bush as long as she felt well, and John planned to stay until the end. However, this would be their last winter at the cabin. For the duration of the lease period, they would return for gold prospecting in the late spring, provided there were no new family members, as having children was now on their radar. Life in the bush was their preferred lifestyle, but Jean's aversion to the long harsh winters and her struggles with depression made this dream difficult.

Work was completed on the emergency shelter, as a bear had broken into the structure over the summer. The cabin also needed repairs to the chimney and roof before winter. However, John had noticed increased waterfowl activity on the lake, and decided to take time to go hunting today. He promised Jean they would be eating duck for dinner, and he returned with three plump ducks in his hands.

After supper they took the canoe out to the lake, a favorite activity. This brought peace of mind to the couple, giving them time to reflect on their lives. On these trips little conversation was had, as personal thoughts dominated their minds. This trip had to be cut short, as a strong north wind came up. They returned to the cabin where they enjoyed a quiet evening followed by a peaceful sleep. Tomorrow they were to catch the plane to Yellowknife, purchase supplies and get ready for another trapping season. Their dreams were full of high expectations, and they slept till dawn's early light.

CHAPTER 47

The plane arrived early and landed gracefully on the lake. John liked to watch the plane's pontoons hit the water, leaving a spray that followed the aircraft to its stop. It taxied quietly to the landing, the pilot greeting them happily. He was their reliable transportation between the cabin and Yellowknife, and because of his good service and positive attitude, Jean and John always tipped him well. The plane's departure was uneventful, and they soon found themselves on their way. John was keeping a big surprise from Jean, trying hard not to reveal it prematurely. He had planned to take her out to dinner tonight and tell her then.

The enthusiastic conversation on the flight, made it seem short and pleasant. John's dad was waiting, and after greetings they loaded their belongings in the truck and headed towards home. John's father made a quick stop at the snowmobile dealer to pick up new parts for his machine. He was hoping John would help him with the repairs, as his mechanical skills were limited.

They soon arrived at the house where John's mother greeted them, hugging both tightly. She did not like John and

Jean being in the bush and worried constantly about their well-being. She was waiting for the day they would move back and start a family. John had informed Jean they were going to treat themselves to dinner out, he had something to discuss with her. This piqued Jean's curiosity, but John assured her it was nothing serious and not to worry about it.

The afternoon was all about Bow, first a trip to the groomer and then to the vet for a physical and his shots updated. This was followed up by a stop at the dog park, where Bow could be off leash, enjoying the company of other dogs. The couple dropped Bow off before heading to the mall for shopping and dinner. The mall, with its availability of products, created a stir to return to city life. But the couple were not ready to give up the silence of the forest at night, the call of the loon from the lake, and most of all, their little cabin in the woods.

After purchasing Christmas gifts for family members, which John's parents would distribute, the couple headed to the restaurant. John had made reservations at a well-known steakhouse. Jean wondered what the special occasion was. After their dinner was served, he told her the news. With his father's help, John had booked a week's vacation in Key West. They were going to Florida. Jean was excited, as she had never been out of country and going somewhere tropical, where the weather was warm, pleased her immensely. After a wonderful dinner they returned to John's parents' place, where John's mom had dessert ready, a pre-planned event. They talked about their trip and their excitement about going to Florida. It was late, so they said their goodnights and soon were in their bed sleeping soundly.

CHAPTER 48

Two days later, John and Jean were at the Yellowknife airport. Their 6:00 a.m. flight to Edmonton was on time and ready to board. After arriving in Edmonton, they would switch planes for their flight to Miami, where they had reserved a rental car for the drive to Key West.

The first leg of the trip was uneventful, but a maintenance problem delayed their plane in Edmonton. The two-hour delay allowed them to eat breakfast and do some shopping. Before long they found themselves boarding the plane and taking off. After the aircraft reached its cruising altitude, and the fasten seat belt sign turned off, Jean relaxed and looked around. She had never been on an airplane this large. Being in this gigantic piece of metal, and the wonderment that it could even fly, made her grasp John's hand tightly, a sense of fear enveloping her. She explained her fear to John who consoled her and pulled her close to him. She snuggled into his shoulder and within minutes had calmed down, the excitement mounting as they got closer to their destination.

The trip seemed long, but soon the beautiful blue waters of the Atlantic came into view. A murmur rose from the passengers, knowing that they would soon be landing. This was John and Jean's first vacation together. They had reserved a hotel on Miami Beach for one night looking forward to seeing the ocean in person. A large city soon came into view, and before long the plane touched down for a perfect landing. The passengers disembarked and made their way to pick up their luggage. After retrieving their bags, they found the car rental booth and were soon driving out of the parking garage into a world vastly different than their own. The temperature was eighty-five degrees and lush tropical foliage dominated the landscape. Jean looked in amazement at the towering palm trees, the warm tropical air rejuvenating her spirit and casting a spell on her that would not lift until returning to Yellowknife.

The couple arrived at this famous beach they had only seen in pictures, thoughts of their life in the wilderness pushed to the back of their minds. After checking into their hotel, and finding their ocean front room, they collapsed in the bed hugging tightly. With passion building, they were soon making love, the atmosphere heightening their desire for each other. The beach was beckoning, and after a quick shower they donned their swimming attire and found themselves a quiet place to lay on the sand, letting the sun warm them as it had never done before.

The ocean was beautiful, the sound of the waves on the shore peaceful. After enjoying this newfound love for the sand and warm ocean water, they decided to go back to the room, shower, walk down the beach to find a place to eat. After a long walk and looking at different restaurants, they decided on a lively patio bar where they enjoyed chicken wings, French fries, and beer. They stayed for an hour just enjoying the atmosphere, it was so unlike their own in the north. Tomorrow would prove to be another great day as they made their way to Key West, designated as one of the most beautiful drives in North America.

Sleep came easy as fatigue, both mental and physical, overtook them. Dreams were of their little cabin and the lifestyle that came with it, Bow, and even their silly raven were being missed. But for now, their vacation was to be enjoyed, before they returned to the harsh environment of their beloved home in Gold Lake.

CHAPTER 49

After enjoying breakfast at the hotel restaurant, the car was loaded and John and Jean's adventure to Key West was about to begin. They made their way to the Interstate, which would take them to US one, known as the Overseas Highway. Traffic was heavy, which was typical of South Florida. Before long they found themselves at John Pennington State Park where they went on a glass-bottomed boat ride over the coral reefs. Tropical fish, brightly coloured coral, and even a sea turtle were observed. John and Jean loved this, it being so unlike the freshwater lakes of the north.. After the two-hour sightseeing tour, the boat returned to the dock, and they continued their journey to Key West.

The Florida Keys are small islands connected by forty-five bridges, the longest being the seven-mile bridge. This one-hundred-mile stretch of road separates the Atlantic Ocean and the Gulf of Mexico. To John and Jean, the scenery was breathtaking. A sign welcoming tourists to Key West soon appeared and they made their way to Old Town, where their hotel was located. They had booked accommodations in a boutique inn with only twelve rooms, preferring this to an overcrowded hotel. Lush tropical foliage surrounded a beautiful swimming pool, steps from their door. John and Jean, who were both avid swimmers, loved this arrangement.

The week flew by, the couple participating in several activities, including visiting the Mel Fisher treasure museum, fascinated by the amount of gold, silver, and other objects, both valuable and common, that had been recovered from shipwrecks. They rode the Old Town Trolley, visiting sites that were unique to the island, enjoying the tour guide's commentary. The couple celebrated sunset at Mallory square, where street performers put on a show, a tradition going back many years. John caught some dolphin when they went on a fishing charter, which the deckhand cleaned, and they cooked for dinner on the barbecue back at their hotel. There were so many things to explore, it was a sad day when they packed their car to leave. Silence overtook them as they drove out of town knowing their vacation would soon be over.

An interesting stop on the way back to Miami was a little tourist village, complete with a restaurant, and an area to feed-the-tarpon off the docks. John and Jean ate lunch there and soon were on their way again. A three-hour trip took them to a hotel near the airport, where they had reserved a room. Their direct flight to Edmonton was scheduled to depart at 9:00 a.m.. Tonight, they would return the car, eat dinner, and spend the evening in their room. Sleep came early, their dreams filled with thoughts of their homestead and the work involved to get ready for the winter. The cabin in the woods was beckoning, and they would shortly return to the seclusion they loved so dearly.

CHAPTER 50

+ + + ◆ + +

Morning found John and Jean on the hotel shuttle to the airport. Excitement was mounting at the prospect of going home. They had enjoyed their vacation immensely but were anxious to get back to Yellowknife now that it was over. The aircraft left right on time. During the flight, John and Jean discussed the errands they needed to complete before they would be ready to leave for Gold Lake.

Jean fell asleep, her head resting comfortably on John's shoulder. John read his book trying hard not to disturb her. The fasten seat belt sign came on as they approached the airport in Edmonton, waking her. Preparations were made for the landing, and they were soon on the ground pulling up to their gate. From here they would board a smaller plane to Yellowknife, where John's father would be waiting for them.

John and Jean arrived in Yellowknife on time, retrieved their luggage and met John's father. They talked of their trip and how beautiful the ocean was, telling him about driving across the seven-mile bridge in the Florida Keys and how it felt as if you were driving across the ocean. They soon arrived at John's parents' house and were warmly greeted by his mother and Bow. Bow thought he had been deserted, never being away from his owners for so long.

The couple were happy to hear that John's sisters, Jean's mother, and an uncle, John had not seen in a long time, were all coming for dinner. John and Jean captivated their audience with stories about their trip. It was a wonderful feeling to reconnect with their family.

Tomorrow the couple would purchase their supplies and reserve the plane to take them to Gold Lake the following day. Sleep was peaceful as they knew they would be home again soon, the reality of the chores needing to be completed before winter arrived momentarily forgotten.

The next day went smoothly and by early afternoon their shopping was completed, and the provisions delivered to the plane's hangar at the airport. John helped his father replace the parts on his snowmobile, and in turn he treated John and Jean to Chinese food for dinner. The next day they were to leave, which created worry for John's parents, as they once again thought of the dangers the couple faced in the bush.

John and Jean arrived at the airport in the morning, helping the pilot load the plane and prepare for the trip to their cabin. They were soon in the air and found themselves back at Gold Lake in a couple of hours, the splendor of the wilderness dominating their senses. After a smooth landing, the cabin came into view, Bow the most excited to be home. They disembarked, unloaded their supplies, wished the pilot well, and watched, with a sense of sadness, the plane disappearing over the horizon leaving them alone once again. The supplies were put away, a fire was lit in the stove, and a sense of finality overcame their tired spirits.

They spent a quiet night together, as the morning would bring reality back to Jean and John. The full moon reflected brightly off the lake, bringing light to the darkness of the forest. The couple slept peacefully as they snuggled closely in the comfort of their own bed. The owl disturbed the silence of the night, but not their dreams.

Bow was awake, a low growl coming from the back of his throat as he sensed danger outside, but even he succumbed to the silence and was soon snoring peacefully. The outside presence was now aware that the inhabitants of this cabin had returned, thinking that something was trespassing on its territory. Jean and John were not aware of this new menace but would soon have an encounter with it they would not quickly forget, bringing a sense of fear to their otherwise peaceful lives.

CHAPTER 51

John and Jean awakened, still tired from their trip home. John let Bow out, where he sniffed the premises to see what animals had visited the cabin while they were gone. Bow picked up the fresh scent of a wolverine. This is what disturbed Bow last night, the animal investigating what had entered the area he now called home. The wolverine was afraid of nothing, including man, and posed a grave danger. John was unaware of this new menace but was soon to discover its presence.

John decided to take some supplies and repair the damage to the emergency shelter. Jean stayed home to clean the cabin and wash the windows. Even though they lived in the wilderness, she still liked everything kept clean. John loaded what he needed in the cart and left for the shelter with Bow. Upon arrival he noticed additional animal activity. The wood the couple had hastily used to secure the cabin was ripped off again. The bear had returned, looking for spoils he had missed the first time.

With lumber purchased in Yellowknife, John was able to secure the door so the bear could not repeat its break and enter. The inside was cleaned up; there was no real damage just a mess. John decided to leave the cart and take a walk to look for deer sign. John carried his gun in case any wayward grouse crossed his path. After a two-mile hike without seeing any sign, John and Bow returned to the shelter to pick up the cart and headed toward home.

The forest was slowly hinting that winter was on its way; the vegetation was dying off, finishing its short life. The leaves of the hardwood trees were turning colors, as the seasonal change was upon them. The daytime air was cool, and the nighttime air was cold, causing John to have a fire in the stove every night. The outside freezer could be used for fowl and fish but was not yet cold enough for deer.

As they pulled up to the cabin, Bow started barking loudly. He could smell the wolverine and he was trying to warn John of the danger. Suddenly, without warning, a full-grown male wolverine bolted from the woodshed. Not seeking an encounter this time, it ran off into the bush leaving John speechless. This was a serious problem, a danger to the trapline, Bow, John, and Jean. Wolverines were fearless when it came to protecting their territory, and to this animal a serious breach had occurred and needed to be corrected.

John entered the cabin telling Jean about this new situation and the need to use caution until they were able to solve it. He would need to shoot or trap this animal as soon as possible. Sleep was fitful as this new problem dominated their thoughts. The animal outside was trying to figure out how to rid itself of these intruders. Bow growled lowly knowing the wolverine was out there.

CHAPTER 52

John thought hard about how to eliminate the wolverine. He decided to ambush it using decaying fish remnants to lure the animal near enough to shoot. Wolverines tend to drop their guard while feeding, allowing John to position himself upwind so as not to be detected. This was the only time it would be possible to get a shot at this animal.

Searching for the perfect location, John found a stand of trees that surrounded a large open area. Keeping to the tree line and using the scope on his rifle, he felt he could eliminate this threat to his trapping season. The couple went out in the canoe the next two evenings. They caught many fish which they cleaned, keeping the remains to bait the trap for the wolverine. John's satellite radio was equipped with a weather station which provided weekly forecasts. He selected a day when there was little wind and clear skies predicted in the evening.

John left before sunset and placed the fish remains in the middle of the clearing. Although there was a light breeze, he chose a spot that was upwind of the bait and sat in a tree. He waited for eight hours, with no sign of the wolverine.

His back and legs were hurting from the uncomfortable position he had been sitting in all night. He walked home disappointed but planned to come back tomorrow, hoping no other animal would find the bait.

The next night found John back in the trees. The bait had not been disturbed, and he hoped the wolverine would be on the move this evening. John waited patiently, three hours went by without any movement, then he caught a glimpse of something dark. He looked through his scope and saw the wolverine heading for the fish. The creature was wary and cautious until his first bite, he then fed without fear. John readied his rifle, his sight aimed at the wolverine's head. A shot rang out hitting the intended target, causing instant death. John sighed with relief, as his nightmare had ended well.

The animal was buried near where it was shot, and peace returned to the little cabin. It was well into fall, and the warm summer was just a memory. Frost now covered the windows of the cabin at night, and the snows could start at any time. This was no worry to the inhabitants of the cabin as they were warm and snug inside, sleeping peacefully, waiting for the arrival of another day.

CHAPTER 53

When winter comes to the far north it usually enters with a vengeance. Preparations for this scenario had been made. John had completed work on the roof of the cabin and repaired the chimney. Items that needed to be stored for the winter were placed in the skinning shed. The sluice box and related items at Gold Creek had been stored in the cave and would be retrieved in the spring.

Early one mid-October morning John awoke to falling snow, filling the air with a whiteness all too familiar. He let Bow outside, who bounded and jumped trying to catch the snowflakes as they fell to earth. Bow loved the snow and would prefer to have it year-round. As the weeks went by the snow accumulated, the lake froze over, and the little cabin became their safe refuge from the winter elements.

John and Jean had been living on a diet of fish, grouse, and rabbit that John had shot or trapped. They also had root vegetables that had been purchased in Yellowknife. A deer hunt was in the making, and John was hoping the deer would be found in the same area as last year. Jean, so far was well, showing no signs of depression. She seemed happy cooking and reading, preferring to stay around the cabin. She would help John more, once the trapping season started. Their raven had disappeared, not being seen, or heard, since their return from Yellowknife. John was not disappointed but wished the raven well. There was no sign that any wolves had moved into this area, but that could change. The trapping season would begin shortly, and they were ready.

CHAPTER 54

Jean woke, feeling nauseous. Minutes later, her head in a bucket, she threw up. John was worried, hoping this was not going to be serious enough for a doctor. They were to put out traps today, but it was beginning to look like it would be just him and Bow. John thought about last winter, being alone and how much he missed Jean, he did not know if he would be willing to do it again. He decided at that moment that separation was no longer an option, if Jean had to return to Yellowknife he would go with her.

John loaded the traps, the bait, and other items he needed in the sled, and with an enthusiastic Bow, headed down the trail. They had decided to increase their number of traps to twenty this year, but today he would only set ten, waiting to see if Jean's illness improved. He had also decided to increase his beaver quota to ten, so two beaver traps would be set in the pond.

The trip was going well until they came upon a half-eaten deer surrounded by wolf tracks. John's heart sunk, memories of last winter and the problems he had with the wolves came flooding back. A new pack had recently moved into this area and would probably winter here in one of the caves that dotted the landscape. These shelters also provided a safe place for their young, which are born in the spring.

John and Jean had staked out their trapping area earlier and marked where they thought the traps should be set. After four-hours the twelve traps were deployed and John and Bow were on their way back to the cabin, setting a half dozen rabbit snares on the way. John had been worried about Jean, but when she opened the cabin door with a smile and warm greeting, he knew she was feeling better. She told John that about an hour after he left, she started feeling back to normal, and now she felt fine.

Jean had not been outside all day, so they decided to don their snowshoes and walk to the area where the crashed plane had been abandoned. This would be their first time to the site, as it was inaccessible through the bush. Traversing the frozen lake would bring them within fifty yards of where the plane had been placed. Forty-five minutes later they reached the plane, which was covered with snow, a variety of animal tracks surrounding the area. It was as if the creatures had come to investigate this strange object that had invaded their forest. The remnants of the plane brought back memories of that fateful day last summer, filling their minds with unpleasant thoughts. They turned around in silence, glad they had a safe home to return to.

Getting back to the cabin, John and Jean stoked the fire and soon the familiar warmth returned. The spirit of the trapper seemed to join them at this time, energizing their spirits with the desire they had for this life. After dinner, sleep came easy, with John looking forward to checking his trapline in the morning.

CHAPTER 55

The wolf pack moved closer, circling the cabin, searching for a scent that might identify who belonged here. Bow growled loudly, alerting John that the wolves were present. John went to the window and observed six large wolves mingling in the moonlight in his yard. He knew they were curious and would probably leave shortly. He saw no sense in retrieving his rifle and creating chaos in the middle of the night. Unlike the last pack, these wolves might keep their distance to avoid conflict.

The sunrise was brilliant, casting its light on the white snow, adding to the beauty of the lake, and the peacefulness of the moment. The chickadees, their song giving away their identity, were eating at the feeder. Jean had purchased it in Yellowknife, having observed the small birds around the cabin looking for food. Sometimes a couple of blue jays also stopped in for a bite.

After a breakfast of rabbit, fried potatoes, and home-made bread, John retrieved Bow, and loaded the sled. He said goodbye to Jean and headed down the trail to check his traps. The first trap held an ermine, a white weasel common in this area and a valuable fur. The next two traps were empty, but the third and fourth held martens, the most abundant fur bearing animal in the forest. The rest of the traps held nothing, but a surprise awaited them at the beaver pond; a large beaver was caught and pulled up from under the ice. It was a good day on the trapline, as John now had enough animals to process. They headed home, picking up three rabbits that had been caught in the snares.

Jean was outside attending to the chickadees as John and Bow pulled into the yard. She had befriended the birds, who now would eat out of her hand. Having these pets helped her deal with the isolation of the cabin. Since it was still early and the winds were calm, John suggested they go for a walk. Jean needed to get out of the cabin, the fresh air and exercise good for her physical and mental health. They walked the trapline as that trail had been broken, the deep snow in other areas too difficult to walk in. This would turn into a daily routine, weather permitting.

Returning to the cabin, John helped Jean prepare dinner. He realized how much a deer was needed to supplement their diet. Little did he know how easily this problem was going to be taken care of. After dinner, John called his father and let him know they were doing fine. His father informed John there was a massive low-pressure system building, forecast to turn into a two-day blizzard and predicted to be one of the more powerful storms they have had in years. John thanked his father and assured him they would stay safe.

John and Jean retired to bed, not knowing a startling surprise would once again test their emotions. They slept peacefully, wrapped in each other's arms, safe in their little cabin.

CHAPTER 56

A loud crash of breaking glass reverberated throughout the cabin. Jean and John, jumped to their feet, their sleep abruptly disturbed in the early morning light. Shattered glass littered the cabin and a dead, bloodied grouse lay on the floor. Apparently, the bird, in the low light, crashed through one of the panes in the window, inadvertently killing itself. John threw on boots to protect his feet. His first move was to get Bow outside, so he would not get cut on the glass that was strewn on the cabin floor. Bow, sensing the danger, and following John's command, had stayed where he was. John retrieved him and safely put him outside. Jean cleaned up the glass while John retrieved a new pane he had bought in Yellowknife just for this type of emergency. Jean added wood to the fire trying to maintain some warmth in the cabin as John replaced the broken window. After two hours, the window was reinstalled, sealed and as good as new. As the warmth in the cabin returned, they were grateful this did not happen during the blizzard that was expected tonight.

Today they would prepare for the storm, making sure they had a three-day supply of provisions on hand. When

John was in the skinning shed earlier, he had lit a fire in the stove so he could thaw and process furs today. The storm was due to hit in the middle of the night. These storms frightened Jean, as the couple were at nature's mercy and even the smallest incident could spell disaster for them.

The furs were processed, John finishing at dinner time. Jean had taken care of the provisions for the storm and had cooked a pot of beaver stew and baked fresh bread. Jean was feeling fine, both mentally and physically. They hoped to make it through the winter with no major upsets. After dinner John wrote in his journal. Jean found that knitting helped to fight her depression. Tired of working at their hobbies they went to bed and fell asleep, only to be disturbed by the howling wind and breaking tree branches which kept them up all night.

The storm had arrived. The couple wondered how their cabin would survive the almost hurricane force winds. As morning dawned, things calmed slightly. The snow and wind were still unrelenting, but not as powerful as during the night. The blizzard lasted two days, coating everything in white that sparkled brightly when the sun returned on the third day. They had survived this test from nature and getting back to the fresh air and trapping was now a priority.

The sun set on the little cabin, a solitary structure built by man to keep him safe and warm even in the most difficult times. The two adults were finally in a deep and relaxing sleep, which they had been deprived of during the storm. The moonlight shining on the little cabin would make a perfect illustration for the book John planned to write after leaving this life. Tomorrow would bring good luck, as their adventures continued in the far north.

CHAPTER 57

John and Bow left early. The two feet of new snow was daunting, especially having to find their traps under it. A long pole was used to find the trap and set it off, rendering it harmless. It could then be pulled out and reset. The traps that contained animals, had to be dug out. John had learned a valuable lesson. When large storms approach, remove the traps from the bush, and reset them later.

After a busy morning, the trapline had been reset, and two minks and a fisher were added to the year's catch. The beaver traps would be checked tomorrow, as John did not like to leave Jean alone for long periods of time, her mental health his major worry.

As the duo made their way back to the cabin, a surprise awaited. While heading down the trail, John made out the form of a large animal floundering in the snow. He urged Bow on, wanting to catch up as quickly as possible. It was a young doe, that had gotten separated from the herd during the blizzard and was now lost and exhausted from trying to get through the deep snow. John stopped Bow and grabbed his rifle. With a well-aimed shot, the deer was now meat for the winter. John could not believe his luck. Typically, it was the wolves who were the victors in a situation such as this. Jean would be surprised and thrilled at the prospect of having a substantial supply of fresh meat.

The deer was loaded on the sled and John and Bow soon found themselves back at the cabin sharing their good news with Jean. They butchered the deer a half mile from the cabin, so as not to leave a scent that would attract unwanted guests, such as the wolves. The remains of the deer were left for these animals. John spent the rest of the afternoon dressing the deer, Bow at his side. When they returned to the cabin, the sled was loaded with meat, which was stored in the outdoor freezer. The sky was darkening as the last items were put away in the skinning shed. The smell of beaver stew dominated John and Bow's senses as they entered the cabin.

After a delicious dinner Jean and John cleaned up and their discussion turned to Christmas, which was just two weeks away. They decided to cut a fresh tree and adorn it with the decorations they had purchased for the occasion. The trapper must have also decorated a tree, as the couple had found ornaments when they moved into the cabin. John had shot a goose right at freeze up and it was stored in the outdoor freezer. This would be Christmas dinner, and along with the presents they had bought each other, and gifts from family in Yellowknife, they would have a good Christmas. Even Bow would have a present under the tree, a giant rawhide bone to chew on.

Pleasant dreams of the holiday dominated their sleep, the little cabin providing comfort and a safe and trusted home in the forest. Tomorrow would be another day of hard work, creating pleasant memories of their life together in a place they both loved.

CHAPTER 58

Bow's consistent barking outside the cabin caught John's attention. He had let the dog out minutes earlier after rousing himself out of bed because of Bow's insistent whining at the door. John dressed to go out and investigate further. Bow was sniffing and barking at very unusual tracks in the snow. The bigfoot had paid them another visit. Many trappers had seen its signature footprints or smelled its odour when working their traplines, but sightings were extremely rare. John put his foot in the track, comparing its size to his own foot. It was at least four inches longer and much wider. Puzzled he shook his head and returned to the cabin to tell Jean. They discussed it over breakfast and decided it was not a threat. There had been no known attacks against humans and the bigfoot was elusive and tried to avoid contact with people.

John and Bow had been busy checking the trapline daily, and the two weeks leading up to Christmas were very productive. A variety of fur was caught, including two beavers, a fox, a lynx, and numerous other more common mammals that inhabited these forests. Jean had been decorating for Christmas and they had harvested a tree for the cabin. They had cut cedar and pine boughs and joined them together making garland that now decorated the inside of the cabin.. The tree was adorned with ornaments, and presents were placed under it; Christmas was almost here.

A light snow was falling making the cabin look magical. Inside John and Jean were enjoying listening to Christmas songs on the satellite radio. It was Christmas Eve. They had enjoyed a small dinner and were now relaxing and enjoying a bottle of wine they had brought for this occasion. They would phone John's parents and Jean's mother tomorrow to wish them a merry Christmas. The night wore on and soon the couple went to bed, both looking forward to tomorrow.

Jean woke first, a feeling of happiness engulfed her. It was Christmas day and she had much to be thankful for, a wonderful husband who loved her very much, and good mental health which was allowing her to stay. John awoke and soon they were opening presents. They had limited the number of Christmas presents to one each. Jean opened hers first, it being a lovely gold ring with her birthstone. Jean collected beautiful rings; she could never have too many. John's gift was a custom-made knife, crafted by the best known knifemaker in Yellowknife. They both loved their gifts immensely.

The day was sunny with a light wind, so John and Jean took Bow and went for a walk. Silence enveloped them as they walked in the solitude of the forest, the only sound was the occasional call of a raven piercing the still air. The walk was enjoyable, but they soon found themselves back at the cabin so Jean could prepare dinner. Roasted goose, smothered in vegetables, was on the menu. Bow would enjoy all the spoils of this meal, just like the humans.

Dinner was served and thanks were given for what they had been blessed with in their lives. A peaceful night was had, the only sound disturbing their sleep was Bow chewing on his rawhide bone. Soon it would be January, the start of a downhill slide toward spring. A feeling of peace filled the little cabin, with the trapper's spirit providing a veil of security over this young family whose life was just beginning. A wonderful Christmas they had, now a memory never to be forgotten.

CHAPTER 59

The month was January, and it was bitter cold. Checking the traps had been scaled back to three days a week, instead of daily. The animals did not move much when it was this cold, including the ones that lived in the cabin, preferring to hunker down and stay warm. An Arctic vortex had moved over the area and was expected to stay in place for two weeks, driving temperatures as low as minus forty-five degrees at night.

The little cabin was warm and cozy. John was making sure the stove was at its hottest all the time. He was glad they stocked enough wood last year for emergencies, as wood consumption can double when it is so cold outside. Inside the cabin, Jean knitted, while John wrote in his journal. They read many of the books they had bought in Yellowknife and played cards to break up the boredom of sitting inside. The frigid weather finally moved out, replaced by much warmer days, so they could go outside to get some work done.

Taking advantage of this change in the weather, John and Jean decided to go fishing to replenish their supply, which was down to one fish. After drilling holes, and setting hooks with bait, they waited. The fish were soon biting, fish after fish came up through the holes. They obviously had parked themselves over a school. Ten walleye were caught, each weighing between three and five pounds. They loaded the fish and supplies they had brought with them on the sled, and with Bow in the lead, headed back to the cabin.

The fish were cleaned, some fillets were reserved for dinner, and the rest went into the freezer, along with the remains of the fish which would be used for baiting the traps. The next day found John and Bow on the trapline. Their bounty included a bobcat, one of the rarest catches. John checked the beaver traps, which held nothing. This season he had been trapping in three ponds and had caught four beavers thus far. On the way back to the cabin John set some rabbit snares to try to replenish the supply of rabbit meat, which was always a nice change from eating venison.

On the trip back to the cabin, Bow was getting restless, causing John to survey the area. What he saw surprised him; the pack of wolves was following them. They were probably hungry, as food was scarce, especially during the severe cold snap they had experienced. John gripped his rifle tightly; hoping to not be confronted by these animals, which was highly unlikely. They followed Bow and John almost all the way to the cabin, at which time the wolves disappeared into the landscape. John would have to keep his guard up, as a famished wolf pack will attack a man and his dog if they are hungry enough. The next couple of weeks went by with no further encounters.

The winter was waning, trapping season would conclude at the end of March, only six weeks away. Thoughts were turning to John and Jean's new life in Yellowknife. They had John's father keeping his eyes open for a house outside of town for them to buy. Life in the cabin would soon be a memory, a suburban lifestyle was waiting. They hoped they would be ready for it.

CHAPTER 60

The sound of a small plane caught John's attention. He watched as the plane landed, throwing up large amounts of snow, making the aircraft invisible at times. The plane made its way across the lake towards the landing by the cabin. It was the game warden doing his last wellness check for the year. John was required to fill out forms on the number and species of animals trapped, and the number of deer he had harvested for food. He was also required to report the number of deer he saw that were killed by wolves. There were forms to be completed which had to be returned to the ministry. Failing to do so would result in a fine and suspension of his trapper's license.

John invited the warden and pilot up to the cabin for coffee. They were happy for the invitation, and soon found themselves seated around the kitchen table eating bread fresh from the oven. After a short visit and an exchange of stories, they checked John's furs. With much thanks for the hospitality, the men were soon on their way.

John returned to the cabin, Jean now laying down saying she did not feel well. Her mental health was on a downhill slide, and the couple decided she should probably head back to Yellowknife early. John arranged for the plane to come get her. She would not need a nurse, nor need to be hospitalized, as this was a proactive evacuation. Even though Jean hated to leave, she knew it was best for her. She would probably not return to the cabin for trapping season again, ending a Chapter in her life that would be with her forever.

The plane arrived two mornings later; Jean was packed and ready to leave. The thought of not having John beside her was breaking her heart. Jean sobbed on John's shoulder, not wanting to let him go. John's feelings were reciprocal, as he remembered the lonely nights without her. The cabin would give up some of its warmth, knowing that Jean was gone.

John watched as the plane left, and the pain in his heart returned as he missed his wife already. Turning sadly, John made his way back to the cabin with Bow at his side. A call a few hours later confirmed Jean's safe arrival in Yellowknife. Jean was going to stay with her mother, but John's mom would visit her often. John was relieved that his wife would be well cared for.

With Bow as his companion, John would make it through the next few weeks and then reunite with his wife to start a new life together. Sleep was fitful for John, as the little cabin had lost its sense of peace with Jean's departure. Time would heal these wounds, as the remainder of the trapping season would be busy, helping him to keep him from dwelling on his wife.

In the morning, John resolved to complete this season. He realized that winters at the cabin would soon be just a memory, and he would be reunited with his wife. In four weeks, a date he was looking forward to, the plane would return for him and Bow, as trapping season came to an end.

CHAPTER 61

As the days passed, John faced loneliness and depression. His day-to-day activities became a blur. He was sick, and it seemed to get worse as time went by. Jean and John's parents were very worried, wanting him to give it up and come home. John was relentless about wanting to finish the season but knew in his heart it was probably not going to happen. The longing for his wife was tearing him apart. He wanted to be with her, and he did not want Jean worrying about him. A decision had to be made. He called Jean and told her he was coming back early. They both wept loudly as they knew they would soon be back together.

Over the next couple of days John packed up. Everything that needed to be stored was put in its rightful place. The perishables, his furs, and personal belongings would go with him to Yellowknife. He would come back in late spring to retrieve the rest of the couple's possessions and complete a final clean up of the cabin.

Bow was sad, sensing that his life in the bush was coming to an end, not knowing what the future held for him. However, he knew he would always be taken care of.

The sound of an approaching aircraft broke the silence. Jean had reserved the plane and it was now approaching Gold Lake, this adventure would soon be just a memory.

The plane arrived and was loaded; the aircraft taking off without incident. John took one final look at the cabin, creating a flood of memories for him to deal with. Conversation was limited on the trip to Yellowknife, the pilot aware of the situation. He followed John's lead, talking only when John initiated the dialog. They arrived in Yellowknife without incident. John exited the plane and fell into the waiting arms of his wife. Their journey was finally over, being replaced by a much easier way to live.

The couple arrived at John's parents house to a greatly relieved mother, who hugged her son tightly, not wanting to let him go. John was exhausted after this experience, his own mental health fragile. Being with his wife, and the comforts of home, would bring improvements to his health quickly.

John and Jean would begin looking for a house, preferably outside of town with some acreage, and a large workshop where John could start a small carpentry business. These were tomorrow's dreams, which would now have to be set in motion, as their lives took on a new meaning and direction. Hopefully, a happy future for these trappers would prevail.

CHAPTER 62

The following weeks found Jean and John ready to buy a home. They had decided on a place outside of town with five acres of land. It had a good well and was on the electrical grid. Jean was thrilled that it had indoor plumbing and modern kitchen appliances. It also had a large workshop that needed little renovation for John's carpentry business.

Upon closing, the couple moved their belongings from storage into their new dwelling. Bow loved his new house, spending most of his time outdoors, running and investigating, his nose constantly sniffing. He was happy he was not kept on a leash, living in a doghouse. John, using his journal and memory, started writing his book, a tale about adventure, survival, and his love for the wilderness.

In the spring, the couple returned to the cabin, retrieving the usable possessions they had left there. Upon leaving, they wondered how long it would be before they returned. John's business worked out well, as his carpentry skills were a much-needed trade in Yellowknife. Some nights, while lying in bed, they would discuss their adventures at the cabin. They were both thankful for the strong character and the respect for nature it had instilled in them. They were now adapting to a world familiar to the people of Yellowknife, but because of their past, they were considered different.

Jean and John raised a family here, and every summer when the kids got older, they would take them on the bush plane to Gold Lake and camp at Gold Creek while John prospected. Gold Lake and their little cabin would never be forgotten, forever engrained in their memories.

When the moon was full, John often thought of the cabin, the tranquillity, and the peace of mind it brought to him and Jean. His new life was also a shining star, which included a loving, furiously devoted wife, and three heathy smart children.

The little cabin in the woods beckoned him, his spirit joining the old trapper's, to lay a veil of peace on the memories that had settled there. The longing spirits that were joined with a special bond, a bond that would never be broken.

YELLOW FEVER

CHAPTER 1

The prospectors lined the banks of the fast-flowing creeks, chasing a dream. Gold pans in hand, they were looking for that one nugget that would change the course of their lives. Unfortunately, for many it was just a dream, leaving most penniless and hungry. This was the beginning of the Yukon gold rush, a time when men would endure hardships beyond belief for a chance to find gold. Most were unprepared, succumbing to nature's elements. Caught without proper shelter, they would die from exposure to cold and hunger. The north was an unforgiving place and showed no mercy.

Jason was a prospector who would succeed. He came from Seattle, a long, hard journey away from Canada's far north. Jason planned to travel to a little-known area where his grandfather had previously spent the summers, his cabin hopefully intact and able to provide shelter. Jason remembered his late grandfather's stories of natural caves and streams flowing from higher elevations, finding nuggets, and panning gold from rich deposits near his cabin. The family never believed the old man's stories, as not one gram of gold was ever seen. Suffering from dementia, there was uncertainty if there was any truth to his tales.

Jason arrived in Dawson City to a busy and violent place; prostitution, gambling, and drinking led to uncivil behaviour, including murder. He was able to purchase a dog from a prospector who, with much disappointment, had given up trying to find gold. His partner had been killed in a dispute with another man over their claim, a common occurrence. The dog was a husky, well-trained, young, and strong. His name was King, and Jason knew he would have to establish a trusting relationship with him. In a short time, they became buddies, looking out for each other's welfare and providing companionship in this lonely place.

A mule was purchased at twice the cost of a horse, their ability to carry supplies making them a valuable commodity. Grandpa's map, drawn up before he developed dementia, would hopefully lead Jason to the cabin. He planned to spend the summer looking for gold and hoped there were clues at the cabin to help him find success.

The trio left Dawson and started their journey, which would take two to three days, depending on conditions. The first night, as Jason sat by the fire, he took in the quiet of the wilderness. With King by his side, his thoughts drifted to what the future had in store for him. His outlook was upbeat, as thoughts of what awaited him sent strong feelings coursing through his body.

The sky was clear, exposing countless stars filling the night sky. His sleep was uninterrupted as fatigue overtook him, dreaming of the adventures that awaited him. One of those dreams would become a reality at first light, making him realize one incident could change his whole direction, a wakeup call to his new world.

CHAPTER 2

Right before dawn, Jason was awakened abruptly by the mule braying loudly and the dog barking. The darkness made things confusing for Jason, who grabbed his rifle and rushed to the chaotic scene. King was growling at the wooded area near where the mule was tethered. Jason's eyes, adapting to the low light, picked up the movement of shadowy figures. A half dozen wolves were looking to turn Jason's pack animal into dinner. Jason took aim, a shot rang out, and one of the wolves went down, dying instantly. The rest of the pack made a quick exit, now knowing the mule was not an easy target.

Jason felt lucky to have averted a tragedy and realized the importance of protecting this asset in the future. He decided to name his mule Brutus, for being so brave at fending off the wolves. He returned to the now extinguished campfire, relit it, and made himself some coffee. He ate some bread and an apple for breakfast, having purchased some provisions in Dawson. Soon living off the land would be his only option for survival.

After packing up camp, the trio made their way deeper into the bush, trying to follow his grandfather's map as accurately as possible. Jason was constantly on the lookout for small game, and soon shot a partridge, a bird noted for its breast meat, which would make a fine dinner. As they continued, the landscape changed, becoming rockier and hillier, with caves appearing periodically. Jason, fearing a storm during the night because of distant thunder, decided finding a cave to sleep in would be ideal.

They soon came upon a cavern and made their camp. Unfortunately, the cave was occupied by a family of foxes, who did not seem willing to share. Deciding to go no further, Jason relocated away from the cave, so as to not disturb the fox family.

The partridge was cooked for dinner, and King was fed dried food, which had been purchased in Dawson. He would survive on this until fresh meat and fish were found. The threat of a storm dissipated, and the clouds lifted. Jason sat in silence, the crackling of the fire the only sound heard. His mind wandered, wondering what they would find when they reached the cabin.

A sudden gust of wind brought Jason back to reality and the hardships he was facing. Fatigue washed over him, followed by deep sleep, sending him back to the comfortable life he enjoyed in Washington. He dreamed of his grandfather trying to convince him to not follow his dreams to Canada. Tomorrow his grandfather's cabin would be found, ending one adventure but setting others in motion.

CHAPTER 3

+ + ✦ ✦ ✦ + +

King's muzzle on his neck woke Jason. He lay on his back, eyes open to the red sky as dawn approached. His thoughts turned to the cabin. He was not confident he would find it with the map his grandfather had given him. If it could not be found, he would have to come up with other arrangements regarding a shelter for the summer.

After breakfast, Jason's supplies were loaded on Brutus and they were on their way. Brutus was the best fed in the party, having an unlimited supply of vegetation on the ground, and foliage above his head, a constant dinner party for a hungry mule. This arrangement worked out well for an animal expected to carry a heavy pack on his back all day.

After a short walk, they found themselves out of the bush and into a large open area, a meadow that was on his grandfather's map. Jason's excitement grew as he realized he was on the right track, the cabin now within his reach. They stopped in the meadow enjoying the sunshine, relaxing in the beauty of the day. Suddenly Jason caught movement in the treeline, it was a large jackrabbit coming to eat in the meadow. Jason quietly picked up his gun and with one quick shot the rabbit was dead, providing dinner for both him and his dog.

Shortly after leaving the meadow, they came across a fast-flowing creek that looked promising for gold. He decided to stop, as yellow fever gripped him. After panning for an hour with no luck, he decided finding the cabin was a more important issue and his time would be better spent on that challenge.

Traversing through a rocky area, the stillness was suddenly disturbed by Brutus, who reared up and brayed loudly in fear, trying to escape a perceived danger. A rattlesnake lay coiled ready to strike. Jason, decided to give the reptile some distance, avoiding a conflict. With the animals in tow, they continued on their journey expecting the cabin to come into view at any time.

The sound of a waterfall caught Jason's attention, leading him to another creek, complete with the remains of an old sluice. He noticed a well-worn path leading from the falls back into the forest. Since it did not appear to be an animal trail, he followed it, hoping it would lead to his grandfather's cabin.

After a short walk, the outline of a cabin came into view. Jason's heart skipped a beat, not because he found the cabin, but because smoke was rising from the outside firepit. The cleanliness and order around the cabin led him to believe someone was living there. He froze in disbelief, wondering how the occupant would react when confronted about the ownership of the building.

Sometimes in the far north, scores like this were settled with violence. He decided to go in and offer his friendship and his rabbit for dinner, hoping conflict could be avoided. A feeling of uneasiness gripped him as he approached the cabin door, preparing himself for what he might find. He knocked and was shocked by who answered the door, changing the course of his adventure in a direction he never expected.

CHAPTER 4

✦ ✦ ✦✦✦ ✦ ✦

A woman stood in the doorway of the cabin, her long black hair and dark skin glistening in the sunlight. She spoke English well and introduced herself as Wendy. She told Jason she was a native, born in the Yukon and raised in Dawson City, after her parents were killed by prospectors. She invited him to stay for dinner, and he offered her his rabbit.

When Jason first saw Wendy in the doorway, there was an immediate attraction. As their eyes met, a feeling of mutual trust and friendship was established. While he cleaned the rabbit, Wendy went to the forest, her backyard garden, to collect edible plants and fungi. This was a skill she learned from her brother, who still practiced native ways to gather wild food for survival. They cooked the meal together, establishing a bond that went beyond friendship, reveling in the mutual attraction they were both experiencing. If this led to a relationship, it would be frowned upon by their families and society, a difficult situation for them in the future.

After dinner they discussed the cabin. Jason told Wendy about his grandfather building it and using it for shelter during the summer, when he came to search for gold and get away from society. He enjoyed the peace the forest offered him, a break from the hectic city life of Seattle. Wendy told Jason her brother often used this cabin while on his late fall hunting trips and had told her it was abandoned. After a tragic accident involving a fire that destroyed their house and took her husband's life, Wendy moved here, making it her new home. It was now completely habitable and comfortable.

The couple continued talking into the night, with Jason sharing his dreams of finding enough gold to allow him to buy a home and start a family. Wendy told Jason she hoped to someday find a partner with whom she could build a life in the wilderness.

As there was no alternative, Wendy invited Jason to spend the night, offering him a pallet on the floor of the cabin. Jason was happy to have a roof over his head and hoped this might be the start of a relationship. In the morning, Wendy asked Jason if he would consider sharing the cabin for the summer, possibly working together. Jason was pleased with this turn of events, as he couldn't imagine a better arrangement.

The couple spent the day getting to know each other and discussing the future. With Jason's help completing the chores needed for survival, such as hunting, gathering edibles, and cutting firewood, there would be ample time to search for gold. They decided to fix up an existing shelter for Brutus, who would accompany them on these outings.

Wendy knew little about prospecting but was willing to help Jason in the pursuit of his dream. Little did she know she was becoming part of his future.

As darkness fell, it was agreed they would share the cabin as a couple, living and working together. At the end of the summer, they would see where they stood in their relationship and if there was a future for them. They retired to bed and without hesitation were soon enjoying each other, resulting in a deep and wonderful sleep.

CHAPTER 5

Jason woke first, lighting a fire to take the early morning chill out of the cabin. It was late May, but it was common to have cold nights this far north, even during the summer. Wendy rolled over in bed, a smile on her face and a feeling of satisfaction caressing her soul. She was so glad Jason had found her, as her love for this man was blossoming.

Jason made coffee that he had bought in Dawson, the aroma stirring Wendy to her feet for a treat she had not enjoyed in months. They talked about going to a nearby lake. Wendy had a canoe there, which they could use for fishing. Fresh fish for dinner sounded like something they would enjoy. Living alone, Wendy did not typically hunt or fish; her knowledge of forest plants and edibles providing the protein she needed.

The hike to the lake was short, and they soon found themselves on the water. The splash of the paddles was the only sound that could be heard. Jason's thoughts turned to Seattle, the family he had left there and when he would see them again. Wendy's thoughts turned to her late husband and the tragedy that had fallen upon them, leading her to move into the cabin, with no clear path forward. She felt that now that she had met Jason, a new and secure future awaited her. Silence prevailed as each of them were caught up in their own thoughts, bringing a feeling of peace.

After a couple of hours, Jason and Wendy returned to the cabin. The fishing had been good, guaranteeing a delicious dinner and a special treat for King. The dog brought a sense of family to the cabin, always willing to cuddle and return love when given. Following a short nap the fish were cleaned and prepared. After dinner, they took a stroll to the waterfall. This would become a favorite place for the couple to go in the evening, during the extended daylight hours of summer.

The pair discussed taking a trip to a creek that Wendy thought had potential for housing deposits of gold. They would set up camp for two nights and explore the surrounding area, with Brutus and King accompanying them. As the sun set, they walked back to the cabin having decided to embark on their adventure in two days, allowing them time to get organized.

CHAPTER 6

Jason and Wendy had awakened early; the day turning out to be sunny and warm. They had Brutus packed with supplies and were ready to go by 8:00 a.m.. King paced the floor, impatiently waiting, sensing an adventure in his future. The couple, finally ready, joined the mule and the dog and left, securing the cabin against any unwanted visitors during their absence.

The first part of their journey took them through rocky terrain and across small streams. Wendy told Jason the creek they were going to was larger and the water ran much faster, leaving backwashes where they could pan for gold. It originated from an underground river about a kilometer from where they would be staying.

The couple stopped for lunch, which consisted of smoked meat and bread. The supplies Jason had brought with him from Dawson were almost gone, making him think about their food supply. Even though they could survive as vegetarians, Jason loved meat and would continue to try to supplement his diet with it.

They continued towards the creek, approaching a treeline. As they drew closer, they noticed movement, and doe and fawn emerged from the forest. Oblivious to their presence, the animals ate until King decided to bark and chase them back into the safety of the trees. Skirting the tree line, Wendy and Jason carried on until the sound of a rushing stream could be heard, leading them to their destination. They found a clearing on the bank of the creek and set up camp. Jason took his fishing rod and walked along the creek, fishing with home made dough balls they had made for bait. To his surprise the creek was full of trout, and within a short time he had enough fish for dinner and for King.

Returning to camp, Wendy had the fire going, sensing Jason would be successful, and they would be eating fish for dinner. After a hearty meal they relaxed around the campfire, enjoying the quiet that nature provided to them. The fire crackled as daylight turned to darkness and the night sky shone with countless stars, bringing a sense of attachment to nature. The forest was silent, except for the sound of the rushing stream, which helped lull the couple into a peaceful sleep.

In the morning, they would try panning for gold. If successful, it would be the beginning of their dream. The couple would let the spirits guide them, as Wendy's ancestors had lived on this land for generations, leaving a presence that could not be disputed. They believed that man was not the owner of the land but given the use of it for their survival. Respecting nature and living as her forebearers had would bring a long and happy life to Jason and Wendy.

CHAPTER 7

The sun was rising, casting a yellow glow over the forest, creating a sense of renewal for the new day. Jason rolled over, wrapping the blankets around him. He moved close to Wendy seeking warmth from the cool morning air. She awoke, reaching for him, and wrapped her arms tightly around him. She was so happy they had found each other. King came over and nuzzled Jason, in return he received a scratch behind his ears. That morning ritual over, Jason rose, and within a short time the fire was going, prompting Wendy to get up. She wrapped herself in a blanket and went and sat by the fire to warm herself in the cool morning air. More trout were cooked for breakfast, bringing a feeling of satisfaction to the stomachs and minds of the happy couple.

After breakfast the panning supplies were un-packed, and the gold seekers got to work. They entered the stream, Jason showing Wendy how to work the pan to find gold. Their first outing was unsuccessful, so they decided to walk the creek toward its underground source, finding areas to pan along the way. After another two hours of working the stream with no success, Jason finally hit paydirt, a small nugget and some flake, proving that there was gold to be found here. Two hours later, with no further success, they decided to return to camp, Jason realizing that finding gold was no easy task. After a late lunch of food gathered from the forest, they lay down for a nap, not waking until King's angry barking startled them.

Not fifty feet away was a black bear, watching the couple. Jason reached for his rifle, preparing for any movement the bear might make toward them. After what appeared to be a standoff between man, dog, and bear, the bear turned and walked back into the forest, leaving a startled Jason to collect his thoughts and settle his nerves. Wendy hugged him, reassuring him the bear was not a threat, and had just found them to be a curiosity.

Jason gathered his hunting supplies, and with King they headed out, hoping to bring home game for dinner. With the dog in the lead there was sudden movement, as a grouse broke cover and tried to make its escape. Jason brought the bird down, guaranteeing them meat for dinner. One more bird was shot, and they headed back to camp. Wendy gathered food along the way to go with the fowl. When they returned to camp, it was evident the bear had returned and gone through their supplies looking for food. Jason was nervous about the bear encounters and would not hesitate to shoot the bear if it became a threat.

The birds were cleaned, and were soon cooking over the fire, the smell making their mouths water. It was also attracting the bear. King noticed him first, barking and sounding a warning. Jason now realized this bear seemed to have no fear of humans, thus presenting a danger for them.

It would have to be shot, or it might attack them in the night while sleeping. Jason picked up his rife and without hesitation shot the bear. Later they would butcher some parts from the animal and take them back to their cabin tomorrow.

The birds were eaten for dinner, and after a short time at the campfire, the couple got ready for bed. The stars shone brightly as their tired souls became one with the heavens, not waking till the first light of the morning sun.

CHAPTER 8

✦ ✦ ✦ ✦ ✦ ✦

When Jason woke, only the call of the hawk could be heard, as the bird scanned the horizon looking for an early morning meal. The bear lay where he had been shot. Upon approaching for a closer look, Jason noticed a large piece of the bear's hind quarter had been removed. It looked like it had been cut from the bear, not ravished by animals feeding off the body. How could this have happened? The only explanation was human activity. Jason shook his head in confusion, backing away from the bear. Deciding not to touch the animal, he returned to the camp to tell Wendy what he had discovered. Unable to explain what had happened to the bear, they decided to go ahead and remove the other hind quarter to take back with them.

They pushed the mystery of the bear to the back of their minds, broke camp and headed toward the cabin. Silence took over as they both reflected on past events and wondered what the future held for them. Jason noticed the wind growing stronger and the air getting much cooler. These were the signs of an approaching storm. They would need to find shelter, as the thunder and lightning in the distance was fast approaching.

Many caves dotted this area, and as luck would have it, a large cave entrance was nearby where they could shelter. The storm came with a vengeance, heavy rain, intense lightning, and thunder. Brutus was anxiety-ridden, so Wendy led him as far away from the entrance as possible. She soothed him, talking quietly, and caressing him, helping take his mind off the events outside. The storm soon abated, and they exited the cave. Brutus had calmed down and began happily munching on vegetation, getting back to his normal self.

The cabin soon came into view, and upon arriving they noticed a greeting had been left. When young, Wendy's brother would go into the forest to collect things and make decorative items with them. One of these creations now adorned her doorway. Her brother had been here to visit, and though she was sorry she had missed him, Wendy knew he would return at another time. They entered the cabin and lit a fire. The day was wet and cool, and the dampness chilled them to the bones.

As the cabin warmed, the couple talked about their trip, agreeing it had been a success. They decided to investigate another creek, which was accessible by canoe, in the near future. Dinner was comprised of edibles Wendy had collected on the way home. A hush fell over the cabin, King in his favorite spot asleep, Wendy and Jason doing likewise. Tomorrow they would smoke the bear and make plans for their next prospecting trip.

CHAPTER 9

—— ✦✦✦✦✦ ——

The full moon shone brightly. The forest was silent with the inhabitants of the cabin sleeping soundly, waiting for the start of another day. Jason and Wendy awoke to the sound of Brutus; he was uneasy about something, which concerned Jason. The sun was just coming up over the horizon as he peered out the cabin window. He caught a glimpse of a shadowy figure disappearing into the underbrush. Jason was not sure what he had seen.

After breakfast they would start the bear smoking and then take the canoe to explore streams that emptied into the lake for signs of gold. They were also going to collect a tasty plant available this time of year, only accessible from the water. Jason was hoping to catch some fish to go with this special treat. After a short hike they reached the lake, loaded the canoe, and set off.

The pristine wilderness was breathtakingly beautiful. The forest, lake, and sky captured the spirit of these young gold seekers, creating a feeling of one with nature. Waterfowl dotted the lake, ducks, geese, and other birds calling this water home during the short summer months.

With Wendy's direction they retrieved the edible plants, and in a stroke of good luck Jason shot a rabbit for dinner. They returned to the canoe and paddled to the area Wendy called Rocky Shores. It was here a fast-moving stream emptied into the lake, creating a possible gold source.

The couple paddled in silence to the site. Upon arriving they pulled their canoe onshore, retrieved their gold pans, and proceeded to a large area with substantial pools where they could look for gold. At first nothing, then a scream of delight from Wendy as a gold nugget appeared in her pan. Jason congratulated her with a big hug. Now Wendy was also touched by the fever, willing her to find more. After two hours of panning, they retrieved another nugget, and a few gold flakes, but nothing substantial. Jason was happy with the day's results and looked forward to returning here.

Upon reaching the canoe, a disappointment awaited them. While gone, something had taken the rabbit which had been left in the canoe. Now Jason would have to shoot a bird or catch some fish, to provide meat for them and King. Luckily, he bagged a large goose, providing enough meat for the next couple of days.

Returning to the cabin, King gave both Jason and Wendy a warm sloppy greeting, relieved they had come home. They had a wonderful dinner and Jason thought once again about his love for Wendy, and the meeting that brought them together. The evening was dark as a storm moved in, the steady sound of rain hitting the roof helped lull the couple into a deep sleep, not awakening again until the sun's early light.

CHAPTER 10

✦✦✦✦✦

The next six weeks passed quicky, with Jason and Wendy continuing to complete chores around the cabin and search for gold in nearby creeks and streams. Both Wendy and Jason carried on under the assumption that Jason would be extending his stay past the summer. They reenforced the fencing of the shelter for Brutus, which provided some protection from predators. Jason visited open meadows and cut tall grass to dry for Brutus to eat over the winter. Wendy gathered forest edibles, drying and preserving some for the colder months. They paddled to areas around the lake where Jason felled dead trees for firewood. They would be collected in the winter when the ice made it easier to transport them to the cabin. The couple found a few more nuggets of gold, but certainly had not attained great wealth.

One morning Wendy awoke with nausea overwhelming her. She rushed to the door of the cabin and made her exit as sickness overtook her. She vomited violently, waves of nausea sweeping over her. A short while later she started to feel better. Initially concerned that it was food related, her instincts told her otherwise. There was little doubt that she was pregnant.

Jason grew concerned. The days passed and the sickness in the morning continued. Wendy now convinced she was going to be a new mother, decided to stick to a strictly plant and fish diet. She felt this would be safer than eating wild meat, which might contain parasites or toxins that could harm the baby.

This was a life changing event for the couple, meaning an exit from the bush, back to Seattle where Jason had family. Their mixed-race relationship would be accepted there, but they would still face prejudices. Finding gold was now a priority, as money for their new life became important. As the days went by Wendy started feeling better, yellow fever returning to both her and Jason as their quest for gold soon dominated their lives.

Tomorrow they would walk around the lake with King and Brutus to a creek they had previously explored when out in the canoe. They decided to spend two days there exploring the area.

Packing for the trip had been completed the night before, allowing them to leave at daybreak. The trip through the forest was slow, as thick brush and heavily wooded areas delayed their progress. They arrived at their destination without incident, found a clearing along the creek, and set up camp. Many chipmunks called this place home also. With no fear of humans, they came to Wendy and Jason, looking for food. To the gold seekers they were entertainment, their constant chattering bringing some life to the quiet forest.

Another resident of the neighborhood was a porcupine, who lived in a hollow tree close to their camp. The first night they were there, Jason and Wendy watched the animal leave at dusk, going on his nightly hunting trip. The night was dark and quiet, the campfire the sole source of light. The couple enjoyed the crackling of the wood, and the mesmerizing flame. The couple lay down by the fire, pulling the blankets over their chilled bodies, snuggling close to keep warm. A peaceful sleep followed, their dreams about gold and their future. The night was black, but dawn would soon arrive, the start of a day that would hopefully bring prosperity to this young couple as survival and their new baby become the focus of their lives.

CHAPTER 11

━━━━━━━ ✦✦✦✦✦ ━━━━━━━

The couple woke, anxious to start their day. Breakfast had to be caught first, so they walked the short distance to the lake, and within an hour returned with enough fish to satisfy their hunger. The meal was cooked on the outdoor fire and enjoyed immensely by the couple and King. After they finished eating, they walked to the creek with their panning supplies, finding a spot that looked promising. After searching for gold with no success, they moved to a different area, but got the same results. They panned for gold again near where the creek emptied into the lake, but again came up with nothing. Discouraged, they returned to camp to talk about how they should continue with this endeavor, realizing they may need a new approach to be successful.

The day was sunny and warm. The couple lay down and soon drifted off to sleep, the sunshine warming them like a cozy blanket on a cold night. When they woke, it was decided to leave early the next day and return to the cabin. Toward dusk a campfire was built, and as they sat around it the couple discussed what to do about their inability to find gold. They could not come up with any answers.

The forest was silent, the stars shining brightly in the night sky as Jason woke up. He sensed something was wrong and woke Wendy fearing the worse. Brutus was missing; but the mystery was how. He had been tied up, and it appeared someone had untied and taken him. A chill ran down Jason's spine as he realized they were not the only ones making these woods home. A clear and present danger now confronted them, and they would have to watch their backs.

The pair packed up the camp in silence, their plans unravelling in front of them. They carried what they could and left the remaining gear to be retrieved at a later date. Without Brutus life would be difficult, but they would adjust. Shortly after leaving camp and rounding a corner, a shock awaited them, there was Brutus! A warm reunion followed, the couple never expecting the return of the animal. Maybe Brutus did free himself, but serious doubt remained.

It was approaching late afternoon when they reached home. They started a fire to warm the cabin, taking the chill out of the air. Wendy had told Jason about an old mine that had been dug by prospectors. The men never reaped the fruits of their labor as they were found murdered in a suspected robbery. The mine had been abandoned and was never worked again. Legend had it that these prospectors had struck it rich, and a horde of gold was stashed somewhere near their camp. In a last-ditch effort, the couple decided to plan a week-long trip to investigate the old mine and surrounding area. Yellow Fever returned as their quest for gold continued.

CHAPTER 12

The couple awoke to loud thunder and a severe lightning storm. Rain pounded on the roof, exposing a leak which ran down the wall of the cabin. King, who hated thunder, stuck close to Jason. The storm was making him nervous. Soon the bad weather moved out, leaving clear skies in its wake. The sky, blue with wispy clouds, welcomed a new day. Preparations would be made today for their adventure to the gold mine. It was a two-day hike and would require shelter to sleep in, as the summer rains had begun. Excitement mounted as the thought of finding gold slipped back into their minds.

The couple's departure date soon arrived; the party left the cabin and started their journey to the mine. They moved in silence, thinking this might be their last chance to make their dreams come true. Finding nothing would mean a return to Seattle broke, with little chance of a future, a struggle faced by many. A feeling of hopelessness was starting to invade their thoughts, as they faced insurmountable odds, success reserved for only a lucky few.

The morning trek was uneventful. They stopped for lunch in a green meadow where Brutus could eat his fill of grass. Jason and Wendy lay down in the warm sunshine, embracing each other, enjoying the love they were feeling. With Brutus finally done eating, they left the meadow, and continued their journey. Wendy told Jason about a lake on their route where they could stay for the night.

Suddenly King ran off. He had smelled the decaying remains of a deer that had been killed by wolves, the bones left for other predators to pick clean. They continued on their journey, soon arriving at the crystal-blue lake, shining in the sunlight. They made camp along the shoreline, the scenery captivating. The lake provided them with dinner, while the forest offered up its share of accompanying delights.

As darkness fell, a roaring campfire was soon burning, casting a warm glow over the couple. The sounds of the forest were everywhere, the wind blowing through the trees, the night owl hooting, and the insects buzzing. Sleep came easily, the darkness sending the couple into a peaceful slumber that lasted till morning. The early morning light and King's activity roused the couple. Another sunny day prevailed, lifting the spirits of these two adventurers, who expected to reach their destination today. Hopefully this trip would be a life changing event, not another disappointment, as they continued in their quest for gold.

CHAPTER 13

———— ✦✦✦✦✦✦ ————

The remnants of an old cabin came into view. The entrance to the mine was one hundred feet from this old structure. The couple had left their campsite early, making their way through the forests and hills of the Yukon wilderness, arriving at their destination just before dinnertime. Exploration of the area was a priority. No sign of recent human activity could be found. The miners' cabin was in ruins. It had never been a well-built structure, and now lay as scattered debris on the property.

A creek nearby provided fresh spring water to drink, and signs of sluicing could be seen, the remnants of the equipment scattered about and abandoned. The old prospectors had originally tried finding gold in the water that flowed from an underground river. Being unsuccessful at this, they decided to dig a mine searching for a vein. It was rumoured that the men had found a sizable amount of gold, which resulted in thieves killing them in an attempt to steal it. However, the gold was never found, leading to the story that the missing gold was hidden somewhere on the property or in the mine.

The wooded area along the bank of the creek was where the couple decided to camp. A tarp was set up to provide shelter, and wood was gathered in hopes that they would be able to catch fish for dinner. The fresh, cold water of these creeks provided a perfect habitat for these elusive fish to live in. Jason was anxious to begin searching for gold, so Wendy agreed to try her hand at fishing while he explored the creek.

Not wanting to wait any longer, Jason took his gold pan and tried his luck. Wading into the water, his efforts paid off, as soon a nugget appeared, followed by another. Less than an hour later Jason was holding four small nuggets, with traces of gold flake in some of the pans he had processed. This led him to believe that they were on the right track, though he tried not to get too excited.

Jason returned to camp and found Wendy cleaning the fish she had caught while he was panning for gold. As he helped her finish, she told him about a figure she had seen in the woods, a shadowy creature that appeared more human than animal. This made her feel uneasy, the memory of their episode with Brutus returning to her. At dinner the young couple tried to think of who or what could be stalking them.

Wendy and Jason were thankful they had King as an early warning system, and they could at least get some sleep without worry. Jason kept his gun loaded, and within reach. It might have been an overactive imagination, but they had to be prepared. Lives in the bush can be changed in minutes; unforeseen danger materializing without warning.

As the darkness set in, the forest took on new meaning, the nocturnal life being in charge. With no moon and a low cloud cover, blackness in the forest was assured until dawn's early light. Jason and Wendy slept peacefully until King's barking jolted them awake. Jason reached for his gun and went to investigate. What he saw shocked him, once again throwing this adventure in a different direction.

CHAPTER 14

The man stood large, a serious look spread across his face; Jason paused, not knowing what his next move would be. Wendy's voice broke the silence. She called out the man's name, they met and embraced. Wendy introduced Jason to her brother, Steward. He was three years older than her, and over the years had become very protective of his sister. On a visit to see Wendy at her cabin, he had noticed the presence of another person. He quietly retreated, deciding to observe, rather than surprise, the visitor. The three of them returned to camp, where Wendy explained the relationship she had with Jason. Steward was not happy, telling Wendy a bond with a white man was something he could never approve of. He hugged his sister and left abruptly, disappearing into the forest.

Silence followed as they reflected on Steward's words and actions. Wendy now knew she would have to leave with Jason. If her brother found out she was pregnant, it could put Jason's life in danger. Honour for his people, and sister, could drive Steward to commit an act of retribution. If they could keep the news of the baby from her brother, Jason would remain safe. Their quest for gold would continue, but Steward would have to be viewed as a threat, not to be taken lightly.

The wind blew through the forest as the couple returned to bed, eventually falling into a deep sleep. In her dream, Wendy was approached by a spirit, who told her the future would be hard because of decisions she had made, but this would not interfere with their success in finding gold. Wendy took this as a positive sign, and in the morning shared the vision with Jason. They sat by the campfire warming themselves, it had been a cool night and the warmth from the fire was appreciated.

Today they needed to find more food, Jason hoped to bag a rabbit or a gamebird. Wendy would collect edible plants from the forest, but Jason wanted meat in his diet. He left and entered the forest, almost immediately shooting a grouse, a plentiful gamebird with a delicious taste. Shortly thereafter another one was shot. He could now return to camp and enjoy the meat he had been craving. He cleaned the fowl, and the birds were soon cooking. Wendy gathered some bittercress, which she also cooked over the fire.

While eating, the couple discussed the mine, and decided to search it in the afternoon. This morning they would go to the forest where Wendy had found ripe berries. They reached the patch and were surprised to find they were not the only ones taking advantage of this free food. A large black bear glared at them; Jason readied his rifle in case of an attack. Fear gripped the couple, not knowing what the outcome of this situation would be.

CHAPTER 15

The black bear paused, its thoughts turning to whether it wanted a confrontation with this unfamiliar species. Jason's heart raced, his finger on the trigger, waiting for the bear to react. With a low growl, the bear turned away and slowly moved into the forest. A huge sigh of relief came from the young couple as they realized how close they had come to a disaster. With the appeal of picking berries gone, they decided to return to their camp. They would regroup and tackle their second task, the investigation of the mine.

The sound of thunder pierced the silence; a cool wind blew, signalling the approach of a storm. Jason checked the tarp to make sure it was secure. He was not a moment too soon, as strong wind, loud thunder, and brilliant lightning dominated the landscape. King huddled with the couple under the tarp, restless but safe. Brutus was tied under a large fir tree, nervous but secure. The storm passed, leaving a silent, misty landscape in its wake. They came out from under the shelter, the bright sun slowly returning, drying the moisture that had been left behind.

Jason caught a glimpse of a fox watching them from a nearby outcropping of rock. Wendy said it was the spirit of her father, keeping them safe. They made their way to the opening in the hill. The prospectors had made this hole in the earth, hoping to find a mineral that would make them rich. Unfortunately, they had ended up dead, their bones scattered around the property by the animals that had made them dinner.

The couple peered into the mine, apprehensive of what lay beyond, apprehensive about entering. They stepped back, surveying the area, looking for any anomalies that would guide them. Seeing nothing, they decided to proceed. After walking just a few yards inside, they recognized it was not really a mine, but a large hole dug in the side of the hill. Jason's heart sank as he realized this adventure was taking them nowhere. They returned to camp, and after a short discussion decided to relocate to a spot Wendy knew of. A lake where they could fish, with a fast-moving stream where they could pan for gold. They packed up and left, once again disappointed at the outcome of this adventure.

After a long walk the pair reached their destination, a small lake surrounded by a lush green meadow. Brutus had discovered the lush grass and was already filling his empty stomach. Camp was set up on a spot that appeared to be made for them, a small rise with a lakefront view. Jason looked out across the water, numerous waterfowl could be seen swimming, a food source if the birds came close enough for him to shoot.

Wendy stayed at camp, using the indigenous skills she had learned from her people to start a fire. Jason went fishing and soon returned with enough fish to feed them, and King, for dinner. The sun was setting as they finished eating. More wood was added to the fire, and peace settled over them. The night was dark, sleep came easy, and a pleasant surprise awaited them tomorrow.

CHAPTER 16

The couple awoke to the sound of a crow, perched high above in a dead birch tree, its shrill call piercing the morning air. King nuzzled Jason, encouraging him to get up, a sense of apprehension in his demeanour. Jason rose, the morning air was cool, causing him to stir the coals in the campfire. He added some dry wood to create some warmth. Wendy stretched, comfortable under her warm blankets. She was in no hurry to begin another day.

Wendy's pregnancy had been progressing smoothly. She had experienced no problems up to this point but was worried that time was not on her side. They would have to soon think about going to Dawson or Seattle to prepare for the baby's arrival, which would be in February. The problem was they had no money, and with no help from Wendy's family, they were on their own. This made finding gold vital to their existence.

Jason left and within an hour returned with fish for breakfast. After eating they would try panning for gold, the nearby creek looking like a good spot. King let out a low growl and moved closer to Jason. The dog's behaviour indicated something was making him uncomfortable. Jason gripped his rifle, ready to deal with any trouble that arose.

The day was cool with bright sunshine, warming the adventurers as they gathered their supplies and headed to the creek. After two hours of fruitless panning, the discouraged couple headed back to camp. They decided to spend the night here and return to the old mine site in the morning. They would not pan for gold there, but rather search for the prospectors' lost gold.

The quiet of the forest was deafening and the light from the campfire mesmerizing, lulling the couple into a false sense of security. Suddenly the calm was interrupted by a frantic cry from Brutus, and King barking and snarling loudly. The dog took a defensive position by the mule. The wolves had been watching, waiting for the opportune time to launch an attack on Brutus. Their plan was foiled by King, who had sensed the danger, warning Jason and Wendy of their unwanted guests. The wolves sensing their plan had been disrupted, slunk back into the forest.

Brutus was tethered closer to Jason and Wendy and watched by King, to make sure this incident would not be repeated. The night passed and the next morning found them on their way back to the old mine. They would spend two more days there, and then return to their cabin. Wendy had a dream, in which her father told her where the missing gold could be found. She did not share this information with Jason, as he did not believe in contact with the spirit world. Maybe tomorrow would bring the discovery of the lost gold, and the beginning of a bright future for this couple.

CHAPTER 17

The small party arrived at the old mine site in the early afternoon the following day. The trip there had been without incident, but in a stroke of good luck, Wendy had shot a rabbit, which would provide Jason and King with meat for dinner. They set up camp, Jason discouraged by the series of events leading up to this moment. Their inability to find gold caused him to worry as to how they could survive without help from his family, something he did not want to ask for.

Before dinner, they searched the old mine, once again finding nothing. Wendy suggested they check the old homestead site again. The remnants of the structure littered the clearing where it had once stood. After a thorough search they found nothing, until Wendy saw something that looked unusual. The end of one of the old cabin's logs appeared to have been sealed with a wooden plug. Jason and Wendy removed the end of the log to reveal a large opening; the log had been hollowed out. Jason reached in and felt a leather bag. His heart was pounding with excitement, as he pulled the bag from its resting place, handed it to Wendy and told her to open it. Wendy reached in and pulled out a smaller bag that was filled with large gold nuggets, enough to give them and their baby a heathy start on life. Neither of them could believe their eyes.

The jubilant couple hugged each other, love and happiness dominating their tired spirits. They returned to camp, examined the gold further, and hid it in a safe place. They wondered where these nuggets had come from. Their appearance suggested they were panned from a creek. Were Jason's grandfather's stories about large nuggets true after all? Were there more hidden at his grandfather's cabin? With their work done here, the couple would leave tomorrow and return home with gratitude for the good fortune that had been bestowed on them.

The campfire that night had a special glow, the fire representing their renewed hope for prosperity in this wild and untamed land. The moon shone brightly, casting a light on the young couple, as if God was bathing them in his protection. But now sleep was on their minds as they prepared for their journey home tomorrow.

CHAPTER 18

The couple woke early, gathering their belongings as they prepared to leave, the gold they had found filling them with joy. Suddenly King started barking and growling. Two men were making their way toward their camp. Fear gripped the couple as these strangers could be dangerous. A man's life meant nothing to most men that plied the Yukon looking for gold. A woman, especially an Indian woman, was considered a prize, usually a target of rape and beatings at the hands of some of these individuals. Jason gripped his rife tightly, ready to take whatever action necessary to protect their lives.

The men approached the couple's camp and held out their hands in greeting. Jason was uneasy and mistrustful as he reached out and shook hands with the strangers. The men looked warily at King, who had taken an instant dislike toward them, sensing danger. The men explained they had come from Dawson City and had heard about the legend of gold and the old mine. They had camped a few miles away and had left at dawn to reach the site. They were surprised to find Jason and Wendy here. Jason explained that they had found nothing in their search for the lost gold and were getting ready to leave.

The men cast an evil eye on Wendy, their thoughts turning to sex, the only thing they felt she was good for. Lust took over, clouding their judgement. One of the men raised his gun, pointing it towards Jason. King attacked and Jason was forced to shoot. Two shots rang out in quick succession, and then there was silence. The strangers lay dead, King's quick actions saving Jason's and Wendy's lives. Shock and disbelief overwhelmed the couple, realizing they had come close to death themselves. They had packed in a shovel, which they used to bury the two men, adding another story to the legend of the mine.

Brutus was loaded with their belongings and they left for home. Silence ensued as the memory of this tragedy unfolded in the minds of Jason and Wendy, a memory that would haunt them forever. The trip back to the cabin was uneventful, and they soon found themselves warming themselves in front of the fire, glad for an inside shelter to shield them from the elements. They had retrieved some food from the now deceased men, and with the grouse that Jason had been lucky enough to shoot, they enjoyed a nice dinner. Survival in this wilderness was the number one priority; taking the dead man's food was not viewed as a cardinal sin.

CHAPTER 19

The storm had raged all night, the thunder and lightning were intense. Jason and Wendy were worried. The cabin sat under large trees, any one of which could destroy the structure if it was uprooted, and fell on the roof, endangering the lives of the couple inside. The wind howled and the crash of toppling trees in the forest could be heard, heightening their anxiety even more. After hours of damaging winds, the atmosphere calmed, and the horizon glowed with the sunrise, promising a brighter day.

The couple exited the cabin, noticing that many trees had been blown down. Worried about Brutus, they checked his shelter which had held up well. He was scared but calm. King had also been afraid, staying close to Jason and Wendy for comfort during the storm. They returned to the cabin, Wendy making her forest tea, which calms the soul when under stress, a remedy used by her people for many years. The decision was made to go to the lake today, retrieve the canoe, and replenish their supply of fish. Jason would also take his gun, as the lake showed signs of beaver, which would provide them with fresh meat, and maybe a nice hat.

They left King and Brutus at the cabin and headed to the lake.

Upon arriving, Wendy and Jason loaded the canoe and launched it into the crystal-clear water, the calm and quiet taking them to another place, and another time. Only the call of the loon could be heard, as the paddles rippled the water, propelling them forward to an unknown destination. Jason nudged Wendy to look. Feeding along the shoreline was a bull moose, it's rack of antlers on display, a symbol of strength in the northern forest. They changed direction and headed toward where they had seen beaver activity; they soon found the lodge and quietly waited.

The beaver, sensing no danger, exposed himself to Jason, and with a quick shot from his rifle, the dead animal was soon sharing a spot in the canoe. Jason hated to kill these mammals, but they provided food, a necessity for sustaining life. The fishing was also successful, and they soon found themselves back at the cabin cleaning fish and butchering the beaver. Wendy would work the hide for use in the future. She gathered some plants from the forest, and soon a large pot of stew was cooking on the stove, a delicious addition to the somewhat bland diet that they had been following.

A knock on the cabin door was startling. Jason grabbed his gun, anxiety and apprehension taking over as they wondered who this visitor might be. King, a low growl coming from his throat, also sensed possible danger. Silence filled the cabin as Jason approached the door to confront the visitor. Unlike their last visit with strangers, this encounter would be more positive. Jason called out and was surprised at the reply he received. He hesitated at opening the door, fearful of what the results might be.

CHAPTER 20

Wendy's brother stood in the open doorway. Jason, sensing no danger, let him enter. Steward embraced his sister, telling her he was on a mission of reconciliation. A visit from their mother in Steward's dream, had revealed Wendy's pregnancy to him. Their mother told her son his support for Wendy and the baby was important and hoped that they would continue to care for one another. His presence indicated he wanted to fulfill their mother's wish. Wendy was elated, hugging her brother, and enjoying the love he once again showered upon her. She knew he would be a protective force while they were at the cabin. After a lengthy visit, Steward left, and a feeling of peace and hope prevailed.

Following the previous night's storm, Wendy and Jason were assessing the damage outside when they happened upon what appeared to be a root cellar. Jason's grandfather had dug a hole in the ground to use for storage, providing a cool, dry place for perishables in the summer and could be used as a freezer in the winter. As the years went by, the entrance door had been covered in debris, concealing it until the high winds revealed its presence. They anxiously opened the now rotted door and entered a small space under the earth.

Their first glance revealed nothing, but a shiny glint in the corner caught Jason's attention. He dug with his hands revealing a small metal box. Excitement mounted as yellow fever struck, the thought that the nuggets his grandfather had bragged about might be inside. Jason's desire for gold mounted as he backed out of the hole, anxious to see what the box contained. Opening it revealed nothing, except a written message.

The couple took the box into the cabin to examine it further, studying the note that Jason's grandfather had left, which indicated it was a clue to finding his hidden gold. The message read, "In the waning days of summer when the waters are low, a treasure can be found at the rushing waters". Tomorrow, they would check around the waterfall, not really believing they would find anything of value.

The day was winding down, the sun setting earlier as the fall equinox approached. King enjoyed the beaver stew, while the couple ate the fish they had caught. The temperatures were getting colder extending the shelf life of meat and fish. The root cellar would also be helpful in maintaining a fresh food supply. The stars shone brightly, the moonlight shining through the window, giving the cabin light throughout the night.

CHAPTER 21

The next day dawned clear and cold. The summer was quickly losing its grip to autumn, which would be followed by a long winter. Wendy and Jason would leave for Dawson soon, but first they had to investigate Jason's grandfather's claim of treasure at the waterfall. With little fanfare they walked to the water, where more land was exposed due to lower water levels. After a fruitless search in the upper rocks, they were just about ready to give up when Jason noticed something unusual. At the bottom of the pool, he caught a glimpse of something shiny. He reached down and pulled a nugget from its resting place. Maybe they had been looking in the wrong place. Were the nuggets in the bottom of the pool the ones Jason's grandfather had described?

Excitement mounted as the thought of pulling more nuggets out of the sand overtook the couple's sensibilities. The pair retrieved the shovel from the cabin and dug down into the now shallow pool. They deposited the first shovel of material on the bank of the river, glints of gold shone in the sun, causing yellow fever to overwhelm the young couple. Further exploration revealed nuggets of varying sizes. Why had this gold never been retrieved? Jason's grandfather had no interest in the monetary value of this precious metal, to him the only value in gold were the stories he could tell about it.

However, the grandfather had known the gold would be of great value to whomever believed his tall tales and searched for the truth. Jason had successfully completed a plan that his grandfather had put in place years ago. The gold was now theirs, but the couple had to safely transport it to a reputable gold buyer to fully realize their wealth. They gathered the gold and returned to the cabin, wondering when they would awaken from this dream.

A flock of noisy crows caught the couple's attention, usually indicating a meal of carrion was available. Upon investigating, they found the remains of a deer the wolves had brought down the night before. It was concerning that this kill was close to the cabin. However, they took advantage of the meat that was still edible, harvesting what they could for King and Jason. This was the second surprising find of the day.

The sky darkened as the night descended on this oasis of peace in the forest. Shooting stars flashed their light across the sky, an endless show put on by the heavens. The power of this celestial event would instill awe for generations to come.

CHAPTER 22

The couple woke to a cold north wind blowing. Wendy and Jason decided it would soon be time to head to Dawson, hoping to leave before a blizzard could block their exit. Travelling with the gold made the couple apprehensive, as many dangers, including robbery, were common in this frontier. Two weeks later they were ready to leave. Brutus was loaded with their possessions, and the cabin was secured. They said a tearful goodbye to the way of life they had come to know. If all went well, it would be a three-day trip, with two nights spent in the bush. With a sadness in their hearts, the adventurers, King, and Brutus left the security of the cabin, for a new life of uncertainties.

The first few miles were uneventful, an easy scenic route through the forests and meadows. Soon things would change, danger would strike quickly, reminding them again about the challenges they faced. Jason sensed something was amiss, King's behavior had changed. He was nervous and restless, signalling imminent danger. Extra precautions needed to be taken until this issue was resolved.

They stopped for lunch, which consisted of fish and venison they had smoked, preserving the meat to provide nutritious food for their trip to Dawson. Many hungry animals populated the bush, also searching for enough food to survive. In their eyes, Brutus was that meal. The travellers were being followed by hungry wolves, the mule being their intended target.

Jason was the first to notice the hungry animals. Led by a black alpha male, an experienced hunter who was in charge of the pack. The natives feared this animal, who was perceived as a sign of darkness and evil. Wendy knew that this wolf could only be stopped by killing him. The black wolf was intent on making Brutus food for the pack. The black wolf would not give up until that goal was reached, even if it meant his own death.

The couple continued their journey, the wolves following at a distance. Tonight, the couple would have to select their camp site carefully, as they needed to protect themselves and their animals against an attack. They would need to keep a large fire going and camp in an open area. Brutus and King would be kept close by, guarded by the couple who would take turns on sentry duty. Hopefully this would keep them safe.

The night was quiet, as a silence overtook the forest. Wendy and Jason had found a safe place to camp and hoped everyone would survive the night. The serenity of the night was deceiving, catching Jason off guard. While on watch, he fell asleep, his rife slung across his chest. The black wolf watched, waiting for the opportune moment to attack. King whimpered, aware of the danger they faced. He nudged Jason to no avail. A successful attack by the wolves would be devastating, as they were experienced killers and had numbers on their side.

CHAPTER 23

King's nudges finally woke Jason. With a start he sat up, realizing the dangerous situation he had put his group in. The forest was silent, thoughts of what lie ahead causing apprehension. Knowing a threat was out there and the situation could explode into violence at any moment, kept Jason's senses on high alert. After hours of silence, his instincts told him the wolves had left. Was this just a trick by the black wolf to lull them into complacency and let their guard down?

The darkness soon turned to light as the sunrise announced the beginning of a new day. The wolves were gone, but the threat remained. Getting to Dawson would free the travelers from this danger, but new ones may prevail. They broke camp early, the calm invaded by doubts as to what their future held. Wendy's pregnancy was entering its fifth month, and she would soon need stability in her life for the safety of their child. The aunt who raised Wendy was still in Dawson, along with a few other relatives. Wendy was sure her mother's sister would help them until the couple had a plan for their future.

The little party slowly made its way forward, visions of a new life with the baby dominating their thoughts. The silence was suddenly broken by King's barking. The wolves were behind them again, watching, waiting, and planning their next move. Jason and Wendy's spirits sank to a new low. They had believed this threat was gone because of the inactivity the night before. The black wolf would have the last laugh, knowing he still had a chance to make his plan successful. Jason and Wendy carried on, the wolves following, instilling fear into the couple as they wondered how this was all going to end.

In the late afternoon, Jason chose a large open area for their camp. He built a roaring fire, and with Wendy's help they gathered enough firewood to last through the night. Jason was exhausted from getting little sleep the night before, leaving Wendy in charge of security while he slept. The activity started with loud barking from King. The wolves were on the attack. The black wolf stayed back, letting his minions carry out his plan.

The pack sprang from the trees, their attention focused on Brutus, quickly bringing him to the ground in a vicious attack. Wendy jumped to her feet, gunshots rang out and the three wolves lay dead. The rest of the pack, realizing the danger, retreated to the woods. Brutus lay still on the ground.

The wolves, with their lust for blood, had ripped out Brutus' throat, causing his death. Sadness filled the hearts of Wendy and Jason over the loss of their beloved mule. The couple got no sleep that night, as they stood guard over Brutus's body. Having no way to bury him, the black wolf was the ultimate winner, his pack able to eat their fill once the couple moved on.

CHAPTER 24

The northern sky was a dark blue with wispy white clouds, the sun's warmth was welcomed after a cold and sleepless night. Jason and Wendy felt no warmth, only grief for the loss of Brutus, their beloved mule. The coldness they felt was toward the wolves, who had killed their companion and helper, leaving them to pack as many of their belongings as they could carry, a formidable task in this wilderness. They had left Brutus where he lay, knowing the black wolf and the remainder of the pack would be back to finish the job they started. A victory for the wolves. a tragic ending for Brutus who deserved much better.

The party was quiet, their thoughts trapped in the moment, until a sharp yelp from King snapped them back to reality. He seemed confused, wandering in circles, whining in discomfort. Jason went to investigate, finding King had stepped on an old trap forgotten years ago by someone trying to eke out a living catching furs. Luckily the spring on the trap was rusted, making it unable to snap shut hard enough to cause damage to the bone. King received only a slight abrasion on his leg. Jason released the trap and King bounded away no worse for the wear.

The sky had darkened, and a cold north wind blew, signalling the first snow of the season. It was a light dusting, which served as a reminder of what was to come. They continued their journey, the buildings of the remote city in the wilderness appearing in the distance. Dawson stood as a testament to the grit and stamina instilled in the men that developed yellow fever, causing them to travel long distances in their quest for gold. Because of the influx of these visitors, Dawson had turned into a crowded, dangerous place.

Luckily for Wendy and Jason, they were headed to the outskirts of town. Wendy's aunt had a large cabin in the woods, where they would be welcomed until the next step of their journey began. Wendy planned on having her baby here, as her Aunt Beverly was a midwife who had delivered many babies in Dawson.

Bev was shocked to see a pregnant Wendy, accompanied by a white man, appear on her doorstep in the afternoon. She welcomed them in and listened intently as Wendy told her how they had met, and the adventures they had shared. Wendy's aunt was pleased to see how happy her niece was, and warmly welcomed Jason to her home.

Celebrating Wendy's return, the couple were treated to dinner, the first food Jason had eaten since breaking camp. He had insisted Wendy have the small amount of food available on the last leg of their journey. King had also gone without, but now it was their turn to eat. The main course was moose, which had been given to Bev by a tribe member, accompanied by a variety of vegetables, a buffet the couple had not experienced in months.

Beverly shared tribal news with Wendy, updating her on members who had passed and babies who had been born. She told Wendy about a 12-year-old boy who had died during a fishing trip when he fell out of the canoe, his father unable to save him. Wendy's aunt informed Jason she knew a reputable gold dealer who dealt fairly with natives, assuring him he would not be cheated. Jason would meet with this man tomorrow, selling the gold they had found. Bev did not want the gold in her home, as she feared the evil it might bring.

CHAPTER 25

————— ✦✦✦✦✦ —————

Dawson was the only city where men could purchase supplies for their gold hunting ventures, most of which ended in failure, sending the men back to their starting point. Jason had found gold, and lots of it. The sale of this precious mineral would provide him and Wendy with enough money to put down roots wherever they chose.

Jason left the house and was soon in Dawson. The city was a hot bed of activity, with the streets full of men with dogs and mules. The gold buyers' storefronts beckoned the lucky few to sell their new found wealth. However, many of these dealers were unscrupulous, often taking advantage of these men. Jason searched for a gold dealer named John. He carried a letter of introduction from Bev, assuring him of fair treatment.

In Dawson City there were many native people. It was common for white prospectors to pair up with Indian women and have children. This created an acceptable tolerance for these mixed-race relationships. John often dealt with such couples when buying gold, so would not be surprised to see Jason with a letter from Beverly. Jason entered John's storefront, finding a large man with a no-nonsense attitude. He read the letter, took the gold, weighed it, paid Jason, and shooed him out the door with little conversation. On his way home, Jason bought a large beef bone for King as a special treat. He would give Bev some money and buy supplies that were needed for the house.

Wendy had been uncomfortable the last few days, she had not felt the baby moving since they left the cabin. She did not share this news with Jason, as she did not want to worry him. A few days later she began having sporadic pains, which was not a good sign. She knew in her heart something was wrong, again not sharing any of this with Jason or her aunt.

The contractions started in the middle of the night. Jason roused Beverly, who rushed to Wendy's side. Both women knew it was too early for a good outcome, so were not surprised that Wendy experienced a stillbirth after an hour of labour. Wendy fared well health-wise but was devastated by the death of her daughter. Wendy and Jason embraced, their sadness overwhelming them. They would pick up the pieces from this tragedy, and Nara, their deceased daughter would remain in their hearts forever.

Jason awoke, the night was still young, the sky dark and starless. Wendy rolled over in the bed and hugged him tightly. The loss of their baby had been a shock, a setback to their plans, a situation that they had to deal with in order to get on with their lives. It had been two weeks since this tragic event and Wendy and Jason were beginning to accept that this was God's decision and no fault of their own. As time passed the wounds would heal, but the memories would never die.

CHAPTER 26

The end of October neared, and tribe members were leaving on a moose hunt. Jason had been asked to join the hunt, which would replenish the meat supply of senior tribe members who were unable to hunt for themselves. Jason had agreed to go at Wendy's request, as a show of cooperation and respect between their two cultures. A group of four men gathered at Bev's house, planning for the hunt to last a few days, not ending until a moose was shot. They left with two horses to pack out meat, a mule for carrying supplies, and King, Jason's dog.

The group's travels took them toward Jason and Wendy's cabin, to a swampy area that the moose enjoyed as habitat. The large animals ate the plants that grew there, but the open area left them exposed to hunters. Toward the end of the day, the party reached the area and set up camp. Snow covered the ground, creating a winter landscape in the forest. A large fire was soon burning, and dinner was being cooked. Tomorrow they would hunt the moose in the early morning, hoping to catch a moose unaware and ending their hunt early. Little did they know an interruption in their plans would take place, opening an old wound for Jason.

The next morning the men were up early, ate breakfast, and enthusiastically left for the hunt. As they approached the area, they saw they were not the only ones interested in bagging a moose. Wolf tracks covered the vicinity. Jason thought of the black wolf and the loss of Brutus, their beloved mule. He wondered if the tracks were from the same predators. Based on the tracks, the numbers made sense. Jason was sure it was the black wolf, giving him a chance to avenge the death of Brutus.

As expected, within a short time a moose was killed, providing a winter's supply of meat for the elderly, an important source of protein to help them get through the Yukon winter. The sun was setting as the last of the moose was butchered and taken back to camp. Jason told the men of his run-in with the black wolf and the loss of his mule. He asked if they would help him eradicate this dangerous predator. The men agreed, although had some reservations because of the folklore surrounding black wolves.

The men covered themselves in the moose's blood so the wolves would not be able to catch their scent and hid in the treeline. The silence of the forest was deafening, the approach of the wolves certain. The animals circled the carcass, the black wolf staying out of sight. Finally, convinced it was safe, the pack leader came out of the shadows to eat. A shot rang out and the black wolf lay dead.

Jason would return to Dawson with the pelt of the black wolf, a rare prize for the people who viewed this animal as an unnecessary evil in the forest. Jason was happy. He had defeated the black wolf on his own terms, bringing peace to his soul, as he blamed himself for the death of Brutus. Tomorrow they would return to Dawson where Jason would reunite with Wendy and continue this journey they call life.

CHAPTER 27

The sky over Dawson was grey, as if casting a shadow over life. The life of a prospector wintering over in the Yukon was desolate and forlorn; nowhere to go, freezing from the cold, their dreams of gold a distant memory. Survival was their main cause of concern, and not an easy task.

The men returned from the moose hunt with smiles of success on their faces. Jason shared with Wendy the story of the black wolf and showed her the pelt he had returned with. Wendy explained it was the animal's fate for harboring so much hate in his heart. A feast was in order as the moose meat was cut up into more manageable pieces. The hunters, and their families, would be the first to enjoy this winter's meat. The meal would be at Bev's house, and everyone was asked to contribute something, if at all possible. Many families could only bring bread, but some had vegetables to offer. Hunger was a problem in Dawson, but it was especially acute during the winter months.

As the families gathered, stories were told, and gossip was shared. The celebration was a welcome change from the hardships of this distant frontier town. After the party, a quiet discussion took place between Bev and Wendy. It was decided that she and Jason would spend the winter here. Bev was most accommodating, knowing that a man's hand around the house could be invaluable.

As Bev lived alone, the tribe assisted her with wood for the winter. Now Jason would be able to secure wood for her, leaving the tribe to help another member. Jason was young and strong, able to fall trees and chop and split the wood. If he ran into trouble getting enough, Jason had money and could purchase wood from one of the many men who eked out a living this way.

Jason thought about acquiring a new mule. Bev's property had a shed large enough for the animal, where he could be protected against bad weather and predators. Bev was agreeable, so Wendy and Jason went to the livery stable in town looking for a healthy mule. The owner had a mule that been purchased in Mexico, taken to California, and then on to the Yukon, where its master was killed in a drunken fight over a woman. The owner of the livery stable took in the mule and had been caring for it since. He was asking a premium price, leaving few customers able to afford him.

Wendy and Jason purchased the mule and thought it appropriate to name him Omar because of his supposed heritage, a not quite believable story. Omar was glad to leave, hoping to enjoy a life filled with love, rather than the life at the stable. In reality, he had been thrust into that life by a prospector who was broke and desperate for money.

The mule settled into his new life with Wendy, Jason, and King, enjoying the comforts of the shelter at Bev's house and people who cared for him. The truth was, Omar was a lazy mule, unwilling to work, or pull his weight. He would need to be taught the right way to do things and the reality of his purpose; a pack animal that was considered family.

CHAPTER 28

It was an unusually warm, late November day in Dawson. The temperature was above freezing, and the snow was melting. This was an isolated event, with the few children living here building snowmen, which would then freeze, and act as town sentinels for the winter.

Dawson was beginning to become familiar to Jason, and for Wendy it was almost home. The thought of building a cabin here and staying was not out of the question. Jason knew the gold rush would eventually end, leaving a civilized town in its wake. As prospectors left to find new adventures elsewhere, land would be cheap, resulting in poverty and hardship for those left behind.

Heavy snows had come in November. Another hunting party had gone out beforehand, shooting a moose. Two deer were also shot outside of Dawson by a small hunting party that just happened upon them. Jason was asked to help to pick up the deer meat and deliver it into town. This was Omar's first test as a pack animal, and he would fail miserably.

Omar had been an entitled mule, living a life of the privilege on a farm in Washington, a pet for someone's daughter. He had been kidnapped and sent to the Klondike where there was a huge demand for pack animals. Omar hated anything on his back, finding it heavy and uncomfortable. Little did he know pack animals that consistently failed to perform their duties were usually sold for meat. Jason did not want Omar to meet that fate, so he would teach him to be a good pack animal. He was sure he could accomplish this task.

During dinner Bev made an interesting proposition. For a small amount of money, and a commitment to take care of her till death, she would give Wendy and Jason the house, which was an offer they could not refuse. Their communal living arrangement had worked out well, leading to this proposal. Bev was old but still in good health, giving Jason and Wendy the freedom to remain independent, at least for the foreseeable future. Other relatives that lived close to Wendy's aunt, were always available to watch out for Bev if needed.

November soon turned to December and the skies grew darker and the days shorter, casting an unforgiving gloom over the land. The perpetual cloud cover and little daylight caused some inhabitants to slip into a depressive state that would not lift until spring arrived. December brought one ray of hope, Christmas, a day of salvation and celebration. It was a time when all the town's inhabitants joined in hopes of a safe and prosperous future, where their Sunday best was worn, and dinners were served.

The community of Dawson, with its enthusiastic spirit and hospitality, was sure to thrive in the future. Wendy and Jason's plans were to become part of this new city in Canada's unforgiving north. A beacon of hope for their future, a new start and eventually a family. A dream almost unimaginable but possible.

CHAPTER 29

The blizzard had raged for two days, the wind was howling, driving the snow into large drifts, leaving the landscape an impregnable wall of white. Bev's house was comfortable. It was a large cabin her husband had built, and they had lived comfortably in for many years. He became sick, and after a long illness he died, leaving Bev to fend for herself. She had been very lonely and was so glad she had found Wendy and Jason to come live with her.

Before the storm had arrived, they had made sure Omar was comfortable, bringing him a warm buffalo rug to lay on, and giving him extra hay that Jason had purchased at the livery stable. This was the first blizzard Jason had experienced in the far north. The power of the storm scared him, making him feel insignificant and small. The cabin was strong, providing a safe refuge from this dangerous event.

Finally, the winds calmed, and the sun returned, shining brightly on the new snow, creating a brilliance Dawson had not seen in many days. The people came out of their cabins, marvelling at the landscape, a sea of white that seemed to never end. Things soon returned to normal, and the Christmas season got underway.

Trees were cut and decorated. Items from the forest were collected in the summer and fall, left to dry and used as ornaments, bringing new life to the dormant trees. Wreaths and garland were made from the evergreens in the forest, draping otherwise forlorn homes in Christmas cheer. Gifts were usually made by hand, a type of folk art that was prevalent in this town. Open houses in the early afternoon on Christmas day was a time for visiting. People called on neighbors, friends, and family, expressing good wishes for everyone's future. This was followed by a meal, with food provided to the needy, ensuring everyone in town enjoyed a traditional feast.

The new year came and went, just another day in town. Jason was asked to join another hunt, this time for wolves, who were competing with the people of Dawson for the few deer in the area. If there was a large population of these predators, the moose would also leave. Wolf pelts could be sold bringing much needed revenue in for the tribe. Traps would be set, and dens would be located, allowing the hunters to shoot the wolves if they could get close enough. The men would stay in shelters that had been built for use on traplines, a profession still practiced by some residents of Dawson. Sharing these shelters with wolf hunters was not a problem, as wolves were a destructive force to trappers, their demise a shared goal.

Wendy and Jason were happy with the way things had turned out for them. They had built trust and respect, making new friends, and had become an accepted part of the community. The wolf hunters were to leave tomorrow, so a good night's sleep was in order. The night was black, the quiet lulling the couple into a deep sleep, until a new day would awaken them.

CHAPTER 30

The hunting party arrived at Bev's house early. They had secured two horses, and food and supplies for their journey. Jason was ready and would take King and Omar on this trip. Omar had learned to be cooperative about carrying things on his back, learning his purpose in life. He was a pack animal, no longer someone's pet. Omar knew he had a good life with Jason, even though he was expected to work, a difficult realization for a lazy mule who preferred to do nothing.

On this hunting trip, the men would also be on the lookout for food, the focus being on rabbit and game birds. The men would set many snares for rabbit on their way to the wolf dens, checking them and collecting the spoils on the way home. They soon reached the first shelter, a cabin large enough to accommodate the three men and King. A fire was soon roaring in the stove, sending a welcome warmth throughout the small space. The men discussed their plans, deciding they would stay and rest in the cabin for the remainder of the day and start their hunt for the wolves tomorrow. They ate venison for dinner, supplemented by a grouse they had shot on the way here. The calm of the forest around them created a relaxing atmosphere, lulling them into an early sleep, not to awaken until dawn.

Jason was the first to rise, letting King out. Upon opening the door, he noticed wolf tracks in the snow. Apparently a single wolf had investigated the hunters' intrusion in his pack's territory. He must have been stealthy, as he had not disturbed the other animals as he went about his business. This was a good sign for the hunters, who could follow the tracks back to the den.

The men ate breakfast and left the shelter realizing the importance of finding these wolves, or the animals would return tonight for the horses or the mule. The tracks were easy to follow, and led them directly to the den, a cave in the rocks. If the men attempted to approach the den from the front, the wolves would see them. Therefore, it was decided one man would climb the rocks from the back, surprising and shooting the sentinel wolf. The other wolves, realizing the danger the gun portrayed, would flee right into the sights of the other hunters.

The first man left and soon a gunshot was heard, followed by another. The remaining two men waited. Sure enough the wolves started leaving, concerned about the danger they were facing, not the trap laid in front of them. Shots rang out, and three wolves lay dead. With the sentinel wolf, a total of four dead bodies were collected.

The men returned to the shelter, everyone happy except Omar who had been forced to carry a bloody, wolf carcass on his back. He thought of running away, but logic prevailed when he realized he had nowhere to go. Jason gave Omar love and affection, as he tied him up in the cedars for the night, indicating he had done a good job. Little did he know Omar would play a role in saving a life during a confrontation with nature tomorrow.

CHAPTER 31

———— ✦✦✦✦✦ ————

A blue sky announced the start of a bright and sunny day, wispy clouds adding an artist's touch to nature's scenery. The men rose, anxious to continue their hunt after yesterday's successes. They had processed the wolf hides and were hoping to add more by the end of the day. Omar was loaded with supplies, and along with one of the horses, the men left the cabin, heading to higher ground where they knew a wolves' den would be located.

After an hour of walking, the men saw no wolf sign. They were unaware they were being followed by the remaining wolves from the pack they had decimated yesterday. Wanting to exact revenge for the deaths of their family members, the wolves planned to ambush the men, hoping to inflict as much damage as possible. They were willing to give up their lives, if needed, so vengeance could be theirs.

The hunting party moved on, a strange calm prevailed. King alerted to possible trouble, exhibiting a restlessness that had proven accurate in the past. The men stopped, surveying the surrounding landscape. Movement was caught along the treeline that bordered the forest; a shadowy figure that no doubt was a wolf. The men froze, now realizing they were being stalked by these predators, the hunters now being the hunted. Their grips on their rifles tightened, sensing an attack was coming.

Three wolves bounded from their cover and lunged towards the men. Shots rang out. One wolf died in the volley, one was wounded, and the other ran off. The wounded wolf lunged at Jason in a vicious attack. In mid-air, just as he was about to pounce on Jason, Omar raised his back legs high and delivered a fatal blow to the injured wolf's head. The wolf collapsed at Jason's feet. Omar was a hero, having saved Jason's life. The mule glowed with the attention he received, comments about his willingness to give up his own life making him proud.

The hunters gathered the two bodies of the wolves, taking them back to camp to be processed. The men then packed up and left for home, the hunt being a huge success. Stopping to check their snares, which yielded six rabbits, the men still made it home before dark. They were all happy to return to a comfortable place after spending two nights in the bush.

Jason hugged Wendy, the couple having missed each other, their love never waning. Jason told Wendy about the wolf attack and how the mule had saved his life. Wendy was proud of the bravery Omar displayed and would now have a different opinion of him. Wendy told Jason there had been a wolverine hanging around the cabin while he had been away. The animal was probably hungry, arriving after smelling the cooking odors from the cabin.

Wendy had a fear of wolverines. In her culture they were cast in a worse light than wolves, taking the title of the most dangerous predator in the bush. This was a new menace that would have to be dealt with if the nightly visits continued.

It was a cold night in Dawson; the full moon and shining stars cast a warm glow over the frozen landscape, creating a serene scene untouched by human hands. The forest slept as the young couple dreamed, tomorrow's adventures unknown.

CHAPTER 32

The cold January days were coming to an end, ushering in February, another month of darkness and frigid cold. This weather kept the residents mostly in their homes, relying on their wood stoves to keep them warm. Wood smoke blanketed the town in a fog, creating a surreal atmosphere, as if the town belonged in another place, in another time.

The lure of gold caused many men to lose their senses, coming to the Yukon unprepared for winter. Some would lose their lives to nature, while others would die at the hands of their fellow man, as personal survival came first, others' lives meaning little. The cold days of February passed. The sick succumbed to the harsh elements; the healthy glad to be alive after an unforgiving winter.

With the approach of spring, Wendy and Jason had some decisions that needed to be made. Jason wanted to go to Seattle to see his family, while Wendy wanted to go back to the cabin, see her brother and live in the wilderness for the summer. Going to Seattle with Jason would not happen, as Wendy knew their relationship would not be accepted there.

Jason had to choose, leave Wendy and go to Seattle, or face the fact that he may never see his mother again.

Jason weighed the situation. His mother had not been well when he left; she could have passed away. It was a long, dangerous journey to Seattle, and may end up being made for nothing. His heart ached as the loss of either of these important women in his life was unthinkable. Deep down Jason knew Wendy would be his choice. She was his life mate, an arrangement made by God, a bond not to be broken. Jason believed his mother was alive and well, and eventually he would be reunited with her. He wrote a letter to her, knowing it may take months to reach her. He wanted to let his mother know he was well and happy.

Jason hugged Wendy, knowing he could not leave her, the risk of never seeing her again too great. They would leave together, spending the summer at the cabin, searching for more gold. Jason thought they needed a plan for next winter, either another stay in Dawson or a trip to Vancouver, a growing city on the coast where they would be able to stay for the winter or beyond. It would provide a refuge from the cold of the Yukon.

Wendy preferred to stay at the cabin, not willing to give up her heritage and past. They would wait until mid-April before heading back to their house in the woods, as the days would be longer, and the sun would be warmer, welcoming them back to their summer home. Jason knew if he wanted his relationship with Wendy to survive, he had two choices, stay in Dawson or in the cabin in the Yukon wilderness.

CHAPTER 33

———— ✦✦✦✦✦ ————

It was mid-April and spring was in the air. As the darkness of the winter days started to retreat, the longer hours of sunlight helped melt the snowpack and bring life back to this frozen piece of land. Jason and Wendy were anxious. The day they would leave Dawson was fast approaching. The rush of potential prospectors would soon overwhelm the town, signalling the start of another summer of gold fever. Many men would lose their lives, while others would lose their minds, as the hardships of the burden they have taken on become a reality.

The day of departure was soon here. A farewell party was held at Bev's house, and the couple, King, and Omar left the next morning. They were happy to leave, preferring the clean environment and air that living in the forest provided them, but they would miss Bev, whom they both loved dearly. They left Dawson in the early morning. A strong cold front had arrived the night before, bringing April snow, not an unusual occurrence this far north. Warm temperatures earlier in the season had melted most of the snowpack, leaving a muddy landscape that froze and thawed daily making travel difficult.

Omar was mad, he had been taken from the comfort he enjoyed at Bev's, and cast into the role of pack animal, which he knew he could never accept or get used to. He had no idea where he was going, but wherever it was he figured he was going to be there for awhile. King felt the opposite, he knew where he was going and could hardly wait to get there. They stopped for lunch and ate some of the smoked moose meat Bev had given them for their journey. They moved on trying to keep to higher elevations, as this part of their trip led them through wetlands which were still full of ice and water. Soon it would be just forest, relieving them of this hazard.

Other perils awaited, such as hungry bears awakening from their long winter sleep. The smell of mule would be tempting to the senses of these omnivores. King's warning of potential trouble reminded Jason to not let his guard down, even for a moment. King's barking alerted him to a bear, which had been following them, keeping out of sight until King exposed his presence. Jason, with a no-nonsense attitude, fired two quick shots off, missing the bear but hopefully sending a warning that it wasn't welcome and should keep its distance if it wanted to survive.

Extra care would be taken at camp to protect Omar. The thought of an encounter with a bear and getting eaten terrified him. The couple stopped early for the night, encountering only a peaceful sleep and dreams about what tomorrow would bring. Reaching their cabin was foremost in their minds, the peace and serenity would be a welcome presence when they arrived.

CHAPTER 34

The sun was rising, a small yellow sphere in an endless blue sky. Jason awoke, his eyes on the heavens, thinking about what the future held for him and Wendy. They would have to settle somewhere, but where? If he wanted to stay with her, his choices were few, Dawson or the cabin. King came over and nuzzled Jason, a show of affection, which he returned by hugging his dog tightly. Wendy stirred, opening her eyes to bright sunshine and a new day.

The couple packed up and left, a clear sky and light breeze signalling a beautiful day. Happiness prevailed as they made their way forward, anxious to reach the cabin. Wendy was looking forward to seeing her brother. She had made him a couple of personal gifts while wintering over in Dawson and was anxious to give them to him. The day passed without incident. They soon found themselves setting up camp on the shores of a still frozen lake. The waters would soon thaw, allowing life once again to flourish there.

The campfire roared, the flames sending light into the surrounding forest. The mood in camp was calm and relaxed. A sudden movement from King startled the campers, his senses were on alert, staring into the darkness. Jason felt he was being watched. There was someone or something aware of their presence. What were its objectives? The forest now seemed like the enemy, dark and silent, about to attack. Wendy and Jason sat in silence, afraid to sleep. They were looking forward to getting to the safety of their cabin tomorrow.

The night passed without incident. They had little sleep as the couple's stress levels remained high, knowing from past events how things can go bad quickly. The morning sun lifted their spirits as they packed to go, last night's events fresh in their minds. Without incident they reached the cabin. A sense of relief washed over them as it looked exactly as they had left it. No one had broken in over the winter. They removed the bear proof barriers from the door and entered. Except for the presence of mice, everything was the way they had left it. They started a fire to get warm and King took up his favorite spot on the rug by the bed and was soon sleeping. Omar was taken care of and bedded down for the night.

The safety, and now the warmth from the fire, sent the two adventurers into a state of relaxation they had not experienced in a long time. They lay on the bed hugging tightly, happy to have this oasis of peace in a chaotic world. Sleep came easily, only the waterfall could be heard with its promise of more gold. The rushing waters made Jason think of his grandfather and the stories he told, which had brought wealth to this fortunate couple. Would the waterfall give up more gold, or had it been used as a hiding place for the mineral that had been found elsewhere? Many questions remained; the answers uncertain.

CHAPTER 35

A low growl from King woke Jason. He listened, the wind blowing through the trees was the only sound breaking the silence. Then he heard something, like the sound of footsteps crunching the leaves outside the cabin's window. Wendy was now awake, and King's growling grew louder. Jason quietly got up and made his way to the window. Blackness was all he could see, the sky darkened by the dense cloud cover and no starlight. Then there was a loud noise. Whatever it was decided to leave in a hurry. King was at the door barking, his hair standing up on his back sensing danger. Suddenly, everything went silent again. An uneasy calm settled over the cabin, Jason and Wendy were trying to make sense of what had just happened.

The morning sun was welcome, and the events of the night before became an afterthought, explained away as a curious bear seeing if anyone was home. Jason had decided to take King and hunt for partridge, a delicious meaty gamebird. It was an important part of a frontier diet, this bird saving many men from starvation. Wendy was staying home to make bread with the flour she had brought from

Dawson. She would also gather some early spring edibles from the forest.

Jason soon returned, two birds in his hand, followed by a happy dog. King felt he was finally back home, once again able to enjoy the freedom of being off leash. Maintenance on the cabin was next on Jason's list of things to do. The stove pipes and chimney needed to be cleaned and the cabin's logs needed to be chinked. The cold winters caused the filler in between the logs to freeze. When it thawed in the spring, pieces became brittle and fell out, creating holes that allowed cold air to enter the cabin. Some work also needed to be done on Omar's shelter, as the windstorms had caused some damage to the structure. Jason also wanted to improve the root cellar to make it more accessible for storing perishable goods

Returning to the cabin after working on Omar's shelter, the smell of hot bread baking, and the game birds cooking stimulated Jason's appetite. It was a special dinner to celebrate their return home. They had carved out a life for themselves in this harsh environment, for which they were grateful. They had purchased candles for this occasion and Wendy soon had the table ready. King joined in the festivities with food that had been purchased in Dawson for him, and a bit of partridge to go with it. They ate until they were full, finishing the meal with an apple pie baked for the occasion.

Jason and Wendy felt it was a good time to talk about their future, each wanting to follow a different path. Wendy was firm on her commitment to stay in this area, her ancestral home. She had no intentions of leaving. Jason was not so sure he wanted to make this commitment. He had a fitful sleep because of the slight rift that had developed between the couple, presenting another challenge to what their future might hold.

CHAPTER 36

━━━━━━ ✦ ✦ ✦ ✦ ✦ ✦ ━━━━━━

Spring in the far north is a slow and subtle affair. As the climate warms there is an explosion of growth and color as the landscape changes from its winter coat of white to a springtime of green. Wildflowers dominate the landscape, their colors bright, a testament to the arrival of warm weather and the end of winter. The ice on the lake slowly melts, ushering in a return of the waterfowl, an important food source.

Jason decided to take the canoe and go bird hunting today. The spring hunt usually provided enough meat that some could be smoked and preserved for a later date. The morning was sunny as the canoe was launched into the calm lake, the paddles breaking the water the only sound to be heard. The silence gripped Jason's spirit like a vice, an overwhelming sense of calm possessed him. The thought of staying in this wilderness entered his mind, the beauty of the moment not wanting to let go.

Jason's thoughts were suddenly interrupted by the splash of ducks landing on the lake, only yards away. He picked up his gun and with a quick succession of shots, four of the unsuspecting birds lay dead. His hunt was successful, a total of twelve ducks were in the canoe when he returned to shore. Jason made his way back to the cabin, stopping at the waterfall on his way home. The water was flowing fast as the spring runoff continued, hopefully trapping more gold nuggets in the pool below. The couple probably would not know until fall what treasures would be found. They had to wait until the water levels were at their lowest point to search the pool thoroughly. He turned away, the ducks in tow and was soon sharing his experiences with Wendy.

The birds were cleaned and soon the aroma of them cooking filled the cabin that sent hungry stomachs churning. King hoped he was also to share in this meal. Wendy had used up the flour, making the last bread they would enjoy all summer. They had just finishing eating when a knock on the door was heard. King ran to the door, a low growl coming from his throat. Jason grabbed his rifle and told the stranger to identify himself. It was Wendy's brother, Steward. With warm greetings he was welcomed inside.

Steward was sad to learn that Wendy had lost the baby but was happy she had returned and would be at the cabin for the summer. He gladly ate the meal Wendy offered him but refused her offer to stay the night. He informed them he was going to Dawson to pick up supplies and would return with flour, sugar, and coffee for them. Jason loaned Omar to Steward, allowing his return trip to be easier as he would have help packing in the supplies. Small gifts were exchanged, and then he left, the full moon and clear sky allowing him to travel through the night.

The night owl's hoot sent a serene feeling through the forest as the couple lay in bed, drifting off to sleep. Their dreams of a future together were now taking hold as Jason's priorities began to change, thinking more of marriage and a future together, not dwelling on himself and his personal priorities. He would soon share these feelings with Wendy and hoped she would feel the same. Another big change in their relationship would be coming, ushering in a bright future and a lifetime of love.

CHAPTER 37

The morning sky dawned bright and cold. Even though it was almost June it was not unusual to have a cold day, a clear sky overnight and a strong north wind had promised a drop in temperature. Jason, warm and comfortable under the covers with Wendy snuggled into his back, did not feel like moving. He thought about how lucky he was to have found Wendy, and how lonely he would be without her. He wondered about his mother and family in Seattle, and realized he missed them dearly. His thoughts turned to taking Wendy to Seattle, a journey she has refused to take.

Jason reluctantly pulled himself out of bed. He let King out for his bathroom break and morning ritual of inspecting the property. He stirred the coals in the fire, adding wood, resulting in a warm cabin within a short time. Wendy, now more comfortable, got out of bed. They shared duck for breakfast, food that they had cooked the night before, as they discussed their plans for the day.

Jason wanted to work on the maintenance of the cabin in the morning and suggested taking the canoe out for fishing and recreational purposes in the afternoon. After letting the fire die back down, he worked on the stovepipes. Smoke causes a buildup of flammable materials inside the pipe, which under certain circumstances can catch on fire and burn the cabin down. Many trappers and prospectors would return home after a hard day of work, only to discover they had no shelter, sometimes a death sentence during the winter. Routine cleaning can eliminate this danger.

After lunch the couple found themselves at the lake, the canoe skimming across the water. They decided to check the beaver lodge for evidence of recent activity. They pulled into shore and explored the small beach area that followed the water line. Beaver sign was everywhere, showing the existence of a healthy colony. They walked the shoreline, finding nothing of interest. Wendy said she would like to go into the forest to look for plants, not an easy task this early in the year. As she was searching for edibles, a white object caught her eye. Investigating further, she was shocked and what she found.

Wendy had stumbled upon the complete skeleton of a man, not ravaged by animals. Wendy yelled for Jason, who upon arrival was just as shocked as Wendy at this discovery. It appeared this person laid down and died, probably from exposure, caught out in the elements unprepared. The remnants of the clothing and the presence of a few traps indicated it was the remains of an unfortunate trapper. They decided to leave the body as it lay, an above ground burial, many years in the making.

The pair returned to the canoe, wondering about the circumstances that led up to this person's death. They paddled back in silence, their moods now changed, no longer wanting to fish. The discovery of the body made them keenly aware of what their own destiny could be. They returned to the cabin solemn, but happy they had each other.

CHAPTER 38

The full moon was bright, casting light on the forest and the cabin. The stillness of the night was a deception as to the reality of the moment. A new wolf pack had moved into the area recently, the former pack having been decimated by Jason and the lone survivor having left. The wolves circled the house, investigating the cabin and surrounding area. A low growl came from King's throat as he listened to the wolves moving around outside. They were also aware of the dog, his scent permeating the area. The wolves left, but their return was certain, as they wanted to kill the dog that had invaded their territory.

The bright sun shone through the cabin window onto Jason's face, waking him. He rolled onto his back letting the sun warm him, his thoughts turned to Dawson in the winter and how he would have appreciated the sun's warmth back then. Wendy stirred, wrapped her arms around Jason and went back to sleep. To her this life was paradise, providing her with everything she wished for except one thing, a baby. She had failed to get pregnant again after the loss of her last child. King was unsettled, his anxiety prevalent, as the events of last night cast gloom on what he thought was an idyllic life. He knew the wolves would kill him if given the chance.

Jason realized except for the remaining smoked duck they had no food left. A trip to the lake today would be on the schedule. Fish would provide them with dinner, and a meal for King. Jason also wondered about Omar, as Steward had borrowed him to go to Dawson to pick up supplies. He believed the mule would enjoy access to all the fresh food he could eat, but not the fact he was expected to carry things on his back.

The couple left the cabin, and soon arrived at the lake. The first thing they noticed was that a racoon had come to visit, leaving empty clamshells and his footprints in the sand. They launched the canoe and were soon catching fish. They took in the scenery. Summer was almost upon them providing a panoramic view of the natural beauty of the land and water together. They soon found themselves back at the cabin, cleaning fish for dinner, King a happy spectator.

Tonight, at dinner Jason had big plans, he was going to ask Wendy for her hand in marriage. If she accepted, they would go to Dawson and be married by one of the elders that resided there. They would have a small party at Bev's, and then they would return to the cabin. During their stay there last winter Jason had a craftsman from the tribe make a ring from a gold nugget he had saved for that purpose. He had been waiting for what he felt was the right time to give it to Wendy.

They ate the fish, a delicious meal leading to content stomachs. Jason's moment was now, he told Wendy to close her eyes, took the ring out, placed it in her hand and asked her to marry him. She opened her eyes looked at the ring and wept. She grabbed Jason and hugged him tightly, not questioning what her answer would be. The young couple celebrated what was now a commitment by both, to make this a lifelong venture in their pursuit of happiness.

CHAPTER 39

The return of Steward came as a surprise. He had informed the couple he might spend some time with Bev before coming back, but changed his plans after having an unpleasant encounter with a drunk when he went into town to buy supplies. The man's language toward Steward was offensive and the man had pulled a gun and threatened to kill him. Luckily the drunk's friend had talked him out of the madness and pulled him from the scene with no apologies. This incident reminded Steward as to how dangerous it could be for an Indian living in Dawson. He finished buying what he needed, returned to Bev's, and informed her of what happened. She understood his wanting to return to the safety of the forest, sad that he would be leaving in the morning.

Steward told Wendy and Jason that Omar had been a cooperative mule, packing in a load of supplies with no complaints or problems. He gave them the sugar, flour, and coffee that he had bought for them. They were grateful and thanked him graciously. He had also returned with a new saw for cutting firewood, a tool desperately needed around the cabin. Steward had shot two partridges on his way to their cabin, offering them for dinner, which the couple were happy to accept.

Wendy decided to bake fresh bread and would serve coffee after dinner. Jason and Steward cut wood with the new saw while Wendy prepared the food. The smell of fresh bread baking, and the birds cooking, sent waves of hunger through the bellies of the two men and the dog who was hoping he would be included in this party.

A sudden wind came up and thunder rumbled in the distance, indicating the approach of a storm. The men put their tools away and went to the cabin for dinner. Minutes later the storm hit with fury, the wind blowing through the trees, with some crashing to the ground. Alarm bells went off in Jason's head with the thought of a tree crashing down on the cabin, destroying it. The storm passed, the thunder now in the distance as it moved away leaving a smell of renewal in the air. They all enjoyed dinner, with King joining them.

Jason and Wendy had decided to keep their marriage plans secret until a date was set, so this news was not revealed to Steward. Wendy enjoyed having the company of her brother, the feeling was mutual. Steward was invited to stay the night. He would sleep on the floor and leave in the morning for his home, which was a day's walk from here. The trio enjoyed coffee, a treat that the couple had not had in a long time. King happily chewed on his bone, an unexpected gift from Steward.

The night was dark, the forest quiet. Sleep came easy until a loud disturbance in the middle of the night shattered their peace, once again reminding them where they were. The many surprises they were confronted with never allowed them to drop their guard, a never-ending series of events that tested their courage and ability to survive in this harsh and unforgiving land.

CHAPTER 40

The wolf pack circled Omar's enclosure, looking for an entry point. They were hungry, the thought of fresh meat driving them into a frenzy of bloodlust. Omar was terrified, even though he was secure in his dwelling, safe from the wolves, he was still scared. He was afraid of getting killed and eaten by these evil predators. Suddenly shots rang out. Jason and Steward heard Omar's distress calls and quickly gotten out of bed, grabbed their rifles, and fired off a few rounds at the wolf pack. One lay dead, the rest had scattered. Omar settled down knowing the danger had passed but was sure the wolves would be back. The men checked the enclosure for damage and finding none returned to the cabin. Jason and Steward agreed that these wolves had to be hunted down and shot, surprises like tonight were no fun.

Upon entering the cabin, the men found Wendy awake and making coffee. They sat around the table and discussed this new threat, knowing the wolves would return, the dog and mule their focus of attention. Steward agreed to help Jason. They would track the wolves back to their den and could use the same method used in Dawson, surprising the animals and driving them into the line of gunfire. They decided to take Wendy as an extra shot. They would only have one opportunity to kill as many wolves as possible.

The trio left the cabin at daylight, first inspecting the area around Omar's dwelling, noticing a blood trail leading into the forest. They had wounded one of the wolves. Steward could follow the blood trail to the wolves' den. After a forty-five minute walk they reached an outcropping of rock, dotted with several caves. The animals were probably in one of them. Watching the rocks, the wolves showed their presence. The animals had picked up their scent and were about to flee. Before they had time to react, the wolves were gone, retreating from the area in a flash. Disappointment reigned as not one shot had been fired.

Inspecting the den, a dead wolf was found. The wounded animal had succumbed to its injuries, further sparking anxiety among the pack, causing them to react quickly with their escape. The hunters took the pelt from the wolf, leaving the remains as a warning to the others to move on or face the same fate.

They returned to the cabin, bittersweet about the success of their hunt. Steward left, silence falling over the cabin as Jason and Wendy sorted out their thoughts. They talked about taking a break and hunting for gold. The streams had dropped enough to allow panning in some areas. The waterfall pool would need another month before it would be possible to check it for gold nuggets. Their thoughts were that there would be nothing more there. They packed a few things for their trip, ate dinner and retired to bed early, not knowing what tomorrow would bring.

CHAPTER 41

Jason awoke to the sound of rain hitting the cabin roof, the sky was dark grey and dampness chilled his body. He collected his thoughts, got up from the bed and stoked the coals of the fire. After adding more wood, the fire was soon warming the cabin. Today the couple were planning to visit a new area that Steward had told them about. There was an old trapper's cabin there, abandoned, and decrepit, built on a creek that he thought could produce gold. They were leaving in the early morning, but the rain had changed their plans.

Wendy got out of bed and put water on to boil for coffee. They appreciated this drink which Steward had brought to them. The sky cleared and anticipation for their trip mounted. King was happy, he loved going on these excursions. His only concern was the wolves who would be looking for him. Omar, much to his dissatisfaction, was loaded with supplies. Off they went on another gold seeking adventure.

It was an easy walk through lush green meadows and hardwood forests, the quiet creating an atmosphere of peace and love for nature. They trekked on until they arrived at a small lake, deciding to stop there for the night. The beauty captivated them; the loon's call the only sound to break the stillness. Jason had shot two rabbits on the way, and along with some fish they hoped to catch they should enjoy a nice dinner. The late afternoon sun and warm air prompted the young couple to go for a swim in the lake, a pleasure they rarely enjoyed. The water was cold, but their spirits were refreshed.

As the sun was setting, Wendy cooked dinner over the campfire. Night soon took over, spreading darkness throughout the forest, only the starlight was visible. After dinner the couple lay on their backs and looked at the sky. The northern lights were on display, a spectacular light show put on by nature, unmatched in its glory. They slept peacefully, rose early, and continued their journey, hoping to arrive at their destination in the early afternoon.

Wendy and Jason were soon looking at an old cabin, uninhabited for many years, it had been left to decay and return to nature. The babble of the creek could be heard, tempting them to camp close by, a soothing sound that would help them sleep peacefully tonight. They set up camp, happy with this place, a feeling of success dominating their spirits.

They ate left over rabbit with bread that Wendy had baked before they left on this trip. They shared dinner with a family of hungry chipmunks, who also enjoyed Wendy's baking. Tomorrow they would pan the creek for gold and investigate the old cabin, looking for any lost treasure left behind. Little did they know that today's dreams, could be tomorrow's reality

CHAPTER 42

The first hint of trouble came from Omar, his distress call recognizable. Jason rolled over and grabbed his rifle; his senses were now on alert. He scoured the area looking for the source of the problem. Then he saw it; he nudged Wendy awake, fear dominating his emotions. Sitting on a ledge above them, watching in the early morning light, was a cougar. The large predatory cat, a rare but known species in the area, posed a grave danger. Jason knew he had to get rid of this menace, otherwise they would be stalked. King was agitated, wanting to rush toward the cat but Wendy restrained him. Jason raised his rifle, took aim, and fired. The cougar dropped, killed instantly with a well-placed shot to the head. Jason realized how lucky they were to have eradicated this threat. The animal's hide would be processed and donated to Bev's tribe. Wendy and Jason would take it with them when they went to get married, their next trip after this one.

After Wendy released King, he rushed off to investigate the cougar and ran into a porcupine returning home from his nightly outing. A fight ensued and King ended up with quills in his face, a painful reminder of the porcupine's defence system. They would have to be removed, a painful but necessary procedure, as the dog could get an infection if they were left in his face. Wendy went into the forest and retrieved some plants to treat the wounds once they were removed. With much drama and pain the quills were extracted and King's wounds were treated.

Jason and Wendy's day had been disrupted. They had no food, so Jason took King, his ego bruised but his health fine, to try and procure some meat. After a short distance, they heard a chattering noise. It was two squirrels, who were soon in Jason's backpack, now dinner. Two grouse were shot, which King retrieved, earning him praise from Jason and a boost to his self esteem. The duo returned to camp and Jason worked the cougar hide and cleaned the small game for dinner.

The day's original itinerary would be put off until tomorrow. Late afternoon approached, the sky changing from cloudy to clear, brightening the moods of these adventurers. The fire was lit, and dinner was prepared. The squirrel meat was enjoyed immensely, a new delicacy given up by the forest. The fire burned softly as the couple enjoyed the peace and serenity of the moment. The sound of the running creek water lulled them into a premature sleep, rest for the weary spirit, challenged daily for survival.

CHAPTER 43

The smoldering coals of the fire filled the air with an odor that was familiar to man for generations; a fight or flight mechanism triggered by the smell of smoke, recognized as both a danger and a means of survival. Jason woke and sat up; the sunny morning prompted hope of achieving their goals today. He looked to the sky, fear gripping him as he noticed a large column of smoke in the distance. There was definitely a forest fire that hopefully would not burn in their direction. These fires were usually started by electrical storms, and the only way they were extinguished was by rain or the fire burning itself out. Jason and Wendy would monitor the smoke to determine if it was getting closer.

Today they were to pan for gold. After a quick breakfast, the couple collected their gold pans and made their way to the creek. Steward had told Wendy and Jason the creek emptied into a small lake within a short distance. They panned all the way to the lake, with no luck. They did the same on the way back but also came up empty. They had worked their way upstream and back, showing nothing for their efforts. Discouraged, they quit, it seemed like a futile mission.

The pair ate lunch and afterwards headed over to the old cabin. All that remained were a pile of logs and an old stone fireplace, untouched as the walls fell around it. They circled the cabin, stopping at the fireplace. Jason cleared debris from the base of the structure, which had deteriorated showing a hollow area underneath. He was intrigued and excited; this looked like a man-made spot for hiding something. He reached into the hole and pulled out a canvas bag. His heart beat faster when the contents were revealed. It held a collection of coins, including American silver dollars and Canadian fifty-cent pieces.

Wendy and Jason gaped in astonishment as to what they had found, the life savings of the trapper who once called this place home. His identity was not known, his body never found, and his grave not in sight. He was another casualty of this unforbidden land. They gathered up their find and headed back to camp, their spirits lifted. Tomorrow they would return home, a successful trip on their minds.

Gathering their fishing poles, they headed to the lake. They had no food for dinner and their options were few. After two hours of fishing, they had a meager catch, but enough to stop the hunger pains that caused their stomachs to ache. The night was clear, shooting stars filled the sky as if announcing to the world the upcoming marriage of Wendy and Jason. Love was in the air as they realized where their future was headed, everything finally coming together as planned.

CHAPTER 44

Excitement mounted as the entourage got ready to leave the encampment. Omar was loaded with their belongings, including the cougar pelt. With a farewell to the family of chipmunks that had befriended them, they left, facing a new day. Omar was led by Jason who would let him stop to eat his favorite grasses on the way. This made Omar happy, leading him to behave in a cooperative manner. They would travel as far as the lake they had camped by on the way here, knowing food was readily available there. Living in this northern wilderness meant constantly looking for nourishment; like the animals of the forest, man needed food to survive.

Wendy and Jason moved on slowly, taking in the beauty that surrounded them. Wendy's mind was filled with thoughts of her union with Jason. Jason's thoughts centered on having to deal with the wolf pack that had taken up residence near their cabin. They trudged on, not in a hurry, Omar taking his time. The monotony of the walk was soon broken when the lake came into view. The body of water glistening in the summer sun, a welcome reprieve from their journey here.

They set up camp beside the lake, watching the activity of the waterfowl. Fish from the lake and plants from the forest provided dinner. The stillness and solitude of the campfire and the dark night soon sent the tired travellers into a deep and peaceful sleep, not awakening until the next morning.

King's loud barking woke the couple. Jason grabbed his rifle and looked closely towards the area King was barking at. Then he saw it, a black bear sitting, watching Omar, probably thinking what a good meal he would make. Jason had other ideas, leveling the rifle he shot over the bear's head. In shock and surprise the animal quickly exited the area, knowing his life could be in danger.

The couple packed up and left, anxious to get back to their cabin. The day went by quickly and by late afternoon they were home. Jason lit a fire in the stove and soon a warm glow filled the cabin, warming their weary bones after their long walk. They finished the fish that was left over from the night before, having no energy, or need, to go out and find more food.

Tomorrow they would discuss their trip to Dawson, what they envisioned for their wedding, and other related issues. The night grew dark, and the bed beckoned, an oasis of comfort enjoyed in a sometimes-chaotic land. Their dreams of marriage and the future filled them with thoughts of what their destiny might be; only time would tell.

CHAPTER 45

Jason lay awake, the rustle of a lone chickadee looking for breakfast the only movement heard. Wendy, upon waking, wrapped her arms around Jason, holding him close. The thoughts of their upcoming wedding had been on her mind. They decided a trip in their canoe, and time on the lake could lead to a productive outcome in planning this event. They took their fishing poles to replenish their food stocks, and the shotgun should any errant waterfowl come their way. They left King in charge at the cabin, and soon found themselves gliding across the calm pristine waters of the lake.

The couple were hoping Steward would be willing to go to Dawson and inform Bev of their plans to marry, then she could plan the wedding. They wanted to get married at Bev's house by one of the elders in the tribe, with a small dinner party held afterward. They would wait for Steward to come visit before any of these plans could be put in place. Their decision made, they made their way back to the cabin, happy with how their day had turned out. Jason had shot two ducks, and they had caught some large fish, providing them with healthy food for a couple of days. Rounding the corner, the cabin came into view. Standing outside, playing with King, was Steward, Wendy's brother.

Pleasant greetings were exchanged, then Wendy took Steward into the cabin alone. She needed to tell him about the wedding and ask him for his help. Not knowing what his reaction would be, she thought it best to talk to her brother in private. He told her he was expecting to hear this, as he had witnessed the love and respect Jason and Wendy had for each other. He told Wendy he loved her very much and would help her and Jason any way he could.

Steward and Jason cleaned the fish and waterfowl, Steward accepting an offer to stay for dinner. The evening was beautiful, so they decided to use their outside fireplace to cook and enjoy their meal under the stars. As night fell, a calm spread across the land like a blanket on a child before bedtime. The day slept; the evening was now in charge. Steward agreed to go talk to Bev and told Wendy she would be happy to hear the news and would be thrilled to plan this special event. He would leave in a couple of days, and after his trip to Dawson he would return to Jason and Wendy's cabin.

Steward also informed the couple that he had recently purchased a trapper's cabin and his dog team, which he would take possession of before winter. The cabin was on a lake with an abundance of fish to feed the dogs. It is a small team of dogs, but they had enough power to take him to Dawson quickly if needed. Steward was able to buy the trapper out with the riches he acquired while looking for gold. He had found a big nugget that was worth a handsome sum of money, enough to get him started in this endeavor. Jason assured Steward that if he needed help financially, they would be happy to assist. This made Steward feel more secure about undertaking this risky venture.

Life goes on in the north. Plans are made, babies are born, and lives are lost in this unforgiving land. It allows man to become one with nature, capturing an inner peace only a higher power can provide, in the Canadian north.

CHAPTER 46

Days passed before Steward returned, informing the couple that Bev was very happy for them, and felt honored to help plan their wedding. She would have everything organized before Wendy and Jason arrived, and once they were safely at her home a final date would be set.

Jason and Wendy had been talking about the winter. Instead of going to Dawson, they thought they would stay at their cabin now that Steward was going to have permanent place close by. He would be able to help provide meat for them and would be available should they have an emergency. Bev was still quite capable of caring for herself, and they would ensure she had all the supplies she would need in the winter. They would hire a couple of young men from the tribe to come and cut a winter's supply of firewood for them. The hired hands would be paid a salary and reside in a tent while here.

A few weeks later, Wendy and Jason were ready. The cabin was secured, and the couple, King, and Omar left for Dawson. It was an uneventful trip and they soon found themselves at Bev's door. After hugging one another, Bev ushered them in and got them something to eat. Bev told the couple she was elated about the marriage. She said twenty-five guests were expected, which was agreeable to Jason and Wendy. They decided to hold the wedding in a week, which allowed enough time to get everything in place.

The big day arrived, and the excitement mounted. People brought food and dressed in their best clothing. The tribal elder took his spot under a large tree with the young couple beside him and the guests gathered around. A traditional ceremony was performed, including a smudging ritual. The elder blessed the couple, wishing them good health and happiness for their future. In a nod to Jason's culture, he pronounced them man and wife. Wendy cried, and kissed Jason. She was looking forward to their wedding night.

Dinner was a feast comprised of a large selection of meats and fish, accompanied by seasonal vegetables, and homemade wine. A traditional dance was held, with Wendy and Jason as the special guests. Soon the wedding ended, and the guests left, leaving only Bev and the newlyweds. Wendy broke the news to Bev about them staying at the cabin this winter instead of Dawson. Bev was upset with their decision, but told them she understood, knowing of Wendy's love for the bush. She assured them she was healthy and fine, and if in need of extra help, she had plenty of people to choose from. She wished them a happy future and hugged both tightly.

The wedding had been a happy occasion. The couple planned to spend a couple of days with Bev and then return to their cabin with Steward accompanying them. A different life now awaited, as their bond of love and friendship was now cemented. A future together was no longer in doubt, as a lifetime of memories would now be made.

CHAPTER 47

◆ ✦ ◆ ✦ ◆ ✦ ◆

Dawson, during the summer, was a hub of activity. Prospectors used this town as their beginning and end in their quest for gold, as well as a resupply stop. It was an untamed frontier where laws were unknown, and simple disputes could end in tragedy. The Yukon is unforgiving, many men came to seek their fortunes, but their lives ended in ruin and early death as the hardships of the north were unleashed on them.

Jason was able to procure two young men from the tribe to come to the cabin and cut wood for them. A promised salary was always a strong initiative to work, as money was scarce among the Indian community. There were still funds left from Jason's nuggets to pay for this help, and the supplies needed to get the couple through the winter. Wendy was happy, her dreams were being realized and her love for Jason was growing stronger. The day for leaving Dawson soon arrived, and with much fanfare they departed, Omar carrying supplies and wedding gifts the couple had received. Steward would accompany them back to the cabin, and then he was going to return to Dawson with Omar, to pick up the supplies he had purchased and left at Bev's house. This would be one of many trips he would make before winter to obtain the items he would need.

The weather was sunny and warm when the trio left but by mid afternoon it had turned cold, as a front moved in from the north. Thoughts of weather entered the minds of Jason and Wendy as they were facing their first big challenge together, surviving the Yukon winter, which was not for the faint of heart. The atmosphere on the trail was calm and peaceful as they left the chaos of Dawson City, a town they would not miss. Their camp that evening was quiet, the forest a welcome reprieve from the excitement of the last week. The flames from the campfire rose high, the warmth on the cool night appreciated. They slept under a star filled sky, the full moon illuminating the forest with nature's light. They left camp early, eager to end what had become a long trip. By late afternoon they found themselves at Jason and Wendy's cabin.

Joy spread through the cabin, a warmth fed by love, not fire. Steward talked of his dreams, the responsibility of the dogs he was to adopt, and the hopeful success of his trapline. The fire was soon warming the cabin, the dampness and chill from being left empty slowly disappeared. Wendy baked some bread and served hot coffee to the men. They ate smoked moose meat for dinner, a gift from Bev when they left Dawson. Steward and Omar would leave in the morning to retrieve Steward's supplies and deliver them to his new cabin.

The darkness of the night fell over the forest as storm clouds moved in, the sound of wind blowing through the trees reminding them of the power of nature and how alone they were. Tomorrow the sun would shine and new challenges would emerge, a never-ending saga. It would be a life of their own choosing, not wanting it any other way; their souls one with the forest and the wilderness around them, a bond that never could be broken.

CHAPTER 48

A few weeks later, the men Jason had hired arrived from Dawson and had successfully started cutting wood for their winter supply. An abundance of dry timber was available for harvesting from the numerous dead trees in the forest. The wood was being cut and would be brought to the cabin with the help of Steward's dog team and Omar. Steward had both a wagon and a sled which could be used for this purpose. Wendy and Jason's primary concern was obtaining enough fuel to last through the winter.

Wendy and Jason had been invited to go to Steward's cabin to see his place and meet his dogs. It would take a half-day to get there and the couple would return with Omar, as Steward was done needing his services. They left for Steward's early, the sun shining brightly, ushering in a warm day. The forest was inviting before taking its long winter nap, shedding its cover of green to one that appears void of life, its long bare arms reaching to the sky as if looking for salvation.

The walk to Steward's was easy, the couple arrived with no mishaps. Omar was glad to see Jason, kicking up his heels and braying a loud greeting upon his arrival. Steward made Omar work hard with few rewards. Omar would be glad to get home, the only thing he would miss was the protection he got from the four dogs that lived here.

Steward's cabin was about the same size as Wendy and Jason's. The trapper, like most men in the far north, rarely did maintenance projects, leading to an eventual deterioration of the property. Steward had been working hard to make needed repairs. The cabin overlooked a beautiful lake, full of fish, birds and other animals attracted to its life-giving qualities. A stand of evergreens sheltered the northside the cabin providing protection against the harsh winter winds, and a dense forest of hardwoods would provide a lifetime supply of firewood. The bush would provide meat and the lake would provide fresh water.

Steward's dogs were Malamutes, sled dogs who did not take well to King, as they felt he had invaded their territory. Wendy loved her brother's place and knew he would be happy and do well here. The scenery was breathtaking, reminding her again as to why she belonged in this country, a surrender of her soul to nature with many rewards given in return. Wendy prepared fresh fish for dinner, caught by Steward earlier in the morning. After dinner they talked, drank coffee, fed the dogs, and enjoyed the solitude of the lake, only the sound of the birds breaking the silence, a peaceful sanctuary untouched by human hands.

CHAPTER 49

The fox sniffed around the cabin, attracted by the smell of fish. The dogs were aware of this small mammal's presence but paid no attention, as they viewed him as non-threatening. The fox found some fish remains left by Steward, who fed this little animal. The irony, this was one of the mammals he would trap this winter, a fox pelt being quite valuable. However, this was one fox he would not catch this season.

Jason and Wendy decided to stay one more day with Steward, helping him get his place ready for winter. They spent the day working on his cabin. They sealed the drafty windows, cleaned the stovepipes, and chinked the logs. With Wendy's help they were finished by early afternoon The couple were planning to spend the rest of the day on the lake in the canoe. Steward was going to take King and go hunting. They would all meet later at the cabin.

The lake was very similar to the one close to Wendy and Jason's dwelling. Most cabins were built on or near a lake, creek, or river, ensuring fresh water was readily available. The lake was also a valuable resource for protein, providing fish, game birds and small mammals to eat. The couple paddled the lake and soon found themselves back where they started. They made their way to the cabin where Steward and King were waiting. Sadly, their hunt had been unsuccessful.

The trapper had built a smoker, which was in fine working condition. This allowed Steward to smoke fish and meat, which is what would be on the menu this evening. Steward was glad he had time to show Jason his dog team in action. They needed regular exercise or they would get lazy and refuse to do anything. Harnessing the dogs brought about barking and mayhem, but soon the dogs were pulling the cart down the trail and out of sight, only to return forty-five minutes later. These dogs would prove to be an asset this winter, providing transportation and companionship, each dog becoming like a family member.

The men returned to the cabin, to the smell of an apple pie baking. This was Steward's favorite dessert, and Wendy was happy to make one with the apples he had purchased in Dawson. They ate delicious smoked lake trout, a delicacy at any time, with apple pie and coffee for dessert. This capped off a wonderful evening, one of many they would enjoy together this season.

Wendy was sad to be leaving in the morning. Steward's new venture worried her, as being a lone trapper in the bush was a dangerous profession, resulting in the deaths of many strong, young men. Everyone retired to bed, the night dark and silent. Like a magnet, the wilderness draws people into this life, becoming one with nature, with no regrets.

CHAPTER 50

The morning was bright, with Wendy and Jason waking to the sun, anxious to get an early start. They were soon ready to leave, thanking Steward for a wonderful time, and heading down the trail for home. The atmosphere was quiet, with little conversation as their thoughts turned inward, the enormity of this life experience weighing heavily on their shoulders.

Soon their home came into view. King bounded toward the structure, glad to be here after spending most of his time inside Steward's cabin because of his dogs and their territorial instincts. The chickadees, a small bird common in the north, were waiting at the cabin to be fed. Jason had been feeding them, creating an attachment and dependency on the food that was being provided. Jason loved wildlife and could never be a trapper, the thought of these animals dying a slow painful death made his heart ache.

The August days passed quickly and soon September was upon them, ushering in the change of seasons. Waterfowl activity increased as the birds got ready to migrate, open water key for their survival. The vibrant green of the vegetation and trees were changing colors, signifying an end to this year's life cycle, and a gradual slide into winter. Jason had rehabilitated his grandfather's smoker and was busy smoking ducks and geese he was harvesting from the lake. Steward visited, and they decided that after the snows came, he and Jason would hunt together, moose and deer the preferred game. With snow on the ground, they could use the dogsled to transport the meat back to their cabins.

It was soon time to check the pool at the bottom of the waterfall. The water was now at its lowest point, providing better access to the gold hunters. Disappointment came, as a search of the pool revealed nothing. His grandfather apparently had used this spot for storage, leaving Jason to wonder where his grandfather had found the nuggets and if there might be more hidden around the cabin. The couple walked the short distance to the lake, sitting in their favorite spot, contemplating their next move. They needed to find more gold, as the money from last year's find was dwindling.

The water on the lake was glistening; the sun's reflection stirring memories of days gone by. The warmth from the sun was diminishing slowly with each passing day. Wendy and Jason fell asleep in each other's arms until King found them and nuzzled them awake. They left as dusk was descending, daylight leaving for another day.

The couple returned to the cabin and soon a roaring fire warmed the cabin to a comfortable temperature. They talked of one more trip to Dawson for supplies, and one last search for gold before winter arrived. Jason wanted to follow the creek to its source, an underground system of caves that were accessible when water levels were low. He wanted to enter the caves and search for gold, thinking this might be the source of the nuggets they had found in the pool. Excitement mounted at this new prospect, giving them hope that their good fortune had not ended, but was only beginning.

CHAPTER 51

The cool morning air blew in through the window of the cabin. Jason had opened it, after the heat from the fire last night had made the room uncomfortably warm. King was at the door, tail wagging waiting to go out. He would scout the property, sniffing for any intruders that may have stopped by during the night. The new wolf pack had not returned since their first encounter, however, this did not mean they would not show up again. Jason made coffee, so Wendy was roused out of bed. They were going on their gold hunting expedition today, hoping Jason's realization would come to pass. They packed up, taking Omar along, giving him time to graze on his favorite vegetation on the way.

The going was slow, Omar was in no mood to be rushed. The weather had been dry, giving the couple a good chance of entry into the caves. Soon the sound of rushing water could be heard as it exited from the ground and moved its way downstream toward the lake. Coming to the cave entrance, Jason peered into the opening. It was large enough for Wendy and him to enter. Some natural light entered the cave through holes in the rock above.

Wendy and Jason left King to watch over Omar as they entered the cave. The water was ice cold. They walked with their eyes focused downward, when a glint of gold caught Jason's eye; a nugget buried in the sand. His heart skipped a beat as he reached down, yellow fever gripping him. Wendy found the next nugget and then the search went cold. They would bring shovels and use their gold pans on their next trip. They made their way home, excited about their find. They envisioned more gold would be found when they returned in a few days. Unfortunately, this was not meant to be, as two days of heavy rain raised the water levels, blocking entry into the cave system. Their dreams were once again dashed, as the realities of life reigned.

Steward dropped by and said he would be going to Dawson soon and wanted Wendy and Jason to stay at his cabin to care for the dogs. Steward could not take the team until there was sufficient snow on the ground. The couple readily agreed, and a date was set with Jason assuring Steward they would be there.

Wendy invited her brother to stay for dinner. Jason had shot two rabbits, as they were easy targets now that the vegetation was dying back. Wendy and Jason loved socializing with Steward; conversation flowed freely, making for great companionship. This relationship worked well for both parties, as they were there to help each other when needed. Steward's help would make getting through the couple's first winter in the Yukon wilderness easier. Only time would tell if it was to be their last.

CHAPTER 52

Wendy and Jason arrived at Steward's place to care for the dogs. Wendy's brother had left early and would be home tomorrow night. His dogs were glad to see these visitors, except for King, who they disliked and wished would leave. The dogs liked Omar and felt it was their job to protect him while he was there. Omar relished the special attention, as he sometimes felt like a forgotten mule at home with Wendy and Jason had little time to dote on him.

Wendy and Jason sat by the lake; most of the birds had migrated, leaving a stillness in the woods. The leaves of the hardwood trees were falling, their resting place a carpet on the forest floor. The beauty of this lake was stunning, a northern jewel, a commodity more precious than gold.

The couple fed the dogs, and then lit the outdoor fire as dusk was settling in. The evenings were getting cold, and snow was expected soon, ushering in the winter season. The flames danced, providing light and entertainment as Wendy and Jason ate smoked meat Steward had left for them for dinner. They wrapped themselves in a large blanket that Wendy's mother had made for Steward, enjoying the comfort and the warmth it provided.

The stars shone brightly, illuminating the path to the cabin. Jason had started a fire in the woodstove upon arrival, its heat filling the building. Steward had worked on eliminating the drafts, allowing the cabin to warm up quickly. The sky was clear, the full moon bright as they retired to bed, a busy day behind them.

The stillness of the night was suddenly interrupted by Omar braying nonstop. The dogs were barking loudly, signalling danger. King knew what the issue was, he had caught their scent earlier as they approached the cabin. It was the wolf pack. King had tried to warn Jason, but he had been ignored.

Jason threw the door to the cabin open, rifle in hand. He had seconds to shoot as the circling wolves closed in on Omar. The mule thought his end was near. Three shots rang out and two wolves fell, the rest of the pack retreating to the safety of the trees. Omar's life had been saved again.

The next day, while waiting for Steward to return, Jason and Wendy prepared the wolf pelts. They would be a gift for the tribe in Dawson, a token of appreciation for the help they had given the couple, and their acceptance of Jason as part of their family. Steward arrived home and was surprised to hear about the trouble with the wolf pack. He figured it was Omar's scent that had brought them to his homestead.

Steward had been able to buy some beef, a rare commodity this far north, a special treat they would enjoy for dinner. He also had some coffee, flour, and sugar for the couple. In the morning, Wendy and Jason would return home, a surprise awaiting them; another stroke of luck, proving again the north can give up secrets of the past.

CHAPTER 53

The entourage was leaving Steward's early and should be home by noon. They planned on working to strengthen Omar's enclosure this afternoon. After his many brushes with death, Jason did not want him to suffer the same fate as Brutus, who lost his life after an attack by wolves. They bid their farewells, and headed down the trail towards home, stopping once at a meadow so Omar could fill up on his favorite grasses that would soon be gone. The day was cold and crisp with a hint of snow. Steward was waiting for winter, so he could run his dogs and sled, and prepare his trapline.

The snow came just as Wendy and Jason reached the cabin, a short intense burst, all that Mother Nature had in her arsenal, but promised to return with more. Soon after, the sun shone brightly, the mood lightening as they ate lunch and warmed up the cabin. They needed to repair the damage to Omar's home, as one of the posts had been weakened by a storm and was now in danger of breaking. The structure would partially collapse if this happened. Jason grabbed a shovel to start the repairs.

A strong replacement post had been crafted by the woodcutters the couple had hired. Jason started digging out the old post, not an easy task as his grandfather had filled the hole with rocks to give the post extra strength when he first built the structure. As Jason dug his shovel hit something that sounded metallic. Further digging revealed the outline of a metal box. Excitement mounted as the box was dug up and could now reveal its contents.

Wendy and Jason decided to set the box aside to finish the repair work, and then take it to the cabin to see what it held. The pair worked diligently on the repair project and within one hour were satisfied with their handiwork. The structure was stronger, offering Omar better protection. The box was retrieved, and they returned to the cabin.

Wendy set the container on the table, a small lock between them and the contents. Jason knocked the lock off the box, opening it to reveal several objects, one of which was his grandfather's pistol. It was wrapped in cloth to preserve it, which had worked well. His grandfather had bragged about winning this pistol in a card game in Dawson, which his family in Seattle did not believe. Next, they inspected a gold pocket watch, engraved with his grandfather's name, along with a locket holding his grandmother's picture. A canvas bag held gold, and lots of it. Good-sized nuggets and smaller pieces, hidden by a sometimes-delusional man long ago, to protect against theft. Also in the bag were forty American silver dollars.

This was Grandpa's life's worth, buried in the ground, forgotten as dementia took the brain of this lifelong adventurer and gold seeker. His treasures left for his grandson to find, the rightful heir to his grandfather's fortune. Wendy and Jason would use these riches to build an addition onto the cabin, as more room would be needed for the family they would soon be ready to start. Wendy's dreams would finally come true, a husband who loved her and a baby she could call her own.

CHAPTER 54

The winds blew all night. It had started with rain after dinner, but as the night wore on the cold front arrived. Around midnight the temperature dropped, and the rain changed to snow. An early winter storm was now blowing, the wind howling, the snow swirling around the cabin. Wendy and Jason were awake, listening. Their home was warm and comfortable, giving them a feeling of security against nature's fury. The couple finally fell into a comfortable sleep but were awakened by the early morning sun shining through the window. The storm had passed, leaving a covering of brilliant white over the once drab landscape. King was at the door, sensing the snow outside, anxious to go out.

Jason got dressed and checked on Omar. He was worried about the mule's shelter and felt that Omar would be better off staying at Bev's for the winter. Jason and Wendy would take him to Dawson when the weather allowed for it. Jason knew someone who loved animals and would be happy to take care of Omar. He would pay this young girl, who could use the money to buy something nice for herself.

The day passed, the warm sun melting the snow, a constant drip coming off the roof. A hawk circled, scanning the ground, looking for movement, a rabbit, a mouse, or a squirrel, all potential meals. This was the game, to find food, a sometimes-fruitless search brought on by hunger and a will to survive.. Jason and Wendy decided they would leave for Dawson tomorrow. The full moon would light their way, allowing them to reach Beverly's within two days.

The couple left before dawn, making their way down a now familiar trail. The journey was uneventful and it was near midnight the following day when they arrived in Dawson. Bev was very surprised to see them, hugging them tightly in a warm greeting. She was fine with the plan for Omar, the barn being empty and unused.

They had coffee and listened to Bev's gossip about what was happening in town. Jason explained to Bev he wanted to rehire the woodcutters to cut some logs for an addition to their cabin. This would need to be done during the winter so Steward could use his dog team to pull the logs through the snow, as close to the cabin as possible. Jason also wanted to visit the gold buyer again to replenish his supply of cash.

The pair did not wish to spend much time here, as the weather could change quickly, making getting back to their cabin a priority. They would spend one more night and leave the following morning before dawn. If things went well, they should be able to see enough by the waning moonlight to make it home without spending more than one night in the bush. They would miss Omar but knew his life would be better here. They would take him back to the cabin in the spring. They retired to bed, knowing tomorrow would be another long day. Soon they would be back in the sanctuary of their cabin, a remoteness they enjoyed, in the wilderness of the great Canadian north.

CHAPTER 55

Wendy and Jason left Bev's house before daybreak, the sky was clear, but a cold north wind was blowing, signifying a change in the weather. They had worn winter gear and had packed extra coverings that would keep them warm in an emergency. Their gear was limited to what they could carry. The urgency to get home was obvious. Little conversation was had as the worry of getting caught in a storm dominated their thoughts, driving them on toward the safety of their cabin. The snows held off and the couple spent the night under a large fir tree, its boughs providing shelter. If they could keep up their pace, they should be home tomorrow. Traveling without Omar made the journey faster.

A wave of relief rolled over them as the cabin came into view, they had made it home safely. They entered, lit a fire in the stove, and allowed the warmth to spread throughout their cold tired bodies. They ate smoked moose meat Bev had given them. The snows came after the couple went to sleep, blanketing the landscape in white that was now here to stay until the warmer spring air melted it.

Wendy and Jason had prepared for winter. They had a good supply of wood, and had readied their outdoor freezer for meat, which Jason hoped to acquire on his hunting trip with Steward. The cabin and windows were sealed, allowing little cold air in, making their firewood last longer. It was cozy and safe.

Jason had been examining his grandfather's pistol. There did not appear to be any damage, no visible rust, which was surprising considering it had been buried for an untold number of years. The cloth it was wrapped in must have saved it. He had purchased ammunition while in Dawson and was pleasantly surprised it was in working condition. It would provide good defence, as it was the easiest firearm to access in an emergency.

Wendy and Jason had been relieved of one of their worries, Omar was now safe, away from predators, and being well cared for. Jason had arranged for hay to be delivered when needed, having paid the proprietor of the livery stable in advance. Additionally, their found wealth allowed Jason and Wendy to realize the dream of building an addition on their cabin. This was something Wendy had wished for. Jason told Wendy when the addition was completed, they could plan to have a baby.

For now, other things were more important, such as organizing the moose hunt with Steward, food being high on the list for survival. Tomorrow would bring more surprises for the couple as some unexpected company would visit from Dawson, bringing something that Jason appreciated and was shocked to receive.

CHAPTER 56

The early December sky was grey, the sun a relic of the past. Winter was casting its shadow on the land, as cold air dominated the region. Wendy and Jason were warm in bed, under the covers with a roaring fire in the stove, life could not be better. King lay in his spot beside Jason, on the bear rug that had been left by Jason's grandfather. He knew if he waited long enough, his owner would reach over and rub his head and neck, causing a feeling of elation to course through his soul.

Jason was waiting for Steward to drop by, they were planning a moose hunt and needed to finalize the date. He had been here a week ago and dropped off some venison, having shot a deer that had wandered close to his cabin. His dogs had alerted him to the deer's presence, the animal seeming to have no fear of the canines, a meal delivered right to his door.

The couple started their day, enjoying coffee and discussing the plans for the new addition. The two men coming to fall trees were expected after Christmas. They would set up a winter camp, a tradition handed down through the generations, a safe place to stay while hunting in the winter. Jason had increased the number of workers to four, the additional two men scheduled to arrive two weeks later and stay for the duration. This made shooting a moose even more important, as these men had to be fed.

Early afternoon brought a surprise, the sound of a dog team approaching. Jason went out to greet who he thought would be Steward, but it wasn't. It was two members of the North West Mounted Police, the new agency assigned to bring law and order to this untamed land. Introductions were made, and the men explained to Jason the reason for their visit. Bev, whom they had met, had asked them to deliver a letter that she felt could be important to Jason. The Mounties had promised to do so, and also brought a gift of coffee that Beverly had sent. The men were invited in for coffee and the letter was set aside to be opened later, leaving Jason to wonder about its contents.

While visiting with the constables, Jason heard another dog team approaching. Steward had arrived, surprised to see two other dogsleds in the yard. He knocked at the door, and was introduced to the two Mounties, whom he was shocked to meet. Steward joined them in a coffee and conversation. It was a nice break from the loneliness of his cabin, where the dogs were his only company. After a few hours, the Mounties left, and Steward headed out. He promised he'd return in a few days to make arrangements for the hunt.

Once they were alone, the letter summoned Jason. It was from his brother in Seattle who informed him that after a lengthy illness his mother had died. She had willed her house to Jason, figuring this would bring him back to

Seattle where she knew he would be safe. Jason's emotions were out of control. He reached for Wendy and held her tightly, waves of sadness coursing through his body as he took in the reality of his mother's death. His decision was made, he would send a letter back to his brother informing him of his marriage to Wendy, his new life here, and that he would not be returning to Seattle. This was the answer Wendy wanted to hear, as this proved Jason's love would be forever, and was not a fleeting romance that would lose its luster during difficult times.

CHAPTER 57

Jason awoke to the sound of an animal on the roof. He remembered the wolverine that had been in Dawson last winter and wondered if this could be one as well. King was aware of its presence, a low growl coming from his throat, letting Jason know he was cognizant of a potential threat. A wolverine was a formidable foe, a destructive mammal with no fear, standing up to the largest predators in the forest. A trapper's bitter enemy, the wolverine would steal or destroy any trapped animal it found. Secretive and cunning it was rare to see and harder to shoot. Jason believed this animal was a threat to King, who would consider the dog a bitter enemy.

Jason rolled over and hugged Wendy tightly. He was lucky to have found her, their love a rare gift from God. It was decided over breakfast that this would be a good day to mark the trees they wanted to have cut down for the addition to the cabin. While in the woods, they would also set some rabbit snares if they saw good sign. The couple dressed warmly, a brisk north wind causing it to feel colder than the actual temperature.

Wendy and Jason selected several trees that could be felled for construction. They marked each with a blaze to allow the workers to readily identify them. The couple also found some snowshoe runways, hard packed trails rabbits make in the deep snow as they traverse from one area to another in search of food. Unfortunately for the rabbit, snare wires can be placed across the runways resulting in a ninety per cent kill rate. After setting some wire, Wendy and Jason headed back toward the cabin, planning a stop at the lake, and the waterfall on their way home.

The lake was frozen, a white plain devoid of life. They stood and stared, the brilliance of the snow making their minds play tricks on them. Movement on the lake caught Wendy's eye. She showed Jason six dark objects chasing a deer. It was the wolf pack hunting for meat, a necessary evil if they wanted to live. The wolves had not been an issue since Omar left, his scent no longer an attractant. They stopped next at the waterfall, their source of water for the cabin. Memories of gold nuggets returned, and the outrageous stories that Jason's grandfather had told him that had turned out to be true. They wondered if there would be more discoveries of riches in their future.

They returned to the cabin, feeling that their lives were heading in the right direction and their future was bright. For most settlers and prospectors, this was not a common outlook. Typically, they came here looking for riches but usually found only hardships. The challenges and isolation of winter were unrelenting, taking a toll on their mental health.

CHAPTER 58

The day was overcast and gray. Jason felt there was a storm brewing, making checking the rabbit snares a good idea. He left Wendy at the cabin and started walking with King. He was startled when he reached the first snare. The fur, blood, and guts of a rabbit littered the snow. Jason knew right away what created this mess, the wolverine. These animals create havoc for trappers and hunters, making survival difficult by destroying a food source. Checking all the snares, Jason found the others untouched by this predator, leaving two rabbits to take home.

Arriving back at the cabin, Jason found Steward there, his dog team tethered outside. A wide berth had to be taken around these snarling dogs who would love to fight King. The men sat drinking the last of the coffee purchased in Dawson and discussed their hunting trip. Having a dogsled was a huge advantage, as the men could travel greater distances and still return to the cabin at night. Steward said he knew an area close by where moose stayed for the winter because of good shelter and an abundance of food. Shooting a deer was a long shot because the fear of wolves made them cautious and aware of their surroundings.

The wind had picked up and the snow had started. Steward decided it was best if he stayed the night, unsure if the storm would intensify. Many men had died thinking they could outrun a storm only to get trapped in a blizzard there was no escape from. Jason told Steward about the wolverine. Now that he had discovered an easy food source and could smell the aroma of cooking from the cabin, he would probably become an annoying pest. The wolverine would not leave until he was killed and his pelt donated to Bev's tribe. This was a job easier said than done.

The wind blew hard, covering the dogs in a blanket of snow, helping to keep them warm on this frigid night. The cabin was comfortable, Jason adding extra wood to counter the cold wind blowing. The woodcutters had done a good job of supplying enough fuel to last this winter and beyond. Wendy, Jason, and Steward ate rabbit for dinner, which was delicious.

King stirred, he heard something on the roof. Jason heard it too. The wolverine, in the middle of this storm, was on the roof of the cabin. In anger, Jason grabbed his rifle and boots, going outside and firing a round off over the roof. He hoped to scare this annoying animal away from whatever his plans might be. Everyone soon retired to bed; the wolverine and the blizzard were fresh in their thoughts. They prayed for a day of sunshine to brighten their moods which were darkening as winter progressed.

CHAPTER 59

The storm had abated overnight, mother nature leaving a fresh white coat of snow as a reminder of her presence. The sun was peeking over the horizon as the trio woke up, their wishes for a bright sunny day obviously taken into consideration. Steward checked on his dogs. He fed them fish and deer remains that he had brought with him. Steward left early, having responsibilities at home that needed to be taken care of. He had not yet set his trapline, his time taken up with other things as he prepared himself for winter. The moose hunt would take place in two days, weather permitting. Without a moose, it would be hard to survive, as there are few options for food during the winter in the Yukon.

Jason and Wendy had a serious conversation about planning for a baby. Wendy had successfully used local herbs for birth control, following the teachings of her elders. They decided to discontinue this practice, hoping the timing was right for their upcoming plans. Wendy was happy with this decision, bringing some much-needed joy back into her life.

The day of the hunt was overcast but calm. Steward arrived on time and they departed after Wendy gave them a worried goodbye and wished them luck. The dogs bounded along and soon they were approaching the area the moose were known to frequent this time of year. Jason stayed with the dogs while Steward struck out on foot. Two hours passed, and then a shot was heard. There was a pause and there was a second shot followed by silence. Shortly thereafter, Steward walked into view. He told Jason he had encountered a bull moose on his way back to the dog team, not far from here. He had shot and wounded the animal, a blood trail marking the snow. They would take the dogs and track the moose, hopefully finding him soon.

The trail was easy to follow and, as expected by the amount of blood loss, they found the moose dead. They cut the two hind quarters off the animal, and with the men walking alongside the sled they headed for the cabin. The dogs strained pulling this much weight, but soon arrived at the cabin, waiting to be fed. They knew what they were pulling. Jason had cut them a special dinner from the moose as a reward for the good work they had done. A return trip in the morning to pick up more meat would be necessary, as the wolf pack would eventually find the carcass and claim it as their own.

That evening everyone feasted, including the dogs. For now, life was good, but change can come fast as Steward was to find out.

CHAPTER 60

——— ✦✦✦✦✦✦ ———

The following day Steward and Jason returned to the moose they had shot. Moving the rest of the meat turned out to be an all-day job, requiring two trips to the cabin with a loaded sled. The strength of Steward's dogs was tested, and they rose to the occasion. After moving the meat, it was further processed and put in cold storage, providing a healthy supply of food for the winter. Steward would take some meat home with him, but most would be left here. He could take whatever he needed at any time. After a long day, the job was completed and the meat safely stored. The winter food supply had now been taken care of, easing Wendy and Jason's worries.

Steward left for home the next morning, anxious to get his trapline going so he could bring in some much-needed income. He was happy to have Wendy and Jason close by, as friendship and good communication were two of the most important things for maintaining good mental health while living in the isolation of the north.

The days slipped by with Christmas fast approaching. Wendy and Jason had invited Steward to come for dinner and he was happy to accept the invitation. Steward had to go to Dawson for supplies and said he would pick up what he could to add to the Christmas meal. Buying anything this time of year was difficult as there was little available, a food shortage gripping the city.

Steward's trip to Dawson was uneventful, he arrived at Bev's and stayed for a couple of days to visit and secure the things he needed. He visited Omar, who was being well cared for by a young native girl who had fallen in love with him and considered him her favorite pet. Omar ate up the attention, never wanting to leave. Steward was soon ready to head home, so he hugged Bev and said goodbye. He was able to secure what he needed for trapping but had little luck with the food except for being able to buy coffee. His return trip was fast, as the snow conditions were perfect.

Steward took care of his dogs, pleased with how they had performed on this trip to and from Dawson. Retiring to the cabin he started a fire to warm up and enjoy some hot coffee. Later he prepared some food for himself, the first meal he had since he had left Bev's. Sleep came easy as fatigue washed over him.

Steward was startled awake. At first, he thought he was dreaming, then he jumped out of bed, grabbing his rifle. The wolves were attacking his dogs. He shot three shots in quick succession to scare these animals, making them retreat into the forest. One of his dogs lay dead, not being able to fight off the five wolves that had attacked him. His other dogs had been left alone. A feeling of seething anger filled Steward's. He would get Jason's help and they would hunt these wolves to their deaths.

CHAPTER 61

Steward's return to Wendy and Jason's cabin was not a happy event. The death of one of his dogs was devastating, like losing a child, the love one feels for their animal the same. Steward had a plan for the wolves. He had kept all the scraps from the moose for food for his dogs, and for bait in his traps. Steward had tracked the wolves to their den, the location was an hour's walk from his cabin. He and Jason would pack in some thawed moose remains, place them in a clearing near the den and wait. The wolves, in a state of near starvation, would throw caution to the wind and hopefully take the bait.

Jason also had a problem at his cabin that had to be dealt with. King could no longer go outside alone because the wolverine had accosted him in the yard. Jason had witnessed the confrontation and luckily had been able to prevent an attack. The wolverine was smart, rarely revealing himself. He was like a shadow in the forest one never sees.

Steward had brought some fish with him. He was experienced with the use of nets under the ice, allowing him good catches of a variety of species. He stayed the night, having fresh fish for dinner with the couple. The men were up at dawn, ready to fight their battle with the wolves. They loaded the sled and headed for Steward's cabin, where the dogs were dropped off. They hiked to the den and placed the remains where they could get a clear shot. The walk had seemed short, the anticipation of getting rid of the wolves occupying their thoughts.

The men hid among a fir's branches for four hours waiting. The wolves could wait no longer, their hungry stomachs overwhelmed by the scent of the remains. They filed out from the security of the forest, ravenously attacking the food, paying no attention to their surroundings. Six rapid shots were fired, resulting in the deaths of five wolves. One escaped but would no longer be a danger, as it would leave this territory deeming it too dangerous. The men looked at one another astonished at their good fortune.

The men went to Steward's cabin, picked up the dogs and returned to the kill site. Jason and Steward skinned the wolves, leaving their remains in the clearing. They dropped the pelts off at Steward's cabin, planning to finish processing them at a later date. When they were finished, they returned to Jason and Wendy's cabin, arriving just before dark.

The men shared the good news with Wendy, who had some news for Jason. When she awoke this morning, she felt nauseous. She just knew she was pregnant but would have to wait to make sure she was correct. After dinner the trio played cards and listened to the wolverine on the roof. This animal was smart and more cunning than them. It would be a battle of wits if they intended to win.

CHAPTER 62

Christmas was drawing near. Wendy and Jason had decorated what they could, with what they had, using things that nature provided. Steward finally had his trapline up and running, a shorter version than he had anticipated. Due to the loss of one of his dogs, it was harder for the remaining three to pull as much weight. He would look to replace the dog this summer.

The best Christmas present Wendy could have hoped for, she received. Her morning sickness had continued, confirming she was pregnant. They were going to tell Steward on Christmas Day about the upcoming new title he would soon receive, Uncle Steward. They were sure this would make him very happy.

Christmas dawned cloudy and cold, the north wind sending an icy chill through the land. The snow flurries and wind swirling around the cabin made for a winter scene that was to last for months to come. Christmas dinner was a collection of meats, moose, smoked duck, partridge, and fish, a smorgasbord of food that the hungry in Dawson would love to be a part of. Jason and Wendy shared the news with Steward about her pregnancy, who was ecstatic he was to be an uncle. The day turned to night and soon the three of them found themselves sleeping, dreaming about what tomorrow would bring. King laying beside Jason's bed, snored quietly, his peaceful thoughts adding to the harmony in the cabin.

In the morning Steward left for home to tend to his trapline. The men arrived from Dawson a few days later to cut down the trees for the addition. They set up their winter camp, providing them a survivable place to stay while doing this work. Jason and the men snowshoed through the forest to see the trees Wendy and Jason had marked. The two workers started, and two additional men arrived two weeks later. Jason worked with them as time permitted.

Many trees were needed. They were cut by hand, limbed, and their trunks cut to size. The logs were left in the woods and would be moved closer to the cabin throughout the winter. The weather cooperated, and the job was completed by the first week of February. Wendy and Jason hosted a dinner in a show of appreciation for the laborers who had worked hard to complete this task. The men left and peace fell over the cabin. Quiet prevailed as the activity stopped, the forest taking back its solitude.

The couple were elated, the trees were cut and ready for construction bringing them one step closer to their goal. Wendy's pregnancy was going well, and the winter was progressing, providing light at the end of the tunnel. The fire burned brightly in the stove, matching the mood of this young couple, their love for one another like the glow of the embers.

CHAPTER 63

King was uneasy, a low growl coming from the back of his throat, The wolverine circled the cabin looking for food, his stomach empty. He had returned after a long absence. The men cutting down trees and working around the property had driven this solitary creature back into the forest. Now that quiet had returned, he was back. The wolverine was mad, his stomach ached from lack of food. He tried to enter the freezer where the meat was stored but had no luck. Frustration mounted as he went back into the forest to continue his search. Jason was awake, aware of the situation outside, knowing that it was the wolverine that was causing King's anxiety. He knew he would have to come up with a plan to get rid of this menace.

The day was sunny, the wind calm. Wendy and Jason decided that after lunch they would go to the lake and enjoy the serenity afforded there. The past weeks had been hectic and they needed time to relax and bring peace back into their lives. The lake beckoned the young couple, its vast expanse of snow mesmerising. The solitude of the lake captured their spirits for a short time, creating a blissful state that only nature could provide.

On their return to the cabin, the couple were surprised to see Steward there. He had been busy with his trapline, so they had not seen him for awhile. He informed Wendy and Jason that trapping had been good, and he felt if things stayed the course, he would make enough to cover expenses and a financial profit was feasible. Steward had brought beaver meat. He had been lucky enough to catch two beavers so far this season, valuable pelts in the fur world and food for the trapper.

Steward and Jason talked about the return of the wolverine. Steward had an abundant supply of remains from the fur bearing animals he had caught. He would bring some for Jason, who could set a trap for this hungry animal. This plan would never be hatched, as something more sinister was to happen.

Steward bid his farewells, saying he would return with the bait for the wolverine in a couple of days. The beaver meat was cooking, sending an odor through the forest that the wolverine could not resist. He waited, watching for his opportunity, which was soon to come. Wendy and Jason decided to accompany King outside for fresh air and a bathroom break. As they exited the doorway, a snarling ball of fur flew past the shocked couple and entered the cabin. Jason slammed the door. The wolverine was in the cabin. Now what was he to do?

Jason realized he had his rifle in his hand and the wolverine was trapped. The animal, now recognising his mistake, was backed into a corner waiting for his fate. Jason thought if he opened the door the animal would charge and probably escape. The only other option was to break a pane of glass out of the window to shoot through. He wanted to shoot only once, to avoid making a mess in the cabin. Anxiety gripped the couple as they were about to act upon their plan, hoping a successful ending was in the cards for them.

CHAPTER 64

Jason stood dumfounded. He found the series of events that had just taken place almost laughable. Now he had to figure out how to solve this problem. Under no circumstances did Wendy want Jason to shoot the wolverine in the cabin. Shooting and killing this animal, its lifeless body laying on the floor of their living space, would make the cabin a place she would no longer wish to reside in. The wolverine could be heard inside, a terrified animal trapped by his own actions. After considerable discussion, the couple decided the best thing they could do was open the door and let it out. As it tried to escape, and once outside, Jason would try to shoot this wary animal, ending this problem that had gotten out of control.

Wendy took King away from the door and held him tightly, not wanting him to instinctively chase the fleeing animal. They were ready. Jason swung the door open. The wolverine and Jason looked at one another, each contemplating the other's next move. Suddenly the wolverine bolted towards the front door, catching Jason by surprise, giving the animal the two seconds he needed to slip past Jason and escape into the woods, without a shot being fired. Jason stood in disbelief at what had just happened.

They re-entered the cabin, glad to have their shelter back with minimal damage. As the couple straightened up, King lay on his rug by Jason's bed trying to let his anxiety ridden body relax and get back to normal, putting this harrowing ordeal behind him. Wendy and Jason found themselves in bed early, their favorite place for discussing life's events, and where plans were usually made. The sky was bright, the starlight and full moon shining through the cabin window, illuminating the inside with a natural light rarely seen during the dark months of winter. Outside a deer browsed on some low hanging branches of green boughs, helping himself to food that that was being offered, oblivious as to the occupants inside the cabin.

The winter months were slowly disappearing. It would soon be time for the sun to shine warmer and longer, bringing a rejuvenation of life to this cold and forgotten land. Early April brought the last big snowstorm of the season. Thereafter, unusually warm weather caused the melting snow to drip off the roof. The lake showed signs of losing its ice, as an early spring rewarded the winter weary residents with sunny days and warm temperatures.

Steward had been busy with his trapline, harvesting a good bounty of fur and having a successful season. He, Jason, and the dogs had worked on moving the logs near the cabin and he was planning on helping with the construction which would be happening soon. The wolverine had not been seen since the episode where he gained entry to the cabin, a memory etched forever into their minds.

CHAPTER 65

Springtime in the Yukon is like a slow reawakening of life on the planet. The warm rays of sunshine melt the snow, starting a process of renewal for the life that has slept all winter. The science of this miracle, never fully understood by man, is necessary for his survival.

Spring meant the return of waterfowl, the migration bringing many types of ducks, geese, and other birds, to the now open waters of the lake. Jason had shot many of these birds, smoking the meat for later consumption. Wendy's pregnancy was going well, the baby seemed fine, always letting you know of its presence by moving around and kicking. It was decided Wendy would have the baby at Bev's house. A lengthy stay there would probably be necessary, as they had a guess as to when the baby was due, but it could arrive early. Jason would make a trip to Dawson to organize his cabin raising crew, and to cash in some gold to buy needed supplies. He would check on Omar and use him to carry what they needed back to the cabin. He would also discuss the birthing plan with Bev.

Jason left the next morning, leaving Wendy at home as the trip to Dawson was a strenuous journey, not safe for a pregnant woman to take. King stayed with her for company and to provide protection. Jason had arranged for Steward to come and spend a night with her, which he knew Wendy would enjoy. It was the morning of the full moon, meaning the forest trail that led to Bev's house would be visible through the night. This would allow Jason to only spend one night in the bush. He would not be so lucky on his return trip with Omar.

Jason's arrival at Bev's house was unexpected but welcomed. It had been a long winter for Bev with little company. Jason told Bev about Wendy's pregnancy and explained the plans surrounding the baby's birth. Bev was thrilled with this news and assured Jason she would make Wendy and the baby's safety her priority. Jason felt relieved; he trusted this woman immensely. His reunion with Omar was happy, until the mule realized Jason's plans, at which time his attitude changed abruptly. He had been spoiled by his handler, the young girl who had done nothing but pamper the mule, leading to this behaviour.

After spending another day and night at Bev's, Jason was ready to go home. Much to Omar's displeasure he was loaded with supplies, and off they went, slowly making their way towards the cabin. After a full day of walking they made camp by a lake, its waters once again free from the confines of ice. Jason lit a fire. The night air was cold, the warmth of the fire radiated through his chilled body. He slept undisturbed; his blanket wrapped tightly around him. The early morning sun woke him. He was anxious to get home to see Wendy, whom he missed greatly. He arrived two days later, at noon, to her open arms and Steward's smile. Fresh coffee was served, with Jason saying he had found six men willing to come and build the addition.

Wendy and Jason's reunion was sweet, as their love for one another blossomed, creating a union that would last forever. Jason was relieved to be home, and happy that Wendy had fared well in his absence. He was grateful that Steward had spent time with her, and King had watched over her.

CHAPTER 66

✦ ✦ ✦ ✦ ✦ ✦ ✦

Spring had arrived in the Yukon, the landscape once a frozen wasteland was now a harbinger of life. Jason woke, he rolled over and wrapped his arms around Wendy, her stomach getting larger from the baby. Sometimes if he laid quietly, he could feel the baby's movements. A new life was about to be born on a planet that would be its home for a lifetime.

Jason dressed and accompanied King outside; he checked on Omar who had adjusted well to his new, but familiar surroundings. It was warm and sunny, a beautiful day to take the canoe and enjoy the lake. He returned to the cabin to share his thoughts with Wendy. She was up, preparing herself for the day. They decided to take fishing poles and replenish their stock of fish. Hopefully they would catch some for dinner tonight and some to be smoked for later.

The lake was calm as they launched the canoe into the still waters. They paddled in silence, taking in the peace and tranquility the moment offered. They watched the waterfowl enjoying themselves, splashing like children in a swimming pool. An eagle dove for its dinner, an unwary fish losing its life to something bigger, a meal for their predator's survival.

The couple discussed the addition on the cabin that was to be built soon and having to feed the six men while they were here. Because the wolves were no longer in the area, the deer had returned. Steward knew a place not far from his cabin where deer congregated, an area with an abundant food supply and good cover for these nervous animals. He was sure he could shoot one of these deer, which would provide enough food for the men. Wendy would cook the meals, while the men did the work.

The fishing was fruitful, but not abundant. Wendy and Jason caught enough for their dinner and for King, but no more. They returned to the cabin, happy with their discussions. They prepared the fish, and with some forest greens enjoyed a meal. The days were getting longer, the extra light allowing Jason and Wendy to take a stroll to the waterfall. It was a serene place where a moment of silence could be observed, allowing them to reflect on the present, the past, and the future. They stayed till dusk, letting the sound of the water cascading over the rocks lull them into a relaxed state. Returning to the cabin they found King sleeping in his bed, oblivious to the fact they had even left.

Wendy brewed some catnip tea to help induce sleep, something she had found useful while pregnant. Tomorrow Steward would come and help Jason get the ground ready for the work to begin on the addition. The crew from Dawson would be arriving soon, and shortly after the completion of the addition, Wendy would have her baby. Decisions would have to be made as to where the baby would spend its first winter, in Dawson or at the cabin. The couple took this thought to bed with them, hoping sleeping on it would allow them to find the right answer.

CHAPTER 67

+ + ◆ + ◆ + +

After two days of hard work the preparation of the construction site was complete. Steward and Jason had retrieved large flat rocks from the creek for the foundation that the addition would sit on. This job completed; their thoughts turned to the deer hunt. Tomorrow morning they planned to leave, taking Omar with them to pack out the meat. For the rest of the day the pair worked on catching and smoking fish, adding some variety to the diet of the men that were coming to work.

The next morning, a sense of excitement motivated the hunting party. Omar did not share in this enthusiasm, being his usual stubborn self. After harsh words from Jason threatening to feed him to the wolves if his attitude did not change, the mule became more cooperative. They started out, and after a long walk reached a heavily wooded area bordered by a large, lush meadow. The hunters concealed themselves and waited. Within a short time two does came out from the safety of the trees to eat. Warily they checked their surroundings; satisfied there was no danger they exposed themselves to the guns of the hunters. One deer was shot, as the men took only what they needed. Steward cut the two hindquarters from the deer, which he and Jason would carry. The rest of the animal was secured across Omar's back to be transported back to the cabin.

Omar was horrified, he had the carcass of a deer strapped to his back, blood dripping down his side. He felt nauseous and vomited, the smell overwhelming his senses. With the blood over him, he was wolf bait for sure. The hunting party left the area, Omar picking up the pace, as he wanted to get this dead animal off his back. Hopefully someone was going to give him a bath when this job was over.

They reached the cabin mid-afternoon and unloaded the animal, which needed to be butchered. The men sent Omar to the creek with Wendy for a bath. Jason and Steward processed the meat and cleaned up the firepit where it would be cooked. They wanted to be ready for the arrival of the men. Wendy was very excited about the addition, as this would make their living space larger, assuring them the room to raise a child. The men coming from Dawson were experienced in building cabins, including additions, adding a sense of security to this endeavor she and Jason had undertaken.

Steward and Jason started a fire to cook some of the venison, which they would store in the underground cooler until the men arrived. They assumed the men would be hungry after their long trek. They also enjoyed the benefits of their labor, eating their fill of the delicious meat, which was shared with Wendy and King.

The night was quiet, a good night's sleep needed in preparation of the hard work that was coming. A surprise awaited, as Jason's grandfather had not given up all of his secrets, continually adding more mystery to his long and sordid life. His dementia had taken hold as he hid his treasures, some never to be found, just the way he wanted it.

CHAPTER 68

————— ✦✦✦✦✦ —————

The men arrived from Dawson right before lunch. They had five horses with them loaded with the supplies Jason had purchased for the addition to the cabin, including a window he bought used, which miraculously made the journey unscathed. The doorway for the addition would be cut from one of the existing windows so another opening was needed for light.

Jason, Wendy, and Steward welcomed the men, one of whom was Steward and Wendy's cousin, a surprise they were not expecting. Jason went to the underground cooler and retrieved the venison they had cooked the night before, along with some fish that had been smoked for this occasion. The men were surprised and grateful for this offering of food. After eating, the horses were unloaded, and the men set up camp. The firepit was reignited and the smoker fueled up with wood. All the raw meat needed to be cooked or smoked, making it less likely to spoil and providing a constant supply of food for the hungry workers.

The night was clear and calm, the forest providing a sense of peace among the men now sitting around the fire, their thoughts their own. Tomorrow they would start construction, expecting it to take a minimum of two full days to complete. The night beckoned, the men slept, the stars the only light.

Work started at daybreak; the men anxious to begin. The old window needed to be removed and saved. Jason would handle this task while the men worked outside. This opening would be made larger to be used as the doorway for the addition. If the window was safely removed, they would create the doorway and enclose it today.

With Wendy's help, Jason carefully removed the window and frame from the cabin's structure. What he found was a big surprise. The log the window frame sat on had been hollowed out and was being used as a hiding spot. A canvas bag filled the opening. Jason with his hands shaking, pulled it out and opened it. Inside was a piece of paper, with his grandfather's handwriting. It read, "these are the winnings of my gambling exploits. I did not lose everything.". The bag contained gold, silver dollars, pocket watches and family heirlooms brought to the gold rush. but sold to buy food or gambled away. No one in Jason's family knew his grandfather had been a gambler; he had managed to hide that secret.

The first day of construction went well. Working until dusk they were close to the halfway point of completion. Wendy was amazed at the speed of construction, and the quality of the workmanship. This project was expected to be completed tomorrow, except for small jobs that Jason and Steward could take care of.

Wendy's dreams were full of happiness, her long awaited addition was being completed, her pregnancy was going well and her love for Jason was growing stronger. She was full of optimism that would be hard to take from her, sensing a happy ending to what was once an impossible dream.

CHAPTER 69

The call of the ravens pierced the silence of the early dawn light, waking the workers from their restful sleep, telling them to get ready for another day. Wendy and Jason had also been roused by the noisy birds, wondering why they were being so vocal? The men were soon up, fed and back to work, hoping to complete the addition today. Wendy worked on making a large dinner tonight. She gathered a couple of the more popular native foods from the forest, to complement the venison and smoked fish they were to have.

The work was progressing smoothly until a sudden commotion from the horses caused a sense of panic. The men could not believe what they were seeing. A wolverine, as if in a drunken stupor, staggered out of the forest towards them. They picked up a rifle that had been set aside for this type of occasion, shooting the wolverine dead. Upon further inspection, it was noted the wolverine had froth around its mouth. Coupled with its bizarre behaviour signified it probably had rabies. Jason took the body away and buried it, not wanting King near it.

The work continued, with the addition completed by sunset. Except for incidentals, the addition was finished, a wonderful job by skilled craftsmen. The feast was served around a roaring campfire and was greatly appreciated by all who were involved in this project. The darkness of night enveloped the party as the coals of the fire burned down. Sleep came easy for the men, returning to Dawson tomorrow occupying their thoughts.

The morning dawned grey and cool as the men left for their trip home, leaving a happy couple to enjoy the luxury of more living space in their cabin. They would build a crib with lumber purchased in Dawson and brought back to the cabin on the back of Omar, their trusted pack mule. Steward also left, leaving the couple alone for the first time in many days.

The couple lay on the bed. Wendy was glad all the activity was over, the quiet sending them into a peaceful sleep until lunchtime. They awoke realizing their food stocks were completely exhausted, the last of the venison given to the men for their trip home. They decided to take the canoe, paddle the lake, and catch some fish for dinner. The lake was calm as glass, the canoe gliding effortlessly across the water, scattering the waterfowl that got in their way. A feeling of exuberance gripped the couple.

Later, at dinner, while enjoying the fish they had caught, Jason and Wendy marveled at how lucky they had been. Jason wondered if it was his grandfather's spirit guiding them to his valuables, making it possible to realize their dreams. Was this thought a fantasy, or another plan by this eccentric man to throw wonder into the lives of this grateful couple? Only God could provide that answer.

CHAPTER 70

The knock at the door came early. King went to the sound growling, the hair on his back standing on end. Jason approached the door, calling out to whoever it was to identify themselves. It was the Mounties warning the couple to be on the lookout for two armed men who had committed a murder in Dawson. While trying to make an arrest the men shot a police officer, wounding him, before they made their escape into the forest. Indian trackers had followed their trail to this area where it was lost when the terrain got too rocky.

This turn of events worried Jason greatly. These men would feel trapped, with nowhere to go. Hungry and desperate, their future looked bleak, which made them dangerous. Wendy thought about Steward, he would have to be warned. The police officers would work their way over to Steward's cabin and tell him it would probably be safer to join Wendy and Jason until these men were caught. Wendy worried about Steward being unaware of the situation and encountering the men.

The day passed without incident and in the late afternoon Steward showed up with his dogs. They would be left outside, providing a warning if strangers entered the property. The trio felt vulnerable, knowing an assassin's bullet could take one of their lives in seconds. They retired to the safety of the cabin and secured the door. They would wait for the police to return to give them an update. Their sleep that night was restless, their calm shattered by this incident.

Morning came and went. Suddenly there was an outburst from the dogs. Jason checked; it was the police returning. The officers had good news, the men had been shot in a confrontation not far from here and had died. Now everyone could safely carry on, no longer afraid to lose their lives to this evil that had confronted them.

It would soon be time for Wendy to move to Dawson. Jason and she would go together, but then he would return to finish work on the addition with Steward's help. As it got closer to the baby's arrival, Jason would return to Bev's to stay with Wendy. The next two months went by, and soon it was time to make the trip. Bev was looking forward to Wendy's arrival and the birth of the new baby.

The couple would leave in the morning if the weather cooperated. They would spend one night in the bush on the way there. They had caught and smoked some fish for the trip and were hoping to shoot a rabbit or partridge on the way. They enjoyed a quiet evening, the cool night air entered the cabin, causing Wendy to get a chill. A small fire was built in the stove to take the dampness away and make her more comfortable. The couple slept, wrapped in each other's arms, as if not wanting to let go of the love they felt for each other. Their lives were about to take another turn, as they would soon be entering parenthood. Hopefully they would be ready.

CHAPTER 71

The entourage left early, Wendy, Jason, King and Omar, the latter being loaded with Wendy and Jason's belongings. Omar knew where he was going, and he wasn't complaining. His life had been rough since he left Bev's. Jason decided they would travel today until they reached the lake where they usually camped. A sudden barking from King warned Jason and Wendy of something amiss. The dog had run ahead and was now alerting them to potential trouble on the trail. Jason halted the party. King continued barking, driving a black bear out of the forest toward Jason and Wendy. Jason raised his rife, firing two shots over the animal's head. Startled and scared, the bear changed direction and ran off into the bush with King in hot pursuit. The dog returned minutes later exhausted from all the excitement he had created.

Wendy and Jason soon found themselves at the lake, their camp set up on the shoreline. The campfire was already burning, hopefully to cook the fish they would catch for dinner. Omar was happy. The mule was able to eat, at his leisure, his favorite grasses and some of the tree canopy he enjoyed but rarely had access to. The fishing was successful and soon the smell of fish and the campfire dominated the atmosphere. As darkness descended, a veil of silence fell over the lake and forest. The stars were twinkling in the early evening light, waiting for darkness to prevail, so they could shine brightly in the night sky. The night was calm, and their sleep was restful, the thoughts of Bev's hospitality present in their minds.

The sound of the chickadees calling woke the couple. They packed up and left early, hoping to reach Dawson by early afternoon. Bev was aware of their coming arrival but not sure of exact date. The couple pressed on and were soon looking at the buildings in Dawson, a ramshackle collection of mostly wooden structures that provided shelter for the hardcore collection of men that called this place home. Jason and Wendy were greeted with open arms, Bev instantly fussing over Wendy telling her how important it was for her to rest after her journey from the cabin, not an easy feat for a woman almost nine months pregnant.

Bev had baked fresh bread earlier in the day and she brewed fresh coffee to go with it. This was a treat greatly appreciated by both Wendy and Jason, who had been cut off from the finer things in life for months. Bev said she had secured the necessary supplies for the birth and aftercare of the newborn, including a cradle.

A few days after arriving at Beverly's a big dinner was planned, with company invited. This was to be a celebration wishing for the safe arrival of the new baby, Wendy's baby shower. The company brought hand crafted gifts for the baby. Wendy was thrilled with all the attention and gifts she received. She couldn't thank everyone enough. The party wound down around midnight, leaving the exhausted couple to quickly fall asleep and prepare themselves for another busy day, a never-ending list of tasks to be completed.

CHAPTER 72

The smell of breakfast cooking roused the couple, who dragged themselves out of bed and went to the table. Bev had acquired a special treat for them, eggs from her friend who raised chickens. After breakfast Jason went to check on Omar. Willow, the young Indian girl who had taken care of him before, was back lavishing attention on him. Omar loved this affection, feeling special when Willow was around.

Jason went to see the gold buyer to sell more gold. He had been told John also bought pocket watches, jewellery, and just about anything else of value. Jason cashed in enough gold and treasure to make a nice donation to the tribe for the help they had given him building the addition and to have some cash for upcoming expenses. Wendy stayed with Bev, doing arts and crafts, making gifts for special occasions such as birthdays and Christmas.

Jason planned his trip back to the cabin to finish up with the addition and build the crib for the new baby. Neither Wendy nor the baby would return to the cabin until the following spring. Jason would spend the winter in Dawson, but occasionally travel to spend time at the cabin over the course of the winter.

The day came for Jason to leave. He had acquired the materials needed to make the addition snug and secure, tied securely on Omar's back. After a two-day journey they reached the cabin without incident. The following morning, after breakfast, they set out for Steward's to let him know they had returned from Dawson. The two men would work a few days together, finishing the chinking of the logs, a time-consuming project if done properly. Jason built the crib and placed it in the addition to await the return of the baby. He also winterized the cabin, protecting it from wildlife that might try to make it their home.

Jason left to make his way back to Dawson, arriving a few days before Wendy went into labour, earlier than she was expecting. Six hours later, a healthy boy was born. They named him Kuzih, a traditional Indian name her father had been given, meaning great talker. The birth of their new son was a life-changing event for the couple, a deeply loved gift from God. Wendy nurtured the baby through the fall and over the winter, working towards a gradual reunification at their cabin in the wilderness of the Yukon. They had formed a family joined by love, with an appreciation of nature, trying to survive in a land they had adopted as their own. This lifestyle would never be taken away, as they surrendered their souls to the north, and their futures to the Yukon in this wild untamed land.

THE NORTH WEST
MOUNTED POLICE

INTRODUCTION

The year was eighteen hundred ninety-six, the place was Dawson City in the Yukon Territories, a boomtown created by the Klondike Gold Rush. These are the stories from the archives of the detachment of Mounties that was set up to police this new frontier. The North West Mounted Police was a law enforcement agency created to keep order in Canada's far north.

The government financed the building of a new police station here, which consisted of the main office, a holding area with six cells, and an additional room for sleeping. It was equipped with the latest furnishings, including new desks and chairs, a woodstove for heat, and a modern cookstove. The two new officers arrived in Dawson with little fanfare, their dog teams tired after the long mush from Fort Edmonton. Two assistants would arrive later to man this outpost when the constables were out on a call or routine patrol. These sub-constables would also help care for the dogs and complete other tasks that arose.

The early days were uneventful, the populace accustomed to settling disputes on their own. This arrangement would soon fall, as the police would now handle such conflicts. The people were happy with this change of events, knowing that lives could be saved with law and order stepping in.

The constables' first law enforcement activity involved alcohol. A native woman came to the station and reported two men had recently arrived in town with a large quantity of liquor. They were trading it to the Indians for their valuable furs, often cheating them. These men were staying at the hotel where they peddled their demon spirits. The constables went to the hotel and confiscated the liquor, The bootleggers spent the night in jail, and were then banished from Dawson forever.

Gambling and prostitution reigned in Dawson, as well as free-flowing liquor and beer. Many proprietors tried to make money off of the gold seekers coming to town. While on street patrol, the constables' main duties were breaking up fights and answering complaints of petty thefts. The Mounties' job also included building trust and establishing relationships. This was especially true for the Indians, who were distrustful of the white men.

Policing was finally being established and the adventures would be many for these two men whose careers would become recognized as the North West Mounted Police, Canada's newest police force.

CHAPTER 1

◆ ◆ ◆◆◆ ◆ ◆

The day was bright and sunny. The sleds were loaded with supplies, and the dogs were anxious to go, pulling at their harnesses and yelping in discontent at what they perceived as a long wait. The sub-constables had arrived and would take care of things in Dawson while the constables were on patrol. On command the dogs lurched forward, the sleds following behind them. The trail was hardpacked, allowing for a fast ride and an easy pull for the dogs. Dawson was soon out of sight as they entered a wooded area, scaring up gamebirds as they moved along the trail.

The Mounties first stop was a trapper's cabin. Old Joe had been living in this wilderness for over forty years. He had taken an Indian woman as his live-in wife, twenty years into his lifelong commitment to the Yukon. As the constables arrived at his cabin, Old Joe's dog was less than welcoming, being confronted by the Mounties' sled dogs. Old Joe was surprised to learn that this part of the country finally had law enforcement officers. On more than one occasion he had to take the law into his own hands to protect his life and home. He invited the constables in, accepting their gift of coffee, a gesture of the friendship that would be established between these men.

They entered the cabin, meeting Joe's wife. Now an elder, she had been born in the wilderness. Being well-versed in medicinal plants, she had saved Joe's life on more than one occasion. One example was when Joe fell through the ice while checking his beaver traps, resulting in a few of his toes freezing. Lena, his wife, removed the dead tissue from his feet and used her herbal remedies to starve off infection. He had also lost fingers to frostbite after being stranded overnight when a part of his dog sled broke on his way home. His life was saved by a small fire and the dogs who helped shelter him from the cold, Lena's medicine again aided his healing.

As the Mounties left, the two parties wished each other well, knowing they would see one another again. The constables continued their journey north, meeting people on the trail who were headed to Dawson. An hour later, as they rounded a corner, a pack of wolves was blocking the trail. The constables stopped their dogs abruptly. It was a standoff, until a rifle discharged over the wolves' heads causing them to take evasive action and run off into the forest.

The constables' shelter for the night soon come into view, a survival cabin with a large stack of firewood piled by the front door. A pleasant warm shelter would be appreciated after the cold day, the temperature never rising above minus twenty-five degrees Fahrenheit. The men were happy to find comfort and warmth, what this shelter assured them.

CHAPTER 2

The survival cabin was small. Built by the government these structures had a small wood stove, two beds, and a table. They were constructed between Mountie outposts, which were beginning to pop up across this rugged terrain. The night was cold and clear. The snoring of the sled dogs was the only sound to break the silence of the forest. The Mounties slept well, warm and cozy in their beds with the fire burning, casting a warm glow throughout the cabin.

The morning sun shone brightly through the curtainless window. The sled dogs were awake and restless, waiting to be fed. The men got dressed and took care of their animals first. They then returned to the cabin and ate breakfast, enjoying smoked duck and goose they had purchased in Dawson. The dogs were harnessed, and they were soon back on the trail heading towards the first Mountie outpost they would visit.

The ride was quiet, the heavy breathing of the sled dogs and the swish of the sleds' runners through the snow added to the beautiful landscape of pristine forest, clean air, and brilliant snow. These men loved their job and the freedom it gave them. But soon disaster would strike, returning them to reality.

Without warning a gunshot rang out and one of the Mounties' sled dogs dropped to the ground, covered in blood, obviously dead. A man appeared from the forest unarmed, sobbing, his mind apparently gone. The Mounties tried to help the man, but he died shortly afterwards. The men followed the man's tracks and discovered a rifle yards from the trail. Apparently, in his delusional state, the man had shot one of the dogs thinking it was food. The bodies of the sled dog and the man were left in the woods, where nature would take its course.

As the sun was dropping below the horizon, the men reached their destination, a Mountie outpost manned by two constables. Their building could comfortably sleep four people. One of the officers was there, the other had travelled to Dawson City for supplies. The three men exchanged greetings and stories; a pleasure not often experienced by these men living in the wilderness.

The lead constable of the outpost told the pair he was having an issue with wolves. They were coming at night, causing the dogs to bark and disturb his sleep. He asked if the men had any ideas as to how to solve this problem. Collectively, they came up with a plan. They would lie in wait, with the dogs in sight, and ambush the wolves.

That night, the men hid, but the wolves did not make an appearance. Most likely the predators were hunting for food. The men from Dawson decided to spend a second night and try again. This time the wolves moved in; unaware their adventure was going to be interrupted. The pack lost four members, and clearly got the message not to return to this lonely outpost in the forest. The wolves' carcases would be donated to the Indians who periodically dropped by when they were in the area.

After the ambush, the men grabbed a few hours sleep before the traveling constables started their return trip to Dawson. The stillness of the night brought peace to the men, making them realize again why they chose this job.

CHAPTER 3

———— ◆·◆◆◆·◆ ————

The Mounties left early, looking forward to their return to Dawson. The morning hinted of snow, with a grey sky and a steady north wind. Instinct told them to wait, but they were already behind schedule having stayed the extra night. They were sure it would not be a problem getting to the shelter, even if the weather turned bad. The dogs were well-fed and rested and should have no difficulty covering the distance to safe harbor.

The trip started uneventfully, but an hour from the outpost their luck changed. Apprehension gripped the men as the winds blew stronger and the snow became a blinding white sheet, obstructing their view and making it hard to follow the trail. Their lives were now dependent on the dogs, their backs to the wind struggling to pull the sleds. After what seemed like an eternity, the little shelter came into view, the men's decision about leaving having a happy ending.

The men entered the shelter after securing the huskies. The dogs would sleep through the blizzard, curling up in the snow, letting it cover them to keep them warm. The men lit a fire and were soon warming their frigid bodies by the stove. They realized how close they had come to losing their lives. If it were not for their faithful and hard-working dogs, they probably would have perished in the cold and snow. The north spares no one, not even law enforcement, from the cruelties of nature.

The storm raged all night, finally calming in the early morning. The sun took over where the storm had left off, leaving a world bright with new snow. The dogs were rising from their white cocoons waiting to be fed as the men left the shelter. Anxious to get back to Dawson, they were soon on the trail, hoping to arrive back at their post by early afternoon.

The dogs worked hard as the snow was deep, but soon the homes in Dawson appeared on the horizon. As they drew closer, a large amount of smoke could be seen in the distance. A house was on fire. The constables made their way to the fire to see if they could be of assistance, but they were too late. The old wooden structure was engulfed in flames, the result of a faulty chimney, the number one cause of house fires in Dawson. Many lives were lost when these wooden buildings burned at night, trapping the occupants in their beds, a death not to be wished upon anyone.

The men returned to the station glad to be back. They never knew if anyone perished in the fire, as it burned so hot any bones would have turned to ash. Life in Dawson City was hard, survival even harder, as nature takes its toll on this frontier town.

CHAPTER 4

The smell of bacon woke the two weary constables. It was a welcome-back breakfast being cooked by one of their assistants. They pulled themselves out of bed and poured some coffee, the steaming aroma heightening their senses and waking them further. The day was cloudy and cold, making the men grateful for an efficient wood stove capable of keeping the cabin at a comfortable temperature.

On the list of things to do today was to see a man in town about the theft of one of his dogs. He knew where the dog was, and he wanted the constables to rescue the animal and return it to him. Dogs were valuable in the north and could be easily sold, sometimes ending up in the goldfields. These kidnapped dogs could be mistreated, especially if they were disobedient or aggressive toward their new owner.

The two constables took their dogsleds and found the man who had lost his dog. He said the thief was an acquaintance of his who had asked to purchase one of his animals. The buyer had no money, wanting to buy the dog on credit, promising payment when he found gold. The dog owner had refused his offer. To his surprise, one of his sled dogs went missing the next morning.

The constables arrived at the supposed thief's home. They were greeted by an angry dog, not happy about having been removed from his pack. The dog had been lured away with fresh meat and went with this man, who he trusted to give him more food. The dog felt betrayed, as he was now locked up and made to go hungry. The constables arrested the thief, his punishment was a week in jail. The rightful owner was glad to be reunited with his dog.

Upon returning to headquarters, one of the assistants informed the Mounties a local bar owner had been in asking for help with an unruly patron. A prospector from the goldfields, awash in cash, had been frequenting his bar, drinking too much, and causing trouble. He wanted this man barred from his establishment before someone got hurt. The officers checked the hotel where the man was staying and were informed by the proprietor the troublemaker had checked out, saying he was heading for Seattle. The Mounties were relieved to hear the problem had been resolved without having to confront the man.

The pair returned to headquarters and fed their prisoner, who pleaded to be let go. He didn't want to be confined any longer. He was now sorry that he had stolen the man's dog. His wishes for freedom were denied, the Mounties keeping him in jail until his sentence was complete. Hoping this would make the man think twice before breaking the law again.

Night was soon upon them, and with the day's record keeping completed, the men retired to bed. Their biggest challenge to date would come tomorrow, as this lawless frontier was being tamed by these men. This was a dauting task; some unwilling outlaws opting to die rather than pay for their crimes, a reality of the far north.

CHAPTER 5

A cold north wind howled. The snow was blowing, as another blizzard showed its face in this harsh wilderness. The people were in their shelters, mostly wooden houses, built in a hurry, that were not well-insulated. The frigid temperatures were unrelenting, creating the danger of freezing to death in one's own home if the firewood ran out.

The Mounties were awake early; the high winds had been blowing debris against the station, the banging noise keeping them awake. The storm was abating but the wind was still blowing, causing the snow to swirl around the building like a tornado. Soon the day grew calm, and the storm passed. The sun was now shining, the white snow glistening, its beauty deceiving. The Mounties readied their dogsleds and set out to patrol in town.

Dawson was quiet; the streets were empty and forlorn. The only visible sign of life was the smoke from the chimneys. The occasional bark from a dog could be heard. The dog team mushed on, and the men soon came upon a collapsed building covered in snow. The hand of a frozen body was protruding, appearing to be reaching out from under the rubble, as if crying out for help. He was a victim of the storm. The Mounties left the area; the body would be recovered later.

As they continued their patrol, the sound of gunshots rang out. Approaching the area where the shots came from, they found a moose lying dead, the snow crimson with its blood. A happy man was sitting on his trophy. The moose had wandered into town, the quiet after the storm leading to its demise, creating a bounty of food that would help people survive.

The constables returned to their outpost to a sight they were not expecting, an Indian with two dead bodies wrapped in blankets on his sled. He said these white men had come across his cabin that he shared with his wife. At first, they were friendly, but things soon turned ugly as they decided to kill him and take his wife as their squaw. Sensing something was amiss, the Indian was ready when they attacked. The knife his father had given him as a young child saved his life, extinguishing the lives of these prospectors. The Indian's story was believed, and it was declared an act of self-defence. He went on his way, leaving the two bodies to be stored for the winter. They would be buried in the spring.

The Mounties' eyes had been opened as to what some of their tasks would be. Death was a common denominator as the survival instincts of humans could lead in different directions. Nature always made the final decision for man, his destiny never his own.

CHAPTER 6

The mouse came out of its hiding place, looking for anything food related that the occupants had dropped. It had moved into this house shortly after it was built. It was its refuge from the cold and snow. Like the mouse, humans have to find shelter from the elements, which are relentless and unforgiving. Nature will take a life with no afterthought; only the brave will survive this lifestyle they have chosen.

The Mounties woke early, a busy day had been planned. The dog sled races were to be held today, an annual event that usually turned into a party, with a carnival-like atmosphere enjoyed by the townspeople. The Mounties appearance at the event would insure everyone behaved, as drinking could become excessive, causing arguments and fights to take place. The day went well, the only issue the Constables had to deal with was a drunk who pulled a knife on a man he had an argument with and had to be jailed overnight to sober up. With the arrival of darkness, the party ended, and everyone went home to warm themselves by the fire, the cold finally taking its toll.

The next morning the Mounties went to see an Indian woman who lived outside of town. They had met her at the town's festival, and she invited them to her place for coffee and some conversation. Her name was Bev, a long-time resident of Dawson, who was here before the gold rush. The morning was cold and clear as the men arrived at Bev's house. They were warmly greeted and offered fresh bread and coffee. Bev turned their conversation to a young couple she adored. They lived in a cabin about a day's journey from Dawson City by sled. Bev asked the constables if they could deliver a letter to them, as it had arrived for the husband and she felt it may be of importance.

Bev also told the Mounties she had the couple's pack animal in the barn, wintering over. His name was Omar and he had a strong back. If the Mounties ever had the need, Bev would be happy to lend him out. However, Omar may not be happy if he was forced to work for these men, as he preferred the easy life.

The Mounties left, assuring Bev they would take the dog sled and ride out to her friends' cabin and check on them. They returned to their outpost where they were informed that after the assistants had released their prisoner from jail, he went straight to the house of the man he had accosted at the festival. They got into another altercation, resulting in him being thrown back in jail for a week to cool off. This argument was over a woman, and the constables worried how this argument might finally be settled.

The night was dark with the stars shining brightly, a lone howl of a wolf the only sound to break the silence. The Mounties slept peacefully ready for the challenges they would face tomorrow, sometimes a task not to be taken lightly in this land they called God's country.

CHAPTER 7

Today the police force in Dawson was expecting visitors, two constables from Fort Edmonton. They were heading to relieve two Mounties who had decided the isolation and hardship of their remote outpost were too much to bear, wishing to return to civilization where life was easier. The constables rode into town, their dogs barking, making their presence known. This was followed by an orchestra of sound from the dogs of Dawson, welcoming their brethren to town. The men were happy that this leg of their long journey was finally over.

The Mounties talked, exchanging stories of adventures they had encountered in this land of hysteria created by the discovery of gold in the Yukon. Yellow fever gripped the souls of men with promises of untold wealth, which many times were never delivered. These Mounties were proud to be participating in a new law enforcement operation whose duty it was to keep order in this wild frontier. This was a job not taken lightly by these recent recruits.

Everyone ate a hearty lunch and discussed the need to harvest meat for the outpost. The men stationed in Dawson had heard from a local of a location where deer were plentiful. The four men decided to go together, readying their dog teams. The deep snow would be in their favor, as it would be difficult for a deer to escape, resulting in an easy kill.

When the men arrived, the deer were nervous from an early morning attack by wolves. The animals panicked at the approach of the dogs, running into deep snow. The Mounties bagged two deer, one more than they had hoped for. The men retrieved the deer and loaded it on the sled to be taken back to the outpost for processing. Some meat would be frozen, and some given away to the neediest residents.

The visitors spent the night and in the morning continued on their way, the men at their destination waiting for their arrival. Some of the venison went with them, as there was no way of knowing how well the outpost they were going to was stocked with food. No meat meant no life, as it was the only food available during the winter months, with the exception of root vegetables that were usually depleted by early winter. Starvation and disease ruled in the Klondike, taking the lives of men unprepared for life in the frontier or gold fields.

In Dawson the mice had come out of hiding looking for leftovers. Their family had increased in number due to the lack of predators, an event noticed by the Mounties that lived there. One constable acquired a cat named Friskers, whose owner had recently passed away. Friskers was a large tomcat experienced at catching mice, a job it took seriously. This animal would prove to become an important asset.

Tomorrow the Mounties planned to go on patrol, checking on trappers in the area. Getting to know these trappers would sometimes lead to gifts of meat, as most of the mammals caught for fur could also be used as food. Quiet reigned as the men finished their daily tasks, allowing them to put this day behind them and get ready for the encounters they would face tomorrow.

CHAPTER 8

The Mounties woke with a start. The dogs were barking loudly, obviously disturbed by something they could see or smell. The sun was just appearing on the horizon as the men went out to investigate the source of the trouble. It was soon apparent by the aroma they could smell. The dogs had an encounter with a skunk and were sprayed by this small, harmless mammal with a bad odor. The Mounties laughed, glad it was just a skunk and not something more serious. They returned to their dwelling, enjoyed breakfast, and began their day.

They loaded the sleds with supplies, the dogs anxious to get out and enjoy a new adventure. The snow was fluffy and deep, the sun casting a bright light over it, creating a visual scene like a million stars sparkling. The cold air stung their senses, invigorating the two men and propelling them into a surreal moment of being one with nature, their souls captured by the peace and serenity of the far north.

After an uneventful two-hour ride, they arrived at the first cabin which belonged to an old, long-time resident of the Yukon; a fur trapper and gold hunter originally from

Seattle. In the summertime a graceful waterfall added ambience to this property, something he was eager to point out. This was his spot of refuge when dealing with the bouts of depression he suffered from. The Mounties were welcomed into the trapper's home. He lived here with his dog, a simple structure that gave him life if he made sensible decisions.

The cabin was sparce; the scent of furs cleaned and stored permeated the air. The smell of body odor from the trapper and his dog, who had been unable to bath in months, added to an aroma common in these old cabins; constructed in the wilderness, left to decay, and become one with the forest again upon their inhabitants' demise. After a short visit, the Mounties prepared to leave, the trapper giving them some smoked fish, a plentiful commodity from the lake that was a short distance from his home.

The trapper and his dog saw the men off, the sleds disappearing across the lake and soon out of sight. The mushing dogs, straining at their harnesses, breathing heavily, and pulling hard spoke to the importance of these sled dogs for man's survival. These animals were rarely disrespected or abused; a good relationship with one's animals vital as to how well they would respect, trust, and protect you in times of trouble. They were a stalwart of the north, dedicated to their own, and man's, survival.

CHAPTER 9

+ ✦ ✦ ✦ ✦ ✦ +

The Mounties drove their sleds in silence, their next stop was one of the survival cabins built for them to use while on patrol. They arrived in the late afternoon, already under the shadow of dusk which arrived early during the winter. They noticed a pack of wolves had been about, their tracks abundant around the structure. The men entered the cabin and lit a fire in the woodstove. It was soon roaring with flames, sending a warm glow throughout this tiny structure in the woods. The wind howled outside; the men were comfortable in this environment they had created. They were cozy, like a child in a mother's womb, protected from the harsh realities of the outside world. They sat around the small table, ate dinner, and played cards, before fatigue overcame them and sent them to bed. The men's dreams were of mushing dogs across wilderness lakes and forests, bringing law enforcement to a land inhabited by few.

A sudden bang at the door startled the men, awakening them from their dreams. The winds had calmed, and they lay in silence, hearing what sounded like footsteps. They listened, the quiet of the night amplifying the sound. The noise approached the door. The doorknob rattled, sounding like somebody was trying to enter. The Mounties froze, and then yelled out. The presence on the other side of the door was startled, leading to its rapid departure from the front of the cabin.

There was no more sleep that night, as the men did not trust whoever it was not to return. They lay awake until sunrise, planning to investigate at first light. What they discovered mystified them. Left in the snow were large human footprints. They led up to, and away from the door. It was apparent this creature picked up its pace, showing it moved quickly as its trail disappeared into the forest. The Mounties looked at one another, not having to explain anything. They had just experienced what other men in the remote forests of the Yukon had reported. Bigfoot, a creature wrapped in legend and folklore, believed to be native in this wilderness, but never proven to be real. Stories like this one were not to be believed and were discounted as tales from crazy men suffering from delusions.

The constables decided to put this incident in the back of their minds. As they loaded their dogsleds, the crows on the roof of the shelter cried out hoping for a handout, which proved to be fruitless. Another bright day greeted the Mounties as they made their way to the next cabin. It belonged to the young couple their friend Bev had asked them to check on. The men were looking forward to meeting them and delivering a gift of coffee they had brought. They would meet in the afternoon, and an interesting story would be shared, making the Mounties question their own sanity, as the north revealed its secrets.

CHAPTER 10

───────── ✦✦✦✦ ─────────

The snow was deep and the trail was unbroken, the dogs strained at their harnesses as they pulled the sleds forward. The sky had turned grey, and a light wind hinted of snow. The Mounties were quiet as they made their way to their next stop, thoughts of home always in the back of their minds. Both men were born in Fort Edmonton, a growing town, and an epicenter for goods to supply this new land. It was the de facto capital of the far north, an important centre for the sale of furs, and a resupply place for those who called this land home. The main headquarters for Canada's newest police force, the North West Mounted Police, was located there.

After many hours of being on the trail, a little cabin appeared. Set in the backdrop of the forest it looked enchanting and well-kept. Smoke billowed from the chimney, indicating that someone was home. The Mounties knocked on the cabin door and were greeted by a tall thin man and his Indian wife. They introduced themselves as Jason and Wendy, and their dog's name was King. The constables gave them the letter and a gift of coffee from Bev.

The couple shared the coffee with the Mounties, which was good, but what the men really enjoyed was the warmth of the fire, and the hospitality that was shown towards them.

A knock at the door ushered in the appearance of another man. He was introduced to the Mounties as Steward, Wendy's brother, who did not live far from here. The constables stayed for an hour sharing stories with their new found friends. With a laugh Steward told the tale of his experience with Bigfoot, the man ape. His ancestors spun yarns of sharing the forest with these large, hairy mammals who were biped and had many of the same characteristics as humans. They became known as Bigfoot because of the large size of their feet, almost twice the size of an adult humans.

Steward said he was out hunting for deer, when he had this intuitive feeling something was watching and following him. Being born and raised in the forest, he was very perceptive, which led him to think something was amiss. He was keenly aware of things such as birds being silent or the breaking of branches signifying activity by a large mammal. At first Steward thought it might be a mountain lion, a stealthy predator who were known, under extreme circumstances, to stalk and kill humans. He decided to conceal himself and see what the mystery was. After a short while his luck paid off. A bigfoot came out of hiding, the legendary creature his ancestors told their stories about.

Steward was frozen, never suspecting the legend was true. He decided the best plan was to scare the creature by shooting over its head, hopefully making it wary of interacting with humans who were invading its territory.

Steward shot off two rounds in quick succession with his rifle. The bigfoot froze, perhaps realizing the danger Steward posed, and bolted into the forest.

Was Steward's story the truth or just another tale to add to the Indian folklore that was part of the culture of the North? The Mounties knew the truth but did not share their story with their company. The men left, saying their goodbyes. An invitation to return again was issued by their hosts, as the company had been enjoyed by all. It was rare to get a chance to socialize in this wilderness, the visits uplifting to the spirits of the lonely souls that occupy a small place in this vast country; a place their souls would never leave or abandon as they sought their place in this new world.

CHAPTER 11

✦ ✦ ✦✦✦ ✦ ✦

The air was fresh and cold, and the winds were light as the Mounties continued on their journey, planning on making it to a shelter that Jason and Steward had built to use while out hunting. It would provide a dry roof over their heads. It had a small woodstove that did not provide sufficient heat to keep the cabin warm and cozy according to Jason, making a stay there survivable rather than comfortable.

When the men arrived they noticed a hole which went under the structure that had been dug by an animal; a fox who had made its winter den here. If it was a female, she probably would have her babies here in the spring. Living under the shelter, the fox could hear the activity over its head, and smell the dogs nearby, which would keep the animal safe in its den until the constables' departure.

As they entered the small structure the men noticed rodents had taken up residence. An infestation had led to mass starvation when winter came, dead and decayed mice carcasses littered the floor. Unfortunately, the bodies were in the very spot where the men had to sleep. This shelter was not comfortable, but it would keep them alive. The remains of the mice were cleaned up, the men glad the dead bodies were frozen, allowing for a more sanitary removal.

The men did not sleep well, the cold outside air seeming to invade every corner of this little building, which sat in the middle of this desolate forest. They were awakened by a crow, who noticed the smoke from the chimney and had come here thinking it was a dinner bell. The bird kept up its call, annoying the Mounties so much they got out from under their warm blankets, went outside and gave this noisy bird a not so welcome greeting.

The men packed up and left early in the morning, thankful for the shelter that had been provided for them. Today they would reach a Mountie outpost; a more comfortable setting, warm and clean, unlike the little shelter they spent the night in. The past night's experience would be a memorable one for these men who were new at their job, an incident that would be just one of many they would have in this career they had chosen.

A snowstorm started as they pulled into the Mountie outpost. They fed and got the dogs ready for the storm and retired inside, out of the worsening weather. The winds were now at blizzard conditions causing snow so intense it made one think they had lost their sight. It was a whiteout, a weather condition that could catch men out in a blizzard, causing a temporary loss of direction, leading to confusion and disorientation. Men had perished this way, getting lost and dying from exposure caused by the cold and snow. Buried in the snow where they fell, their bodies would not be found until spring, sometimes their remains eaten by predators. Many men came here hoping to find gold or fur, but gave up their lives in a land that showed them little mercy.

CHAPTER 12

The men realized the seriousness of their situation when they entered the Mountie outpost to the screams of a tortured soul. A man, living alone for many years, suffering from mental anguish created by the loneliness, had finally succumbed to the illness called insanity. Dementia and the death of his dog had pushed the man over the edge. It happened on a cold grey morning, the man sensing the time was near for him to surrender his life. It must have been God's plan for the Mounties to intervene.

One of the Mounties, having noticed the man's declining condition, visited him often to keep an eye on him. When he found the man talking but making no sense, he realized he was suffering from a mental breakdown. The Mountie took this tired and weary soul to the station where he would be kept safely in a jail cell until they could figure out what to do with him. If he had been left alone, he would have met certain death in his cabin or in the bush, as the wilderness would have taken him, reuniting his soul with his maker.

The man was found hanging in his jail cell the morning after the Mounties' arrival; taking his own life to end his suffering. It was a rational decision made by an irrational mind. The jail cell had proven to not be a safe haven after all. The Mounties' jobs were making men out of these boys, as life in the far north was a different experience than what they were expecting.

The mood was somber as the body was cut down and taken to a building out back where all of the unclaimed cadavers were kept until their burials in the spring. The day was dark grey and cold with a strong north wind blowing, suggesting more snow was on its way. Except for going out to care for the dogs, the men spent their day inside. They discussed their different law enforcement experiences, and the required writing of detailed reports, which were to be sent and reviewed by the government to determine if this new force was being successful.

After a busy day of conversations, the suicide of the ill man in the jail cell became less concerning. The oldest Mountie explained that to be a good police officer one had to accept all kinds of unpleasant situations as a normal part of the job. The men ate dinner, the pantry was well stocked with canned food and the underground freezer full of meat.

A storm raged outside, the snow swirling and blowing, the cold unrelenting. Inside the fire was roaring, creating a warmth that spread among the men, bringing them together. Their spirits were joined in a mutual satisfaction from sharing the same experiences, their destinies now laid out in front of them with no way of looking back.

CHAPTER 13

The Mounties left the following morning, their adventure somewhat spoiled, their lives changed at a moment's notice. The haunting images of the old man hanging in the jail cell were ingrained in their thoughts forever. They mushed the dogs down the trail with the sun shining brightly, the air crisp and cold. The dogs exhibited their strength and loyalty, as their breath rose like steam from an old locomotive chugging down the tracks. The constables planned to stay at the shelter they had used on the way here; the one belonging to Jason and Steward.

After a difficult journey the little building came into view, a welcome sight after struggling through deep snow all day. The fox sat at the entrance to its den, watching the arrival of the uninvited company. It had no fear, sensing the visitors meant no harm. The animal retired to its underground shelter, safe and secure. The Mounties had not forgotten about the little fox and had brought the animal some food as a token of their friendship.

Soon warmth spread over the cold bodies of the men as the fire roared to life, and they started to relax from the difficult day they had just endured. They ate dinner and retired to bed, exhaustion taking over. Sleep came quickly. The full moon shone, bathing the forest in light, stimulating activity among the nocturnal animal population. Their search for food was necessary for their survival. Hunger was the common bond that held this diverse group of wildlife together. The men slept soundly, their dreams of bringing some sense of order to this uncivil land the product of their imaginations and hopes.

The bright sun and the fox antagonizing the tethered dogs woke the Mounties, their dreams now just thoughts that were forgotten upon waking. They packed up and left early, planning on making one more stop on their way to Dawson. An old Indian woman in Dawson had a brother with a cabin in the bush, nearby. It was located just off a main trail, hidden in the forest. She had not seen him in over a year and feared he had died, as he always came to town for supplies, but the past year he never showed. The Mounties, spending more time than they should have, located the cabin, and were not prepared for what they found inside; a completely bleached skeleton of a man lying on his bed. They gathered a few of his personal belongings for his sister and then left, closing the door behind them, his cabin becoming his crypt. They would report to his sister that he appeared to have died of natural causes, a man who gave his soul to the north in his everlasting search for freedom and spiritual cleansing.

CHAPTER 14

The Mounties secured the cabin door, they did not want animals to get in and disturb this man's sacred burial ground, scattering his bones and desecrating his remains. They headed back to Dawson, the dogs pulling hard at their harnesses, their hot steamy breath a testament to their hard work. They had taken a slightly different route, which took them to a large frozen lake. Upon crossing they were surprised to see a cabin with a fire burning, smoke billowing from the chimney. They stopped and discussed paying the man a visit, as getting to know the people who lived in these remote areas was a top priority for these police officers. His dog saw them coming and alerted his owner by barking aggressively.

A burley man came to the doorway, rifle in hand. He was not friendly, cautious over the arrival of these strangers. The Mounties introduced themselves and the man relaxed, holding out his hand in greeting. He said he went by his Indian name, Greywolf, his father insisting he follow the culture of the Indian, not the white man. When he became an adult, his father and brothers built this cabin for him.

This allowed Greywolf his independence and taught him to use the survival skills he had learned growing up in the wilderness. He was a skilled hunter, an avid trapper, and was even known to do some gold panning in the many creeks nearby. The small stash of gold he found was hidden and saved for a rainy day.

The men enjoyed some hot tea, brewed from a forest plant rumoured to have health benefits. It made the Mounties feel lightheaded but relaxed. The man was glad for the visit, wished them well and sent them on their way. He watched as the dog sleds disappeared across the frozen lake, becoming but a speck on the horizon.

Just as the sun was setting, the houses in Dawson City came into view. A short time later the constables pulled up to their headquarters, glad to be home after such a long and hard journey. They made themselves some dinner and left the care of the dogs and unloading of the sleds to the other men that called this outpost home. After completing these chores, the sub-constables joined the returned travellers for coffee.

Their ensuing discussion turned to murder. Two men, who once worked as a team on a claim in the Klondike, had a violent disagreement. Coming here as best friends, they grew to hate one another, their friendship ruined by the greed known as yellow fever; an addiction gripping those who find gold, their lust not satisfied until they find more. Their argument was about a theft, one man taking more than his fair share of gold from the other. A fierce struggle ensued, resulting in the stabbing death of the most unfortunate of the two. The survivor robbed his former partner and friend of all the gold and left town. The sub-constables had picked up the body and put it in the storage building out back where it would stay frozen until spring. It was a never-ending series of events, most not pleasant, that were not easy for anyone who challenged the north, where only the strongest survived.

CHAPTER 15

+ ◆◆◆◆◆ +

The next morning the Mounties visited Bev. When meeting Bev, one instantly feels an attachment and love for her, her kind heart and honest soul a rare find. The men told her the good news, that Jason and Wendy were fine and doing well. They shared that the couple appreciated her gift of coffee and had sent a scarf that Wendy had knit for her. The Mounties also brought Bev some meat, their freezer well-stocked with moose and venison, with another hunt in the planning stages.

The Mounties asked Bev if they could use Omar, as they had a task that required a mule. Bev was more than happy to oblige, thinking Omar would enjoy the exercise. She was wrong, Omar would rather stay in the comfort of his own home than go out in the cold and snow and haul heavy things on his back. He just wasn't into it. The Mounties left, telling Bev they would be back to pick up Omar when he was needed.

They stopped at the livery stable where a few horses and a couple of mules were being housed for the winter. The owner told the constables that he suspected a man who had been hanging around his property was responsible for the theft of one of his mules. These animals were a valuable commodity, used for hauling supplies by gold prospectors and fur trappers in the summer months. Mules can easily die of exposure if out in the frigid cold for an extended period of time. The proprietor of the stable said he had not seen this man since the mule went missing. Many times, when such crimes were reported the culprits were long gone, usually with no witnesses. This left the Mounties virtually no clues to work with, resulting in the thief getting away with his ill-gotten gains. They found the stolen mule in town; the man trying to sell it to make enough money to get back to the U.S. where his ill-fated journey had started.

The constables next stop was at a man's home who was selling bootleg alcohol. It had not been distilled properly, and he had poisoned three natives, killing them. Although he had quit selling the tainted spirits, it was too late, the deaths could not be taken back. The man responsible was arrested, not for murder but for criminal negligence. He would spend a short time in jail for the terrible choice he made, resulting in the deaths of three men. Men die in a variety of ways, their demise determined by powers they have no control over, their destinies sealed and their fates decided.

CHAPTER 16

The man looked out his window, the sky was dark and full of snow. Depression had overcome this resident of Dawson, the blackness seeping deeply into his soul. His spirit was broken, his will to live no more. He reached for his gun to end this hell. A shot rang out. No one would notice, or care, what he had done, his body would not be found until spring. Suicide was a common way to die in the north as the lack of sunlight and the unforgiving cold and loneliness took its toll on these men and women who called this place home. In the spring their corpses were found, the odor of decomposition leading to the discovery of their bodies, victims of this untamed land who had died alone during the winter months.

The days were moving on and it would soon be Christmas, a time for sharing among the residents. The hungry would be fed on this special day, as people prayed for a better life. The Mounties were working on a special project. The nearby river had an over population of beaver that needed to be thinned out. It seemed unusual to the constables that no one had been trapping this beaver-rich area. The dams they had built had allowed water to flood areas that encroached on some nearby cabins. The men had set two beaver traps days earlier, and today they would check them.

This was the Mounties first attempt at trapping, being shown how by Steward, who had come to town to find supplies. He had stopped by the Mountie's station acting upon their invitation that had been extended when the men met earlier at Jason and Wendy's cabin. The Mounties mentioned their trapping project, and their inexperience. Steward stepped up, offering to teach them about trapping, as this was one of the ways he made his living. He had been taught by his father and uncles, and was now seasoned at this art. An accomplished woodsman, he would prove to be a benefit to the Mounties, helping them overcome obstacles when they needed direction.

To their surprise, both traps contained beaver. They removed them and reset the traps, hoping to catch two more. The traps would then be moved to a different area, until the desired number of beavers were caught. They planned to give these animals to their friend Bev, who would share the fur and meat with her tribe, the neediest first.

It was the week before Christmas, and the spirit of the season was upon them. The sub-constables cooked large amounts of moose and portions were picked up by the hungry, a welcome protein to help rejuvenate their tired spirits. The fires crackled in the houses of Dawson City, keeping the occupants warm; their bodies no match for the cold outside that could kill them. A week before Christmas, for the sake of nostalgia from their childhood and helping lift other people's spirits, the Mounties took the dog sled and went out and picked the perfect Christmas tree for their outpost. When the people heard it was a tree for everyone to enjoy, they brought decorations. Some were made during the cold nights of winter, while others were mementos from their past. A wonderful Christmas was in store for all, in this frozen land they called the north.

CHAPTER 17

Christmas Eve was here, a joyful time for the majority of people in Dawson. For some, the decorations were sparce and the joy of Christmas was replaced with feelings of hopelessness and regret. These citizens longed to return to a more civilized way of life, not having to struggle daily for survival. However, these were usually only fleeting thoughts, their reality quite different.

On Christmas day the Mounties greeted everyone that came by the station with a hot cup of coffee, a helping of moose meat, and a special treat, fresh apple pie, made from apples that had been delivered earlier in the season. If stored properly, this fruit could be stored for months before spoilage. Christmas ended quietly with a million shining stars filling the night sky. The homes in town were mostly silent; the acrid smell of burning wood filled the air, a welcome aroma to travellers ready to get out of the cold. The forest was quiet as the cold sent the animals to their shelters.

The Constables woke early. They needed to replenish their stock of meat, as their Christmas present depleted their supply. They headed to Steward's cabin; he was familiar with the territory the moose kept in the winter and would be their guide on a hunt. The men spent the evening playing cards, a favorite way to pass the time and enjoy good conversation around the table. They discussed that in the morning they would take two dogsleds to an area close to where Steward had seen moose many times. It was his experience that these large animals were easily scared off by his dog team. They would need to shelter the dogs a distance away and walk in on snowshoes to surprise the animal for an easy kill.

The trio left early and soon reached a good area of cover for the dogs, the men continuing on snowshoes. An hour later, they approached the tree line. Steward stopped the Mounties with a hand signal. He told them to go low as he had seen movement ahead. A moose was eating boughs from a tree, paying no attention. The men needed to move closer for a good shot. They only had one chance.

The Mounties were ready, the sounds of the gunshots instantaneously echoing through the silence of the forest. Then it was quiet as the moose staggered forward, a shot in the heart fatal. Silence ensued as death once again prevailed, an animal's life given to sustain the life of others.

The men rejoiced; their luck was good and the reward huge. A bull moose, when dressed, would feed many hungry people for a long time. They had brought the tools to butcher the moose and get it back to Steward's cabin before dark. The crows, upon hearing the gunshots, arrived almost immediately, eating the eyes out the moose, which they considered a delicacy. The men's hard work paid off and the sun was setting as the last of the moose meat was stored safely away from hungry animals looking for a free meal. They would process it further tomorrow, but tonight their dogs would be rewarded. The hard-working animals had been going crazy all day, the odor of fresh meat making their stomachs ache with hunger. Such stories of success were few, as this land showed little mercy, but sustained life when needed.

CHAPTER 18

A celebratory mood had overtaken the men as they transferred the moose meat from the kill zone to Steward's cabin. After a good night's sleep, they spent the next day dressing out the animal and then treated themselves to a large dinner from their favorite parts of the moose. The dogs again shared in this bounty, eating their fill, blood covering their muzzles as they feasted. These animals worked hard and getting an all-you-can-eat buffet of moose was something they rarely enjoyed.

The Mounties and Steward had become close friends. He had proven to be a hardworking and decent man, respectful and well-mannered, traits his mother had instilled in him as a child. Steward had felt a responsibility towards his sister, Wendy, after their parents had been killed years ago. This sense of duty is why he was alarmed when he discovered she was in an intimate relationship with a white man. Now he trusted Jason, as he had taken Wendy as his wife and was a good husband. He treated her well and took good care of her. Steward was happy with this arrangement and trusted Jason like a brother.

The Mounties left the next morning, their sleds loaded down with meat. They would return at a later date to retrieve the rest of the bull moose they had shot. They would keep half of the meat and distribute the rest throughout the community. The men made it safely back to Dawson. Their trip had been a success, their moose hunt the blessing they had hoped for.

There had been another house fire in Dawson while they were away. It was believed to have been caused by a faulty chimney. Unfortunately for the owner, his remains were found in his bed, burnt beyond recognition by the hot flames. The smoke curling out from the chimneys of the homes in town belied the fact that these wooden structures were like kindling, perfect fuel for a fire out of control.

When the Mounties returned to their station they were surprised to learn from the sub-constables that one of the sled dogs had been attacked by a fox. This unusual incident indicated the animal was rabid, and it had bitten the dog numerous times before the fox was shot and killed. The men had quarantined the animal to watch for signs of rabies. The dog would have to be euthanized if it exhibited any symptoms of this disease. The fox's remains were removed from the area and left to freeze; hopefully the body could be buried in the spring before it thawed and decomposed.

Life goes on in this land of little opportunity. The call of the north beckoned men with an extended hand, inviting these hardy souls to join this life of adventure offered to few.

CHAPTER 19

The chained sled dog that had been attacked by the fox was exhibiting unusual behaviours; snarling and growling at anyone who came near, its eyes flashing red with the look of the devil, and its mouth foaming, froth dripping on the ground. There was little doubt that this animal was infected with rabies. It had to be shot and its body handled carefully, so as not to spread the disease. The Mounties decided among themselves who would shoot the dog. The most senior officer did the deed, as sadness gripped these men. Like losing a family member, they wept, letting their emotions take control. Soon afterwards they returned to their duties.

The Mounties' reports were due for the month and that task took up the rest of their day. The men finally finished, with the younger of the two sworn officers working late. He had always wanted to be a writer. He decided he was living a story that he could share with people in the future; the story of his many adventures living in Dawson and being one of the first Mounties stationed this far north. He was planning on taking this information and writing a book when his career in law enforcement was over, as he did not see policing as his lifetime vocation.

The men slept soundly. Going into the coldest months of the year created untold hardship in Dawson. Deaths from exposure were common as firewood supplies ran out. Not readily available, wood stored for personal use was not given up at any cost, forcing those who ran low to brave the elements in search of this vital resource. The desolation and darkness of January could have a profound effect on even the strongest minds; the isolation leading to illusions and thoughts that were not real. These irrational notions, if dwelled upon, could take control, causing insanity and creating additional victims of the north.

The following day the town awoke to the sound of melting snow dripping off the roofs of their homes. A rare, but much appreciated, thaw was upon them. This short period of melt during the winter months was a reprieve from the cold and provided an opportunity for the populous to go out and enjoy the warmer air, not knowing when they would be so blessed again.

That night was silent, the fires burning in the homes of Dawson City warming the weary bones of the people waiting for spring. The snow fell softly, the puffy clouds hiding the full moon. The tranquility of the forest was striking as the moon tried to make its entrance known, illuminating the dark cold forest like daylight. Nature slept, waiting for the first rays of light to appear in the morning, promising another day to those who called this enchanting place home.

CHAPTER 20

--- ✦✦✦✦✦ ---

The Mounties needed to go to Whitehorse, a gruelling week-long trip. They were to attend a regional meeting that required all the constables to be present. The men would receive updates on the progression of their new force, and how it was perceived by the people it served. They would also pick up supplies they had requisitioned. It would be a difficult journey. The many shelters that had been constructed by the government along the way did not shorten the trip, but provided warm and safe places to sleep. These small cabins dotted the northern forests. Built as shelters for the patrolling officers of this new police force, which had been successful beyond expectations. They would leave for Whitehorse as soon as preparations were finished.

The night was cold, and the howling wind was raging through the forest. This was not a good sign for the start of the men's trip tomorrow into the wilderness. The winds calmed as dawn broke. The dogs pulled on their harnesses loudly exclaiming they were ready to face a new adventure. They left Dawson under bright sunshine; the animals finally glad to be on the trail.

Once underway, silence again stole the moment, creating a euphoric feeling only residents of the north experience. Some smoked meat and fresh moose had been packed, but most of their food would be hunted while on the trail. The first day was uneventful. They arrived at their lodgings earlier than expected. The trail had been well-packed, making it easy for the dogs to travel. The shelter was situated on a large lake, which was frozen in time. There was little life on its surface, all of it living under the ice. Many of these shelters were built on interconnected lakes, providing the Mounties a way to travel in the warmer months. They would use canoes to explore and map new lakes for the government, providing an idea of what this vast land offered.

The men started a fire. The cabin was well stocked with wood, which was replenished by government workers during the summer months. They cooked dinner on the small woodstove, the smoke rising up the chimney, slowing winding its way upward till its demise in the heavens a short time later. This is the way of the Yukon, capturing one's heart and soul in all its tranquility.

CHAPTER 21

＋＋◆◆◆＋＋

The dogs were restless, whining, and unsettled. Wolves encircled the huskies, who were now starting to panic, as these larger animals intimidated them. The wolves moved closer; the dogs afraid to bark, fearing that it would give the wolves a reason to attack. Suddenly two gunshots rang out. The Mounties had heard the dogs, and after watching the area they had noticed a movement that was similar to that of a dog. They instantly knew what they were looking at, a pack of wolves. They readied their guns and on command each fired once, to be assured of hitting their target and not their own dogs. The pack scattered and the men checked the area where they found two dead wolves, their ambush successful. They dragged the bodies away, leaving them for the scavengers to eat, the wolves becoming the prey rather than the predators.

The men returned to bed and slept well. They were up early and on the trail by sunrise. They crossed the lake and came to a tree line where a small doe, a female deer, was feeding on boughs, unaware of the approaching danger. One constable grabbed his gun and quickly shot the deer;

it died where it fell. This would provide meat for the dogs and themselves for the duration of their trip to Whitehorse, a lucky break for these men. As they continued on, the sky was grey, and the feeling of snow was in the air.

They approached another lake, the wind and snow telling them a storm was coming. The Mounties scanned the horizon searching for an answer to their situation. Being stranded in this wilderness with no shelter was a serious problem. Then a miracle happened. A man, and a dog pulling a sled seemed to appear out of nowhere. The man's beard was caked in ice, his sled was loaded with fur. He stopped his dog, and his surprise was mutual. After a brief conversation the man gestured for the men to follow him, leading them to a cabin snuggled into the woods a short distance from the lake. They secured the dogs and went inside. The stranger introduced himself as Red, telling them he was astonished to be in the company of law enforcement from Dawson.

The trapper told them his father had built this cabin and had lived here with an Indian woman whom he had taken as his wife. Red lived here with his parents until their deaths. At that time, he took possession of the cabin and his father's trapline, which he was still working to this day.

The storm picked up steam, the wind howling, snapping limbs off the trees. The snow was blowing so hard it was creating whiteouts. Red offered the Mounties a warm place to sleep on the floor. They took him up on his offer, spending the night beside the woodstove, its warmth keeping them cozy with only a light blanket. Inside the cabin, the sounds from the storm were accompanied by Red and his dog both snoring, and a mystery sound from the woods that never could be identified by the men. A restful night's sleep was had, as the Mounties readied themselves for another day in this wilderness they called home.

CHAPTER 22

The following day the Mounties woke to bright sunshine. The storm had left a blanket of white snow that covered the trees like a wedding veil. Red cooked some venison for breakfast, the smell of the meat filling the cabin, creating a feeling of hunger among the men. Red was glad he had crossed paths with the Mounties, having enjoyed the company they provided. The men said goodbye, waving farewell, their sleds soon disappearing from sight. The encounter last night with the storm, and their rescue by Red, made the Mounties realize how quickly death could come if caught in a blizzard with no shelter. It was a miracle their meeting had taken place.

The men's minds drifted, as the whiteness of the snow was mesmerizing, creating a feeling of being one with nature and a sense of calm and peace to prevail. The men continued on, the dogs straining, pulling the sleds through the snow. They decided to follow a route that would cross many lakes, which would make the remainder of the trip faster and safer for the Mounties. The occasional cabin, built by fur trappers or a native Indians, sometimes could be seen. The landscape, stripped of its foliage, revealed these buildings that were usually hidden among the trees. If they would have come across one of these structures that showed signs of life, the men would have stopped for a brief visit.

The day wore on, and the Mounties were making good time. Their next shelter soon came into view. As they drew closer they noticed the front door was open, banging in the wind. They blamed a bear for this intrusion, probably while looking for food. Further inspection revealed no damage to structure, but the inside furnishings were strewn about. The Mounties were glad they had arrived fairly early, as cleanup and prep for their stay took until the daylight hours were waning. They started a fire in the stove and within a short time they were removing heavy clothing, basking in the warmth of the cabin. The night was calm, the outside air still. The mice came out of hiding looking for food, little of which could be found.

The next two days were uneventful as the Mounties trip became focused more on their desire to arrive at their destination than their journey. The monotony of the sleds underneath them, and the constant whiteness of the landscape started to be an annoyance to their senses. The days wore on and they arrived in Whitehorse the day before the district meeting would take place. They checked into the hotel that had been prearranged for them. They would be staying in the same hotel as their fellow Mounties. The two men took a much-needed bath, changing into clean clothing they had brought with them. Then it was on to a sit-down dinner in the restaurant, a privilege they had not enjoyed in a long time.

Tomorrow the meeting would start at midday, but first they would pick up the supplies they had requisitioned. They retired to their beds, which got them off the ground for the first time in a week, guaranteeing them a peaceful and comfortable sleep. This would help prepare them for their social gathering and meeting tomorrow, an event that the Mounties were looking forward to. Their struggles would continue and their adventures would never end.

CHAPTER 23

The Mounties were up early, excited about the day they were going to have. They went downstairs where other constables were gathering for breakfast. A feeling of comradery was shared among the officers during a breakfast of ham or bacon and eggs, potatoes, and hot steaming bread just out of the oven. The two men shared a table with two other constables who were stationed here in Whitehorse but had been born and raised in Winnipeg. These tablemates had made the long journey here last summer. The Northwest was opening up and they wanted to be a part of it.

The next task on the Mounties' itinerary was to check on the supplies they had ordered. They picked up updated lamps for better lighting and various other sundries, their list of needed items almost completely filled. To their surprise, their order also included new uniforms and sidearms. These weapons were to be worn while on duty. As the number of people had increased in this frontier, so did the danger for law enforcement. Criminals, many of them running from the law, came north looking for easy scores, such as thefts to support their gambling and drinking habits. The Mounties needed additional protection, as some men on this new force had lost their lives at the hands of these outlaws, caught without a firearm for safety.

The constables' meeting was very informative. There were about thirty people in attendance from a number of different districts. It was a good representation of the group, but not every Mountie was present due to other commitments. They discussed policing in the north and how the continuing alcohol sales to Indians by unscrupulous and dishonest men were taking a toll. By feigning friendship, the natives were being swindled out of their furs while drunk, causing hunger and poverty to adversely affect their families. This problem had become the Mounted Patrol's main concern. Stiffer penalties had been enacted by the federal government and these new laws were to be strictly enforced. The organization was continuing to build outposts and new shelters as their law enforcement arm expanded north.

After the lengthy meeting, the men were to break for an hour and then come back together for dinner, a roast beef buffet to cap off this special event. The Mounties were treated well, an important gesture from their bosses. It was a show of appreciation for their dedication and loyalty to the country, as they tried to establish law and order in a land where most men did not understand that term. After dinner, it was time to hit the bars for drinks and a night on the town.

The men went to a show featuring dancing girls, something Whitehorse was known for. The Mounties spent the evening with the two officers they had shared a table with earlier in the day, exchanging stories of their many adventures, some happy, some sad. This was a common theme in this natural, but sometimes deceiving, world of the north. It offered adventure and a new life that would often morph into something completely different, presenting surprises that were never expected.

CHAPTER 24

The Mountie convention had ended, and the constables were leaving town. The sleds were loaded with new supplies ready to be taken back to their posts. Every Mountie got a new uniform, including the sub-constables. However, the sub-constables did not receive new guns. Due to budget constraints, the men of lower rank were not going to get these new weapons until next year. The new rules set out by the federal government stated that no unarmed police officer would be sent out on calls that were perceived as dangerous. They could accompany an armed constable to calls where a weapon might be needed.

The Mounties were soon out of town, leaving the civilized world behind. They hoped to make the first shelter before dark, this one being the furthest distance, taking longer to get there. The men arrived well before dusk, as the trail was good, and the dogs were well-rested. They ate dinner in silence, pondering the long journey back to Dawson, wishing it was over and they were sitting in the comfort of their own outpost ready to crawl into their warm beds. Their treatment in Whitehorse had spoiled them, getting back to the reality of living in the bush would take some time to readjust to.

As darkness set in, they lit a candle which threw some light into the cabin, the full moon providing the rest. A deer on the lake was in a life-or-death struggle with a pack of wolves that had chased it out onto the vast open space. Here it would be easier for the pack to take the deer down, sometimes not an easy task if the animal was strong and healthy. The men in the cabin heard the wolves' victory howls, reveling in the glory that they would eat tonight. The wolves fed on the small doe, leaving only the bones and hide for the ravens to pick clean. Giving up one's life to save another was an accepted way of life in the north.

The night once again fell silent. The stars shone brightly, their light reflecting off the snow, creating a glow that illuminated the forest. A weasel walked around the cabin, looking for food. Typically, if there was activity at a cabin it meant a trapper was there. The weasel associated this with food, as these men usually cleaned their furs outside, leaving a smorgasbord for small animals to eat. Foxes were also known to visit trappers' cabins at night, aware of these free meals.

The sleds were packed early, and the men were off, continuing their trip back to Dawson. The cold air was bitter as the end of January approached. Spring would be welcomed, a reprieve from the cold that numbed one to the bone, breathing new life into their tired souls.

CHAPTER 25

The dog sleds moved forward, the yell of the Mounties quickening their pace. The North West Mounted Police dog sled teams had an average of six dogs and were able to traverse fifty miles per day, depending on trail conditions. In the winter these dogs were the main mode of transportation for travelling longer distances and were used to haul supplies. Dogs were one of the north's greatest assets.

The panting of the animals was the only sound to be heard, the quiet allowing the men to reflect on what a future in law enforcement held for them. They both had talked about cutting their careers short, this job not being what they had expected. The suffering of the people, the cold, hunger, and sickness taking its toll on their mental health.

The days passed by and because of good weather conditions they found themselves back in Dawson much earlier than they had expected. They immediately went to the Mountie station, glad to be home. After a welcome back from the sub-constables, all of the men helped unload the sleds. The assistants were pleasantly surprised to receive their uniforms and were looking forward to receiving their sidearms next year.

The Mounties were told it had been busy at the police station while they were away; many problems had come up that needed to be dealt with. The most serious of these was the removal of a burnt corpse from a house after a fire in town. Also, a native had been found frozen to death after he drank too much alcohol. Apparently he had passed out in sub-zero temperatures, which eventually killed him, another victim of alcohol abuse, a common cause of death in the Yukon.

A man had come in for first aid after cutting himself with an axe while chopping firewood. Having no one to help him, he came to the police station looking for assistance. The sub-constables said they were happy to have helped this injured man, providing him with the assistance he needed. The most unusual thing that happened when the Mounties were in Whitehorse was a dogsled appearing one day in town. It was being controlled by the dogs, the musher dead, found frozen on the sled. No explanation was forthcoming, turning this story, with more elements added to it, into a legend.

The Mounties were also informed that their friend Steward had dropped by looking for them. He had left two rabbits, dressed and ready for them to cook. The men decided to eat these delicacies for dinner as they had not eaten anything but dried meat on their return trip to Dawson, and the change of taste would be greatly appreciated.

The spring, even though still a long way off, would soon be thought about more and more as the days grew longer and warmer, signalling the start of a rebirth in the Yukon. One would not think this possible while viewing the frozen landscape, a place where only the hardiest of souls survive.

CHAPTER 26

------◆◆◆◆◆◆◆------

The month of February passed quickly; the brutality of the winter would soon end, and the Yukon would take on a new atmosphere. The spring season would slowly bring activity back to this frozen wonderland, a place unique to the planet where life of all kinds learn that survival is not a game.

The middle of March brought Dawson it's first warm front of the season. The melting snow dripped off the eaves of the homes. The people were appearing outside, enjoying the warm air for the first time in months. Mother Nature was sending her magic north, not forgetting about the Yukon, one of her last stops.

The Mounties were enjoying being posted here and everything had worked out with the sub-constables. The pleasant work environment and the compatibility of the men made their jobs at the station pleasant. The snow was melting, the landscape getting dressed in its summer clothing, providing a splendid display of colour native only to the Yukon. Small colourful wildflowers dominated the ground, projecting life on an otherwise barren environment. The lakes and rivers would soon be free of ice, allowing boats to traverse the Yukon River, making it easier to move goods. Water allowed a better passage than ice for bringing large amounts of product to Dawson. The boats would also bring summer residents here, people who enjoyed the solitude of the north but not the winter cold. Some would stay, but only the strongest would survive the winter, not understanding it until they experienced it.

The Mounties were facing a problem. The Yukon River had developed an ice jam, backing up the water to flood stage, delaying the season for cargo to be shipped up the river to Dawson. This jam would have to be blown up with dynamite. They had the dynamite, but no expertise as to how to use it. It would be a dangerous job that should be handled by a professional. The Mounties put out word of what they needed, and the importance of solving this problem. Within hours a man appeared who had worked in mines handling dynamite, a man experienced in explosives. He was offered the job and would be paid extra because of the danger he faced. Falling in the ice-filled river or mishandling the dynamite would mean a certain death.

The people of Dawson lined the riverbank, the excitement of watching this daredevil standing on unstable ice setting explosives was palpable. A hush fell over the crowd as he maneuvered himself into position to set the first charge. This chore would have to be repeated again, if it did not work the first time. He successfully finished his job and told the crowd to get back, fearing a shard of ice could do as much damage as glass in an explosion.

The Mounties waited for the blast; it never happened. The man who had handled the explosives waited also, and then his impatience took over. The explosives expert approached the ice jam, and a murmur went through the nervous crowd. He moved slowly to where he had set the charges, multiple sticks of dynamite wired together, set to go off as one. A low rumbling sound informed the crowd what was coming. Within seconds a violent explosion occurred, throwing the man onto the remnants of the ice jam which shredded his body like a grinder. The water bloody, body parts washed down the river with the blown ice. It was a horrible way to die for a man who was just trying to help.

The Mountie's plan had been a success, except for the poor chap who gave up his life to save his town from being flooded. Now looked upon as a hero, his death will always be remembered by the crowd that witnessed it. This was the way of the north, opportunities were given and then taken away, a mystery beyond comprehension.

CHAPTER 27

＊＋◆◆◆＋＊

It was the middle of May and commerce had started in earnest on the Yukon River. Products, such as building materials for new homes and supplies for the fur trappers and Indians, arrived daily. Most people living in Dawson could not afford the high cost of shipping goods this far north. There were others, such as rich capitalists from the United States, willing to invest money in saloons and dancehalls. They set up gambling dens and planned other devious ways to make money off of people passing through, speculating there would be a rush to the goldfields of the Klondike, which were still a fairly well-kept secret.

As soon as the trail dried, the Mounties were going to take Omar home to spend the summer with Jason and Wendy. Unknown to Omar, he was going to pack a fifty-pound bag of flour on his back, available now that the supply boats were arriving daily. He was not going to be happy about this upcoming adventure, but Wendy would be thrilled. If she could keep the bugs and rodents out of it, she could use the flour for baking for a long time. The Mounties would also bring the couple some beef jerky, a delicious product made in Seattle and sold throughout the North and Northwest. It was used by many men while travelling on dog sleds, an unperishable protein source that was safe to eat for a long time.

The leaves had started to show, explosive green pleasing to the eyes of the beholder. The forest had awakened; an abundance of birds looking for mates and a safe place to nest were among the first sounds of spring. The animals of the forest were out with their young. These babies had been born either in early spring or during the long winter months. Bev got Omar ready for the Mounties to pick up.

The men arrived shortly thereafter. The constables had purchased two fifty-pound bags of flour. This quantity would not be available for long; when it was sold out the supply would not return until the next year. They took Omar to retrieve the flour and delivered the bags to their outpost. They planned for Omar to spend the night at the livery stable, where they would get him in the morning for their trip.

Omar would have rather stayed where he was. As much as he loved Jason and Wendy he felt his life was in danger. He had not forgotten his close brushes with death by the presence of wolves and bears near his shelter at their remote cabin. The animals in the woods intimidated him. He knew Wendy and Jason would never forgive themselves if he got eaten by one of the predators that considered him nothing more than a meal.

The trip to Jason's cabin would begin in the morning. Omar had sensed something like this was going to happen and he was not very happy about it. He would participate, but not willingly. He knew the trip was not really that bad; his attitude was just for show, a way to be treated with extra kindness and get treats for being a good mule. For once the Mounties were making a fun trip and not one for work, a welcome break from their very structured routine.

CHAPTER 28

The trip to Wendy and Jason's had to be postponed a day. The Mounties were expecting to receive two horses that were coming by barge up the Yukon River. Arriving two weeks earlier than expected, the men were lucky they got the news of their arrival before they left on their trip. The horses were picked up and taken to the stable to be fed and watered. The animals were unsettled from the rough trip on the barge in the Yukon's turbulent and fast-moving water. The Mounties decided to take the horses on their journey to Wendy and Jason's house, thinking maybe a quiet, stress-free trip would be good for the horses, helping to calm their troubled spirits. It would also allow for the men and animals to get accustomed to one another.

The early morning light was just creeping over the horizon when they reached the stable where they picked up Omar and the two horses. The mounts had been trained for police work; many constables being assigned these horses for the first time. The horses had arrived with two saddles and an extra set of reins. The men gathered up the animals and left the stable. They then loaded the horses with the

Mounties personal belongings and Omar with the flour and other provisions.

The constables mounted their horses and proudly rode through Dawson, waving at people passing by. The trail soon led out of town; the forest was thick with new growth, the fresh aroma of nature permeating the spring air, greeting their senses. The horses were wonderful, as they got the Mounties above ground level and allowed them a better view of their surroundings. Omar seemed quite happy; tied to one of the horses he trudged along behind, in no hurry to go anywhere.

They would spend the night in the bush and were expected to arrive at their destination tomorrow afternoon. The day wore on, the boredom building among the men and animals alike. The Mounties decided they would stop at a lake halfway to the cabin. Spending the night there should easily allow them enough time to reach their destination before dark tomorrow.

The lake soon appeared. It was a beautiful oasis of water filled with waterfowl. The lake was teeming with fish and the air was fresh and clean. They made their camp, gathered firewood, and soon had a blazing fire going. They would sleep on the shore close to the campfire, as the nights this far north were still cold this time of year. The Mounties lay under their blankets, the night sky full of stars. The call of the loon, native to these remote lakes in the Yukon, created a feeling of loneliness. The Mounties slept well, their idea of heaven under their feet. These men were proud to be part of this new police force of the north, giving their lives, if needed, in the name of law and order in the policing of this young nation.

CHAPTER 29

Omar was annoyed. A small bird kept landing on his back, apparently looking for small bugs that lived on his body. He wanted to sleep knowing he had another day of work ahead of him, and this bird was not making it easy. The feathered friend finally left, leaving Omar in a bad mood to start his day.

The Mounties ate breakfast, packed up the mule and horses, and continued on their journey to Jason and Wendy's cabin. The sky was clear with the sun shining brightly as the entourage left the lake and continued on. After travelling a short distance, they came upon a large meadow, the grass lush and green, a good place for the horses and Omar to eat their breakfast. They stopped and let the animals graze but not to excess, as over eating would make them feel sluggish and they might not want to continue walking. Luckily a nearby stream provided them a drink after their meal.

The weather in the Yukon this spring had been dry; not a lot of mud or fast flowing creeks to cross, making for an easier journey. The Mounties had noticed an abundance of partridge, continually scaring them into flight as they travelled through the more wooded areas. One of the men had bought a shotgun while in Whitehorse. It had a custom carved stock, and the mechanisms were the most up to date available.

The gun had been owned by a fur trapper who had died. He had carved the wildlife scenes into the wood, working on it during the long dark nights of the Yukon winter, his dog his only companion in his lonely cabin. The gun had become his most prized possession. Upon his death, it was left to his son, who needed money more than he needed the firearm, so he sold it to the Mountie. It also came with a custom-made waterproof case that the trapper had made from the hides of the animals he trapped. This would be an opportune time to test it out and see how well it worked.

The men stopped the horses and the Mountie struck off into the woods. Within a short time, gunshots rang out and shortly thereafter the victor appeared with two birds. This maneuver was completed again farther down the trail, resulting in the shooting of two more birds. There now would be enough food for dinner tonight.

Dark clouds rolled in, the sound of approaching thunder made the horses nervous, but not Omar. The thunder and lightning did not cause the mule to display any fear, compared to the higher-strung horses. The Mounties found cover under a large outcropping of rock that was nearby. The storm was relentless, the sky was black, the thunder was deafening. The animals stayed surprisingly calm, perhaps knowing the storm would soon be over. It quickly passed, the sound of the thunder now in the distance. A calm lay over the forest, the air was still, nature's show was over.

The cabin soon came into view, signifying the end of this journey, their destination reached. The men's appearance was a welcome addition to this lonely cabin in the woods, in the wild and untamed land they called the Yukon.

CHAPTER 30

Jason and Wendy opened the door to the cabin and greeted the two Mounties as old friends. Their reunion with Omar was sweet, the mule burying his head between them braying loudly while they hugged him. Omar was glad to be home.

Wendy was thrilled to get her flour and put it to good use by baking bread for dinner. Everyone enjoyed the coffee the men had brought with them, a commodity in the north one could never have enough of. It was more than just a hot drink, as it created a feeling of friendship between people that sat around a table enjoying conversation.

The afternoon sun was shining brightly, and a warm breeze caressed the faces of these settlers of the far north as they enjoyed the brief warmth that mother nature gave them. Wendy showed the visitors her vegetable garden. A large variety of vegetables could be grown here, but they only thrive with the addition of nutrients to the soil, usually compost. What Wendy could grow well here were sunflowers. The one she had planted a few years ago had spread from a single plant with many flowers to a garden that now encircled the cabin. Many insects visited her garden, assuring the flowers they had a friend they could lean on.

Jason and the Mounties cleaned the partridge, while Wendy baked the bread. King, the couple's dog joined the men, along with a noisy crow on the roof, both waiting patiently for a hand out. The blue sky and the wispy clouds made for a beautiful day. The smell of fresh bread coming from the cabin stirred the men's appetite, just as the smell of the dead birds did for the dog and the crow. Daylight was waning as they moved into the cabin.

The birds were cut up and fried in a large frying pan delivering a flavour unmatched by any other fowl, their breast meat fought over. The lingering smell of the bread added more pleasure to the meal, having been deprived of this aroma which now seemed like a long-lost friend. The dinner turned out wonderful. The conversation was spontaneous, the friendship between the Mounties and the couple now a trusted relationship, like that between siblings.

The night was noisy as the wolves howled, their hunting party on the prowl. The horses were uneasy knowing these animals were predators, something they needed to be fearful of. Omar was terrified, placing himself in between his new found friends, whom he had ignored on his trip here. He now decided becoming buddies with the horses was better than not liking each other. He hoped the horses had not decided otherwise; not wanting to be his pal, ignoring his fears, and not wanting to help him. Omar would have to think less selfishly if he wanted his life to be fruitful and productive, instilling a decency in him that others could not ignore.

CHAPTER 31

--- ✦✦✦✦✦ ---

The Yukon was ablaze in color, wildflowers of many varieties dominated the landscape, their short burst of color a reprieve from the white blanket of winter. A breeze blew through the trees, the leaves of the aspens and poplars sparkling in the bright light of the sun, casting a magical feeling over this unusually hostile land.

Wendy was up early making coffee and bread for the men for breakfast. Being such a beautiful evening, the constables had gathered up their sleeping gear and spent the night under the stars. The coals from their campfire still glowed from the night before, sending little wisps of smoke into the cool morning air. The Mounties sat up, Wendy's call to come in for coffee inviting. They checked the horses and Omar who all seemed fine, obviously happy with their living arrangements.

The men went to the cabin. Jason was up, drinking coffee and snacking on last night's leftovers. The Mounties accepted some of Wendy's home-made bread, which was fast becoming a forest favorite. After breakfast, the men returned outside. They planned to complete various repairs around the property and, when finished, they would go and show Steward the new horses. He could also have a visit with Omar at the same time. The constables had planned a rabbit hunt with Steward. This would give the one Mountie a chance to show off his new shotgun, which had become his most prized possession.

The sound of hammers prevailed, loose boards were secured, and the winter sheds were cleaned. The doors and windows of these buildings were left open, to try to air out some of the stench from the fur bearing mammals caught on the couple's trapline, that had been cleaned and stored here for the winter. Unknown to any one but Jason, while he was fixing one of the loose floorboards in the fur cleaning shed a canvas bag appeared. Jason's heart stopped, as he reached in and retrieved it. The bag was similar to one he had previously found in the cabin, which had contained a variety of coins. Upon opening it and seeing what was inside, a smile spread across Jason's face. He hid his find, planning on showing Wendy the contents later. He thought they had found all the treasures his grandfather had hidden, but obviously he was wrong.

The men finished the jobs on hand and readied the horses and Omar, while Jason and Wendy packed a few things and closed up their cabin. Soon everyone, including King, were on their way. Two hours later they arrived at Steward's cabin. He was busy chopping wood for his stove, trying to get a jump on his winter supply. He was already thinking about the cold and the insatiable appetite for wood his stove possessed.

Omar ran to Steward throwing his back legs upward and braying with excitement. The Mounties also received a warm greeting from Steward, big hugs, and a welcome slap on their backs, for these trusted and now good friends.

Life is hard in this land, an untamed wilderness that man will never conquer. Friendships made here are lasting, treasured because they are so rare. They were not cast aside like something that can be replaced; a friendship ruined is a friendship destroyed, often never to be repaired.

CHAPTER 32

◆◆◆◆◆◆

The seasons were changing. Soon summer would be here in all its glory, a short lifetime of splendor supplied by God, appreciated in a land that gets so little. The mother bear and her cubs were hungry. The animals found a berry patch, the mother teaching her young how to eat the ripe berries from the stems of the plants. The cubs enjoyed this outing and liked the idea of being given the responsibility of finding food to eat on their own. This was the cubs first lesson in survival, learning to take care of themselves, not depending on anyone else to be there for them. These were the ways of the north.

The Mounties checked their guns. They both had shotguns, as these firearms were kept at the outpost as both a law enforcement tool and for the hunting of fowl and small game. Of course, the Mountie with the custom-made gun would use it on the hunt, bringing this special firearm for its accuracy and balance when shooting. Wendy and Jason were going to stay at Steward's and watch over the animals. However, Jason's dog King would go with the hunting party. Being trained to hunt rabbits, he would chase them into a

407

clearing, making it easier for the men to kill them for food, an accepted way to hunt here.

They left on foot, King leading the way, aware of the purpose of this journey; rabbit for him for dinner if they were successful. Sometimes rabbits were plentiful in the Yukon; at times to the point of there being too many. They provided a valuable food source for a number of predators, including raptors and humans. The hunters found that today was no exception to the rule, as many rabbits were seen, making them easy prey for these marksmen. A total of six rabbits were shot in under two hours, and the men deemed it a successful hunt. They returned to Steward's cabin and cleaned the bounty. They would have a nice dinner tonight and the Mounties would say farewell in the morning.

Steward prepared dinner outside over the fire, using a method his father had taught him as a young man growing up. Wendy had gathered edibles to make their meal complete, except for dessert, which was a challenge to make as ingredients were hard to find. The smell of the cooking rabbit caused King's mouth to salivate at the thought of eating one of his favorite meals; rabbit so fresh its body barely had time to get cold, cooked over a camp fire and delivered hot and ready to eat. And that is exactly what King had, even though he was last one to be fed.

The sky was clear, and the moon shone brightly as this small group of friends sat around the fire. They discussed their futures and their pasts, remembering days gone by when life was much easier until they surrendered their souls to the north; a decision not one of them regretted.

CHAPTER 33

✦ ✦ ✦✦✦ ✦ ✦

The Mounties left in the early morning, their time off work had been both fun and relaxing. With a tearful farewell they left, not knowing if they would return before winter. Even Omar was sad to see them go. He would no longer have the protection of his big buddies, the horses, to look out for him. He was now alone, left to defend himself from all the hungry animals that wanted to eat him. He did not care that Jason thought his enclosure was safe and would protect him, because Omar thought otherwise.

The horses were loaded with the Mounties belongings, and they started the journey back to Dawson, leaving Jason and Wendy at Steward's house. Within a short distance they entered a meadow where they stopped and let the horses graze. The horses had worked out well for the Mounties and would provide great benefits in the future for this new mounted force, becoming the face of this organization.

The day was cloudy and cool, the sky dark with a hint of rain. The forest was silent, only the leaves on the trees rustling in the wind, and the horse's hoofs hitting the hard ground could be heard. The Mounties loved the peace of mind and restful spirit this job created for them. It was a hard life that was full of challenges, but a satisfying one.

Suddenly the horses stopped, they were restless pulling at their reigns. They had smelled something that they perceived as danger, putting their senses on high alert. The Mounties studied their surroundings looking for clues. Then they saw the problem, a large black bear had picked up the scent of the horses and was investigating if this smell might turn into a meal. The scent of the men made the bear think otherwise, leading the animal to disappear into the bush, avoiding a confrontation. The men rested the horses, waiting for their disturbed spirits to settle down as the fear of the predator passed.

Their journey continued; the trail easy to traverse. They would soon reach the lake they had previously camped at, which is where they would spend the night. It was roughly the half way point on their journey to Dawson, and always turned out to be a restful place to sleep. Steward had given them some venison, which they would enjoy for dinner.

Soon the lake came into view, the waterfowl plentiful on its surface. An eagle circled the lake, its telescopic vision looking for fish he could call his own. The Mounties secured the horses for the evening, and collected wood for the fire, knowing when the sun went down its warmth would be appreciated. They sat around the fire eating their venison, enjoying the quiet of the evening and the now clear night sky. The fire burnt down, the men asleep under their blankets, not waking until the morning dawn, the sound of the songbirds announcing the beginning of another day, in this land they called God's country.

CHAPTER 34

The cool breeze moved across the faces of the constables as the morning sun rose over the horizon. The men were awakened by the noisy crows who equated humans with food. They waited, hopeful for some kind of handout, which rarely ever came. The Mounties had a supply of smoked beef, which would be their food for the rest of the trip. They had brought this non-perishable item with them from Dawson before they left, and it is what they ate for breakfast.

The lake was peaceful. Its pristine waters were untouched by human hands; an ecosystem that was undisturbed, left the way God made it. The men sat, their gaze focused on the lake, their thoughts caught in the moment as a feeling of total relaxation swept over their souls. This was the feeling of the true north..

They packed up their horses and continued on their way, expecting to be in Dawson City by late afternoon. The rest of their journey was uneventful and by early evening they were looking at the outline of the homes of Dawson. Soon they were at their headquarters being welcomed by the sub-constables, who had taken over their duties in their absence. The men unloaded their personal gear and then returned the horses to the livery stable where they were being boarded.

Returning to their office, they found they had a few issues to deal with, the biggest one being a dispute over the ownership of a cabin. The cabin had been built many years ago and then abandoned, after its owner was killed in a rare bear attack. The man and his dog had surprised the mother and her cub. Thinking her baby was in danger, the mother bear first attacked and killed the man's dog. Then, still in a fit of rage, she attacked and killed the man. His cabin had sat abandoned for five years but was finally rescued and restored to a livable state by another settler. That settler had lived peacefully in the cabin for a number of years, until a stranger had shown up at the police station reporting someone was living in his cabin and he wanted them evicted.

The stranger said he was from Vancouver and had found out about the cabin and its location after cleaning out a house which belonged to one of his late uncles. He had discovered papers that indicated his grandfather was the owner. He had come to Dawson to claim this property thinking it belonged in the family, and he was the rightful owner. The man had been waiting in Dawson for the Mounties and upon their return, was at the police station complaining about his problem.

The two police officers looked over the man's paperwork and decided that since the man had no title or deed for the property, only the paperwork he had found in the old trunk, his claim for ownership was denied. The man returned to

Vancouver, disappointed and not happy with their decision, but willing to accept it.

Life in this country was an ever-changing series of events, with surprises around every corner. A never-ending story of a people that would never be tamed; a land not easy to forgive or forget.

CHAPTER 35

─────── ✦✦✦✦✦ ───────

The eagle circled, its eyes fixed on its target, a baby rabbit which would make a tasty meal for a hungry raptor. The eagle struck without warning, the small rabbit in the bird's talons, a feast for this mother and her baby.

The Mounties woke to loud pounding on their locked front door. One of the dancing girls from the saloon was frantic. She had been tricked by a man who seemed friendly and trustful, but was not. She had accepted his invitation for a drink in his room, but soon after arriving his demeaner changed and his hatred for women became apparent. He kept her a prisoner in his room, sexually assaulting her and beating her until his sick desires were satisfied. The man had then hurriedly left town, not bothering to check out, leaving no witnesses as to which direction he went. The woman was frantic but would live to dance another day in this sometimes-dangerous profession. Unfortunately, the culprit was never caught, living to commit the same crime again.

The Mounties patrolled the streets of Dawson on horseback, the townspeople always waving a warm greeting as they passed. The barges came up the Yukon

River supplying Dawson with the products it needed for its continuing growth, and its ability to have the needed goods for the populous that called this flourishing city and surrounding area home.

The constables decided to take a couple of days off from their busy schedule and visit a wilderness lake, rocky and deep, its pristine waters were full of fish. They would take their horses and enjoy the peace the lake would offer. They left early the next morning, a beautiful sunny day, warm and pleasant with a light breeze. Their route was difficult, but having the horses made the journey easier. They arrived at the lake finding it surrounded by rocky shores, allowing the viewer to look down and spot the large trout that lived in these clear cold waters. Some of those fish were going to make a delicious dinner tonight.

The men found a nice place to camp on a higher piece of land overlooking the water. They made a campfire and gathered firewood knowing the night air would be cool. They had brought fishing supplies, and the rewards were many, as the fish were hungry and waiting to be caught. The smell of fresh fish cooking and the cool evening air cast a feeling of peace over these men, the reason why they were here.

The full moon shone down upon the Mounties, their burning campfire the only other sign of life in the dark forest in which they found themselves. The silence was punctuated only by the call of the loon, a mysterious bird whose reputation was entwined in Indian culture and folklore. The Mounties slept, the quiet creating a peace that could only be felt here, in this little piece of paradise they called home.

CHAPTER 36

The Mounties spent one more night on this pristine water, naming it Silent Lake, an appropriate name for such a peaceful place. They returned to Dawson resuming their police duties, which were more numerous during the summer months. The northern frontier was starting to open up, as rumours of gold in the Klondike stirred the imaginations of men thinking it would be their way to easy riches. The north would teach them otherwise, causing the unnecessary deaths of an untold number of prospectors, who dared to take on the challenges.

The Constables had seen an uptick in disturbing the peace incidents, including assaults and drunkenness caused by these newcomers. Some spent the night in jail for their unruly behaviour. The warm weather would soon come to an end. August, the last consistently warm month of summer, would soon be over ushering in a new season. The trees would soon change colour and drop their leaves, their bare limbs signifying a long winter's sleep was ahead of them. The flight of the migratory birds leaving the north, cemented the fact that soon winter would return, proclaiming its dominance once again.

The Mounties were surprised at how much produce they were given by the townspeople. The gardens produced a bounty of food in the summer; the root vegetables lasting until after Christmas if stored properly. The men had talked to their friend Bev about canning some of the donated vegetables for them. This would assure the police at the outpost of some healthy additions to their diets during the winter. The Mounties gathered up the needed supplies and gave them to Bev so she could do this for them. She was happy to help as a thank you for the law and order they had brought to Dawson.

The dog days of summer were upon them, monotony taking over; until one day a trapper looked out his cabin window and witnessed the first change of the season, a golden yellow leaf floating silently to the ground. Thoughts of the cruel reality of winter set upon him, a season he knew only the strongest could survive.

The Mounties were soon answering an increase in calls involving encounters with bears. The interactions of these large mammals with humans expanded in the fall; the bears on a constant search for food as they readied themselves for hibernation. These encounters sometimes resulted in the death of the bear at the hands of the Mounties, if it continued to pose a threat to humans.

Men were out hunting this time of year as they prepared for the long winter. Scores of migratory birds leaving the far north were edible, and there was a short window of opportunity to harvest this bounty. Unfortunately, it also brought out many inexperienced hunters, who clumsily handled their guns causing them to shoot themselves, or another hunter, in a careless accident. Every year there was at least one fatality and this year was no exception. The Mounties had already been to the forest collecting an unclaimed body, shot in a hunting mishap. This was another lone soul, whose spirit had joined its creator, a special resting place for a man who just wanted to call this place home.

CHAPTER 37

✦ ✦ ✦✦✦✦ ✦ ✦

Fall in the Yukon is a busy time for nature, as it slowly winds down the life it offered in the summer. When this short season ends, this land will be in the grips of what it knows best, winter. Fall is a season of change, the leaves on the trees turning from their summer coat of green to a cascade of colours. Floating to the ground, the leaves cover the forest floor like a carpet. It was September, a busy month for migratory birds, and the Mounties were ready to get in on some of the action.

The men took their horses and traveled to a lake that was a short distance from Dawson. It was a prime habitat for migrating birds to visit on their way south. They were planning on staying overnight, as the birds were most active in the early morning. This was when they would hunt for these game birds.

These men loved to wilderness camp, the lakes of the north drawing them like magnets to an iron bar. This lake was marshy, attracting a variety of waterfowl because of a high volume of food, the vegetation making it more like a swamp than a lake. This warm weather pastime would soon end as the land and water froze, the Yukon becoming like a snow swept plain.

The horses slowly poked along, the Mounties in no hurry to reach their destination. After a pleasant two-hour ride, the lake came into view. The tall grass and undergrowth around the shoreline provided good cover. A multitude of waterfowl flew in and around the lake, suggesting a successful hunt. They found a clearing on the shore where they built a fire and made camp. The nights were getting cooler, so a warm fire was called for.

Countless species of wildlife called this place home. Muskrat, a fur bearing mammal, were abundant, their homes plentiful in this swampy habitat. A beaver lodge could be seen in the distance. One of these animals swam by the men as they sat quietly at their campsite. The fire burned down. The night air was cool, as silence enveloped the men who slept peacefully under the stars.

A commotion on the lake awakened the Mounties. The noise of the waterfowl grew louder, the birds' activity increasing as they tried to find their way forward in this mystery called migration. After a breakfast of beef jerky, the men retrieved their shotguns and were soon shooting birds that flew over their makeshift cover. Two hours later, they had shot and retrieved thirteen fowl. Some they would keep and the rest they would give away to the natives that frequented the police station. These guests would come for visits and warm themselves beside the ever-present fire.

The trip back to Dawson was uneventful except for the rain the men got caught in, soaking them and the horses to the bone. It was a small trade off for the game birds they were returning with, a gift of food that would soon not be available, as the ice and snow take over.

CHAPTER 38

The Dawson City area could expect its first snowfall in mid-September and this year was no exception. The Mounties awoke one morning to a light dusting of snow on the ground. The middle of the month had just passed, the prediction of snow had been right on schedule. The constables' horses had been sent back to Whitehorse, where they would spend the winter. They would return in the spring after the ice left the Yukon River, and the barges could make it to Dawson. The exodus of the summer visitors had also taken place, with a few of them waiting to see the first snow.

The Mounties had recently visited their friend Bev who had told them that Jason and Wendy would soon be returning Omar to her for the winter. Steward would be accompanying them, and they planned to have dinner. An invitation to join them was extended, and the constables gratefully accepted. They were looking forward to a good meal, almost as much as the company.

The meat supply at the police outpost was getting low. At this time of year moose and deer meat could not be easily transported from a kill site deep in the woods. Such hunting would have to wait until the snows were deep enough for the dog sleds to be operational. The occasional animal that was shot near one's dwelling could be packed home but required a number of loads on one's back. And so went life in the Yukon, a constant game of staying ahead of your adversary, nature. Life would soon switch back to a game of survival as the harsh realities of winter set in.

The Mounties dropped by Bev's house to see if her guests had arrived. Hugs were given as this group of friends was reunited. The Mounties went to the barn to welcome Omar back. Omar loved the Mounties; they were like family to him. He was glad to be back from the wilderness, his home here safe and warm, compared to his forest habitat. There he felt he had too many close calls and his life was always in danger. At Bev's, he would be treated like royalty. There was a young girl who adopted him as her own in the winter, taking care of him like a mother caring for her child. This was the life Omar preferred.

Bev served coffee and it was decided that they would have dinner together the following evening. The Mounties left, glad that they had made such good friends. They returned to their headquarters where they were informed a body had been pulled from the Yukon River in their absence. There was clearly a bullet hole in the back of the man's head. He could not be identified as a local man, so it was assumed he had been shot elsewhere. His body was most likely dumped upriver, the cold water preserving it. The killer would never be found.

The Mounties then had to answer a call relating to a man shooting another man's dog, a grave crime to commit in the north. The shooter said the dog jumped him in an unprovoked attack and had savagely bitten him. He showed the constables his wounds claiming he shot the dog in self defence, fearing for his life. This dog had a history of aggressive behavior and its owner had been warned that if he did not keep better control of his dog it would be seized and destroyed. That action would no longer be necessary, as the dog was dead, another casualty of this untamed land. The north's victims were both man and beast, the Yukon did not care.

CHAPTER 39

——— ✦✦✦✦✦ ———

The snow was falling lightly as the Mounties made their way to Bev's house. She was preparing lake trout, that her brother had dropped off, for dinner. The Mounties pulled up the hoods on their coats, the cold wind biting the exposed skin on their faces. The cold was early, soon they would be wearing their heavy parkas, trying to keep warm during the harsh Yukon winter.

Bev was glad to entertain her friends whose company she enjoyed very much. As the dark days of winter progressed, visits became less common, the bitter cold making it less likely anyone would venture outdoors unnecessarily. The fish was good, served smoked, with fresh root vegetables and cabbage, which were still available. The conversation was non-stop, as stories were told about the different experiences everyone had while living in the Yukon, a land of many surprises, some good, some bad.

Jason and Wendy said they were planning on adding another ten traps to their trapline this winter. They had mastered the art of fur trapping and now would try to make some money at it. Steward would work the same number of traps as he had last year. As a single person, he had reached his limit on the number he could take care of. The night ended and the Mounties said their goodbyes, promising they would visit them again during the winter months.

The sky was full of snow, the accumulation on the ground was growing. The snow would probably melt, as it was too early in the season for winter to completely dominate this land. The men walked back to their post, the fire beckoning them to sit and get warm. Cold ruled this barren land, with winter being its longest season. It seemed never willing to give up its grip, proven by the bodies of those unable to survive. This land showed no empathy for the downtrodden and weak.

The Mounties had enjoyed the evening. Having friends was important when living in the Yukon. Loneliness was the number one cause for depression, potentially leading to suicide. Last winter the Mounties had removed a suicide victim from a trapper's cabin after he took his own life. No longer able to deal with the pain from a back injury he had received while working his trapline, and no longer able to chop firewood or feed himself, he felt he had no choice but to end his life. The Mounties had grown accustomed to answering calls of all types, many of them to offer assistance when there was no one else available to help.

The cold October wind swept down the deserted streets of Dawson City, a town that would soon explode in population as word spread about gold being found in the Klondike. Tens of thousands of men would pass through Dawson, and a boomtown it would become. A big change in the Yukon was in the future, changing the fabric of this territory forever.

CHAPTER 40

A grey sky prevailed, the morning offering a mix of snow and rain, promising a cold wet day. The mid-October weather had a hint of what was coming, snow and cold. The leaves were dropping rapidly, as if in a race to see which tree in the forest would be bare first.

The Mounties were to have a busy day. A man had been reported missing, lost in the bush after going hunting alone. His dog had returned to camp but there was no sign of him. He had been missing for two days. With the help of his friends, the Mounties were able to get a good indication as to what direction the man had headed off in. They searched the area, his friends joining in, but came up with no clues as to his whereabouts. Silence gripped the Mounties, a feeling that the man was dead, occupied their thoughts. The lost man was experienced at surviving in the forest and most likely he had met with an accident, unable to get help. These assumptions were proven true when another hunter found the man's body days later. Apparently, he had accidentally shot himself in the leg, and bled to death.

The days were getting shorter, and the nights were getting colder. Early November brought the first blizzard of the season to Dawson, a big storm that spread eighteen inches of snow over the landscape. After the storm ended, the first dog sleds appeared, the huskies glad the winter season had returned. The Mounties picked up their sleds the next day, eager to hunt again as their meat supply was critically low.

The snows were here to stay, the winter season was upon them. Trappers who had been waiting for the season to open could now proceed, their dogs ready to pull their sleds through the deep snow, allowing the men to set their traps. The Yukon is beautiful when the first snows appear, bathing the landscape in a veil of white, covering the drab landscape with a sense of renewal. The land becomes a system of highways, the dogs packing down forest trails into roads. Sled dogs are invaluable in the north, responsible for providing transportation, moving goods and meat in the winter.

The Mounties relaxed, the blazing fire keeping the men warm in their comfortable headquarters. They sat around the table they had pulled closer to the fire, playing cards, and enjoying a loud and boisterous conversation with their co-workers. So, life went in the Yukon, where nature was in control. One had to play the hand he was dealt, left with few other choices.

CHAPTER 41

⟡ ✦✦✦✦ ⟡

The winds swept across the barren land, the darkness descending on the Yukon early, as the winter months marched forward. Dawson City had been quiet but was expecting an influx of people in the spring, gold seekers struck by yellow fever, willing to risk their life and soul for a little piece of yellow rock. There was rumour of gold in the Klondike, a murmur of easy riches to be had for a little bit of labour, these men never understanding what the consequences of their actions would be.

The Mounties were required to make one visit to each wilderness cabin in their district before Christmas. The men living here were typically fur trappers, a rugged breed of men refusing to abide by societies' norms, choosing to live on their own terms instead. The constables decided to turn this excursion into a hunting trip, as their meat supply had almost run out.

The day was sunny and mild as they left on their trip into the bush. The old fur trappers they planned to visit were private people with few friends, but they welcomed company if it was somebody they trusted. The constables usually brought a pound of coffee for each trapper, which went a long way towards forming friendships. The trail was fresh with new snow, a small storm passing through the area last night leaving a fresh coat of white over the landscape. The Mounties planned to visit three cabins on this outing. Being the acting game wardens, they also were to check licences, making sure all fees had been paid. The Mounties did not like this chore, knowing the men they were going to visit did not like their privacy invaded by strangers.

The first cabin came into view, an old building in need of repair. They were greeted at the front door by Old Joe, a trapper they had visited last winter. He invited the Mounties in, wondering if they had brought coffee for him again. The Mounties gave the trapper his gift and they were soon all enjoying the hot brew. Old Joe told them the fur season had been good so far, except for the fact that a wolverine was eating animals from his traps, destroying the furs. He had not found a way to rid himself of this problem yet. The conversation was pleasant, but it was soon time to go. With waves goodbye they left and continued on their way.

When the Mounties stopped at the next cabin, no one was home; the trapper was probably out working his trapline. Their last stop was interesting. After they knocked, a man in the cabin staggered to the front door, his dog in tow. He was drunk and not expecting visitors. He was instantly belligerent with the Mounties, telling them to leave his property, turning down their gift of coffee and slamming the door in their faces. The Mounties left, not wanting to deal with this man while he was in this drunken state, behaving erratically. The afternoon light was waning as they reached the small shelter they stayed in last year. The men anticipated a good night's rest, the quiet rejuvenating their spirits for another day.

CHAPTER 42

＋＋✦✦✦＋＋

The shelter was cozy, the woodstove throwing sufficient heat to keep the little building warm. The Mounties slept soundly, the cry of the wolves not disturbing them. The wind had picked up, blowing the snow which covered the huskies, like a thermal blanket, keeping them warm. A wolverine was curious, he had come across this shelter earlier in the week and had made it his mission to get inside. Now there were humans and dogs in his way. He crept up to the shelter, staying at the back of the building. The dogs, having not picked up his scent, did not awake. The wolverine was able to climb onto the roof. He watched the dogs, asleep under their banket of snow. He turned, exiting the roof the way he had come. He went into the safety of the forest, planning on returning when the company left.

The sun shone brightly through the grimy windows, waking the Mounties from a deep sleep. Usually up at dawn, they had slept longer than usual. They got up, dressed, and ate breakfast. They fed the dogs and packed up their sleds, planning to make the return trip to Dawson today. The dogs seemed motivated, and their trip back home should be fast and uneventful. The trail beckoned, the silence of the north overwhelming the spirits of the two men. A feeling of good will towards the creator took hold.

Two miles from Dawson the dog teams rounded a bend in the trail and, there, one hundred yards away was a bull moose, his rack of antlers an instant giveaway to his gender. A full-grown male moose would feed many people for a long time. The men stopped the dogs and tied them to trees off the trail. One man stayed behind with the dogs, while the other grabbed his rifle and slowly made his way towards the large animal. The moose was busy eating, unaware of the danger he was in. His inattention would cost him his life.

The Mountie approached, his prey coming within range of a good shot. The rifle took the moose down, killing it instantly. The other Mountie joined him at the fallen animal. It was late in the day, so the men decided one would stay and begin gutting the animal. The other went into town to get firewood, a few lanterns and one of the sub-constables. They returned before dark and worked until the wee hours of the morning dressing the moose and transporting it to town.

The sub-constables had been busy while the Mounties were gone. They had to deal with two bootleggers after it was reported they were trading liquor for fur with the Indians. The police confiscated all the men's alcohol, dumped it out in the snow and chased them out of town. Another call dealt with a fox who was acting peculiar and had no fear of humans. The sub-constables found the fox and shot it, fearing the animal had rabies. The stories of the north are endless, an unrelenting series of situations that must be dealt with daily.

CHAPTER 43

After a few hours sleep, the Mounties were happy to hear a few local natives had successfully butchered the moose and the meat was stored in the winter vault. This was a perfect example of reaping the rewards of having developed honest and trusting relationships with the people of Dawson.

As the afternoon turned into evening, the winds grew stronger and snow started to fall. The men knew a blizzard was in the making. Their help had left earlier carrying packages of meat, a gift for the work they had done dressing the moose. The men in the outpost stayed up until midnight. The wind was blowing hard, and the snow was unrelenting as they finally were able to get to sleep, not awakening till the sun rose in the morning. It was a good beginning for another day in this frozen world of beauty.

Typically, a blizzard is followed by bright sunshine, a reward for putting up with nature's fury the night before. Today the Mounties would take some meat to Bev's house and pick up the preserves she had made for them. Leaving the sub-constables in charge, the men left the station and headed to her home. In a short time, they were being greeted by their friend Bev, who was always glad to see them. The Mounties gave her the meat and some coffee, the latter item being hard to find outside of the Mounties supply lines. They enjoyed a nice visit and when it ended they promised to see each other again soon. The men gathered up their preserves and headed back to the station.

Upon arriving, they found two men in Mountie uniforms awaiting them. These men were from an outpost further north and were headed to Fort Edmonton. From there they were to be transferred to a different area of the country. The visitors felt glad and lucky, knowing that soon the face of the Yukon would be changed forever. It was rumored that a multitude of men were waiting for spring to flock to the north to quench their appetites for gold. Dawson City would become the epicenter to start this new journey.

Eventually, tens of thousands of men would stream into Dawson carrying the one ton of supplies they were required to have before being allowed to proceed on their journey to the gold fields. This migration to the north would start in the late spring as men found their way from the cities in the western part of the United States to Dawson. They would arrive on steamships and any other means of dependable transportation to get there.

The Mounties welcomed their comrades and offered accommodations for the night, as well as invited them to share the evening meal. Their new friends gratefully accepted their offer. Over dinner they talked of the changes that were to come to the north. Yellow fever would bring many people into the Klondike on an adventure they never imagined. The quest for gold may overpower these fortune seekers sensibilities, leading to many conflicts the Mounties would have to deal with. The men left for Fort Edmonton the following day, leaving the Mounties to wonder if they would also be transferred out of Dawson, as rotations were common in this new law enforcement force.

Christmas day arrived. The townspeople had decorated their homes with what they had on hand. The bounty of moose meat guaranteed that everyone had a small piece waiting for them at the police station. The day was cheerful as this small town shared what they had together. The spirit of Christmas was enjoyed in this precious moment of peace, Dawson serene and undisturbed on Christmas night.

CHAPTER 44

The January weather was cold, the cloud cover making the day even gloomier, creating a feeling of loneliness to sweep over the residents of Dawson. The streets were deserted, the people staying in their homes to keep warm. The snows were deep, and the winds cold as winter tightened its grip on this small enclave in the Yukon.

The Mounties patrolled the quiet streets of the city, the occasional yelp from a dog the only sound to break the silence. They felt their time in Dawson would soon come to an end, becoming just a memory lost in time. Thousands of gold seekers would flood Dawson in the late spring, bringing a new contingent of law enforcement officers to deal with the crowds. The two Mounties time here was well spent; they introduced law enforcement to the far north and brought a sense of law and order to a formerly untamed land.

The Mounties were transferred to new assignments, the townspeople throwing a farewell party in celebration. The entire town was in attendance to see them off and wish them well. One of the constables was assigned to a new post in Whitehorse, where he continued to serve until he reached the age of retirement. The lead constable went to Fort Edmonton, and after five more years of service he decided to pursue other interests. He went on to write a book giving a colourful account of his career as a North West Mounted Police officer, a title that could never be taken away from a man who committed his life to the north.

ACKNOWLEDGMENTS

I would like to extend my thanks and gratitude to my sister, Hilda, who read each chapter of these stories as they were being written and continually offered her words of encouragement. Also to my brother, Dave, and his wife, Judy, who have been extremely supportive, reading everything I've written. And finally, to my wife, Ruth Ann, without whom this work would have never made it to publication.